BRETT JAMES

THE DEADFALL PROJECT

FALLACY PUBLICATIONS • OAKLAND

COPYRIGHT © 2009 BRETT JAMES

FALLACY PUBLICATIONS

http://thedeadfallproject.com

ISBN 978-0-9850864-1-1

Third Edition

PRINTED IN THE UNITED STATES OF AMERICA

4 5 6 7 8 9 0 1 2 3

BOOK DESIGN BY MOBIHUE
ORIGINAL DESIGN BY ENAMEL
Set in Garamond & Franklin Gothic

For Tom, who inspired this path

1

*L*arge red numbers flashed. The timer counted down:
Twenty.

Nineteen.

Eighteen.

The device swelled with power, set for a devastating burst.
Amin chanted feverishly, prepared to ride its destructive wave
to salvation. The counter hit ten.

Nine.

Eight.

Seven.

Amin drew a deep breath and held it. He closed his eyes
and pressed his forehead against the timer.

Three.

Two.

The device sizzled like a match dropped in water. The
fluorescent lights on the high ceiling sputtered out.

Amin el Fassid looked up just as the dark enveloped him.
He was kneeling prostrate on his rug, facing toward Mecca

and, incidentally, the large bubbling device in the middle of the basement floor.

The device was a bomb, a collection of chemicals and electronics. Although Amin had assembled it, he hadn't the faintest idea how it worked. What was clear to him—as the bomb's glowing display faded—was that it hadn't worked.

Amin blinked, hoping his eyes had made a mistake. The room remained dark, the bomb a silent shadow. His stomach trembled with panic. He was ready to die, but unprepared for failure. This dark room was alien and cold, and he was too far from the desert. Too far from home. His body shivered.

Amin clasped his hands together and squeezed reassurance into them. He forced himself to focus.

Still on his knees, Amin groped into the black air that surrounded him. His hands found a thin tube and traced it back to the bomb's core, a copper tub. The copper burned his fingertips. He ignored the pain, pressing his palm flat against the side. He could feel the liquid bubbling inside, but it was tapering off, growing still. He pulled his hand from the searing metal, moaning as much from failure as pain. At the very moment of his triumph, success had been snatched away.

He laid his stinging hand against the holy mark on his forehead. The mark was a waxy scar the size of a silver-dollar, creeping down from his turban, pale white against his dark leather skin. Allah put the scar there fourteen years ago, singling Amin out and giving him a destiny. The scar had brought him into the service of Il Siyâh and they had led him here, to this strange distant land. Tonight his destiny was to be fulfilled. He was to become a martyr the likes of which had not been seen since Sumayah herself. But now that was lost. All lost.

He rose to his feet. He wasn't a tall man, but the turban added inches. A full beard of black hair masked his face but for his brown eyes, which searched the dark room like those of an abandoned child.

He took a careful step, feeling with pointed toe, trying to remember the room so recently lit. His galabiyya, a simple robe, hung loosely over his wiry frame. It was damp with sweat and cold against the bare skin underneath. Two more steps and his foot knocked against something heavy. He brought his hand down, finding his duffle bag. He unzipped the top and dug through metal tools. At the very bottom, his hand closed around a cheap plastic flashlight.

The duffle had been prepared for him, but the light hadn't been included. He'd found it in the glove compartment of the van he used to transport the bomb here. His instructions had strictly forbidden him to bring anything not provided by his contact, but the flashlight looked useful so he brought it anyway. Allah favors the prepared.

He slid the switch, then banged it against his palm. He was rewarded with a dim orange light. It wasn't much, but he was glad to have it. He traced the light over the bomb. Its jumble of wires and tubes looked foreign to him now, like he'd never laid eyes on them before. A single bubble rose from the tub, its soft gurgle punctuating the silence. Amin tapped his index finger on the dull display, half hopeful, half helpless.

The flashlight faded. A small window, set high in the far wall, funneled faint light in from the sidewalk above. A metal grate secured the window, but a few hours ago Amin had sawed the lock off. He hadn't planned to need an escape route, but was thankful he had taken such precautions.

His eyes adjusted, bringing shapes out of the darkness. His nose caught the acid smell of burnt plastic. He followed it to his left, where the building's circuit-breaker panel lurked in the shadows. He took three steps and froze, foot hanging in mid-step. Something had tickled in his ear. He strained against the hollow silence, wondering if it was a noise or his imagination. But there it was again: distant footsteps.

He lowered his foot softly, holding his breath. He looked first to the staircase, framed in an open doorway, then to the bomb that sat in the center of the floor. Even in this dim light, it would be the first thing anyone would see. He had to hide it.

Against the wall, he saw a gap between two elephant-sized heaters. Their churning fans had fallen silent with the lights and their metal skins crackled as they cooled.

He knelt and tested the side of the copper tub; it had cooled enough to touch. He placed both hands against it, coiled his legs and pushed. The metal bent under his hands—sloshing liquid to the floor—but the tub didn't move. He cursed himself for assembling the bomb on the floor. If he had just set it on the rolling cart it would be easy to hide. Now the cart held nothing but empty bottles, their contents poured into the tub, making it too heavy to move.

It was too late for these thoughts, too late for anything but regret—and no time for that, either. The device was placed to achieve maximum destruction, not to avoid discovery.

The footsteps grew louder. Closer.

Amin's heart raced, pounding blood to his head. He yanked a white sheet off the cart and kicked it away, its wheels squealing against the concrete. He stretched the sheet over the bomb. In the dim light, it resembled a melted ghost.

The metallic clink of a door latch echoed down the stair-well. The beam of a flashlight danced in the doorway as feet shuffled down the steps. Amin heard whistling, someone bolstering himself against the intimidating dark basement. Amin reached under his arm and drew a heavy long-barreled revolver from its leather pouch. The gun was another thing he wasn't supposed to have, but he would no sooner have left it behind than come naked. He was calmed by the familiar supple wood handle, polished by the palms of three generations of his family.

Amin slipped across the room, flattening himself against the wall by the doorway. All fear was gone. He knew what he must do.

The whistling grew louder and the footsteps shuffled to its rhythm. Feet hit the landing and the light bounced upward, flashing in Amin's eyes, blinding him. His finger tightened on the gun's trigger, but he held back. A blind shot would be useless, dangerous. An instant later, the flashlight moved on. He hadn't been seen.

Orange spots obscured Amin's vision. He saw the shadow of a man, backlit by the oval beam of his flashlight. The whistling stopped when the flashlight found the bulging sheet. The man bent down and raised the corner.

Amin could wait no longer. He stepped forward, extended his arm.

"Qu'est-ce que c'est que ça?" the man muttered, inspecting a nest of plastic tubes.

Not trusting his eyes, Amin pressed the gun's barrel against the spine of the man's neck. The man jumped, first from the surprise and again from impact as the gun kicked a bullet into him.

The man crumbled forward, lifeless even before he slapped against the floor. The gunshot echoed, a tuneless requiem for an unknown man.

Amin stared dumbly at the body. Guns had been his whole life, but he'd never before killed a man. The gunshot's echo faded, replaced by yelling and scrambling footsteps. The door at the top of the steps was opened and a name was called down.

Amin made himself move. He holstered his gun and sprinted across the dark room. It was sheer luck nothing tripped him. He targeted the small window and leapt with all his strength. He body-slammed the wall with a grunt, but his hands found the windowsill and held him off the floor. Gripping with one hand, he flipped the grate up with the other. He got his shoulder under it and punched through the window. Glass tinkled outside, and cold fresh air poured over him.

Footsteps drummed down the stairs. Amin reached through the fractured window and grabbed the sill outside. Glass dug into his arm as he pulled himself up the wall. Shards of glass broke against his shoulders. His robe shredded and grew thick with blood. He ignored the pain.

When his shoulders were through, he set his palms flat on the sill. He locked his elbows to his hip, balancing his body above the tendrils of glass that could effortlessly disembowel him. He tipped forward, curled his body gracefully and rolled his legs out over his head. His feet came down on the hard cement of the sidewalk and he dropped into a crouch.

Panicked voices inside; the body had been found.

Though Amin stood in the middle of a city, the night air was fresh after so many hours of containment. He inspected himself. His arms and shoulders were lacerated, but his galabiyya was absorbing the blood; it wouldn't drip and leave a trail. Bending low, he dashed across the street. The road was abandoned. He ducked behind the row of parked cars that lined the far curb, using them as cover as he made his way down the sidewalk.

A cartoon of a well-fed maid in a skimpy outfit peered down at him from the side of a white van. Blue italic letters declared *Premier Rang: Service de Ménage*. A bubble rose from the maid's mouth, affirming, *"Nous sommes au premier rang!"* The company was real, but they knew nothing of this van.

Amin drew his revolver and flipped it around, holding it like a hammer. The barrel was warm as flesh, as if it had stolen not just the man's life, but his heat as well. He smashed the window, scattering gleaming chunks of glass over the bench seat. He popped the lock and slid over to the driver's side. The key was in the ignition, just as he had left it. The van started easily. He laid the revolver at his side and put the van into gear. Despite the urgency he felt, he kept his foot light on the gas pedal, steering the van into the street at a sluggish idle. He used the mirror to watch the empty street behind him as the vehicle puttered away.

Amin had no idea what to do next. He wasn't even supposed be alive, much less trying to escape. He decided to head to the DeGaulle airport, where he could park the van and come back into the city on the train. International flights arrived at all hours and he could use their crowds as cover. Then, once he was sure it was safe, he'd call in and confess his failure.

After two blocks, the van turned down a thin street, edging between the cars parked on either side. It puttered through two more byways and arrived at the bank of the Seine, the wide river that split Paris in two on its long journey to the English Channel. The van idled at the red light, then accelerated down the wide avenue that traced the river's edge. It blended anonymously into the city's traffic, which persisted even at this darkest of hours.

The clock atop the Musée d' Orsay watched the van pass like the eye of a giant. That eye had seen two world wars and tonight it had almost witnessed the start of a third. Hidden somewhere in the dark neighborhood behind it, a normally sleepy bank was a flurry of activity. Security guards were calling police, and the police, once apprised, were calling higher authorities.

II

*T*he phone rang just seconds before the alarm beside it began to chirp. The cacophony filled the bedroom, but didn't disturb its owner's sleep: the bed was already empty.

The room was small and overfull with beautiful furniture that didn't match. A brass bed sat between modern Swedish end tables. The Art Deco wardrobe looked overdressed next to the muted Italian bureau, and the colonial English secretary looked a little nervous, as if it had stumbled into the wrong part of town. They were packed into the small dumpy room, a memoir of larger apartments and bigger budgets.

Under the electronic din, the sound of running water trickled through a crooked doorframe. Steam escaped at the gaps, bringing a soapy smell to the musty bedroom. On the other side of the door, Grey Stark squeezed into the tiny bathroom, bent over the stained porcelain sink, and inspected his face in a cheap gilt mirror. Half of it was smoothly shaven, the other coated with white cream. His fingers circled slowly over the shaved half, searching for stray hairs and making strategic attacks with a metal safety razor. It wasn't that he wanted a perfect shave so much as he was wasting time. And he wasn't so much wasting time as he was smothering the life out of it. He paused to wait out the phone, then straightened up and took stock of himself in the mirror.

Once upon a time, he had been six-foot two, but the years had robbed him of at least an inch; it was too depressing for him to measure. He stood straight-backed—his good posture a remnant of the military service in his early history—but, despite rigorous exercise and a strict diet, his stomach pushed out. His body still swelled with muscles, thick and solid, but the skin over them had lost its firmness, softening his edges.

Two thick scars cut a diagonal path from his chest to his waist, not quite parallel and too jagged for a surgeon's knife. His right shoulder had two quarter-sized pockmarks—bullet scars made over twelve years apart. Only one of them had been avenged. His nose, broken three times, didn't rise off his face as it once did and his black hair was dabbed with silver. Grey would still pass muster at a distance, but closer inspection revealed the wear and tear of hard use.

This particular morning he was blessed with dark puffy crescents under his eyes. His night had consisted of lying in the bed and staring at the ceiling, intermingled with tall glasses of straight whiskey. For that, he had been rewarded with one short and unsatisfying nap. The bottle had given out two hours ago and he gave up all pretense of sleep. He dedicated the rest of the dark morning to his toiletry, which he intended to drag out until sunrise.

The phone started complaining again.

The best Grey could muster was a sigh. He dropped his razor in a lump of spent shaving cream—ashen from his black stubble—and cut the water off. He jerked open the door and walked to the bed, whose sheets were twisted disproportionately for the use they had seen. He pulled the phone from its cradle, holding it up to the chirping alarm to emphasize the smallness of the hour. It was 6:26 in the morning, and the October sun hadn't even started its overture. Grey switched off the alarm and raised the phone to the shaven side of his face. His tone was the only thing polite:

"What?"

"I could use your expertise this morning, if you've got a moment."

It was Denis. Grey's eyes rose involuntarily toward his forehead. Denis was the Director of Operations of the DST, which was short for the verbose *Direction de la Surveillance du Territoire*. The Directorate, as it was called, was France's internal intelligence agency, roughly equivalent to the FBI.

Denis was efficient and friendly, honest and smart. All good qualities that were far too rare in the intelligence community, but in the twelve years Grey had been assigned to France, Denis had been little more than the bearer of paperwork and the patron of puerile assignments. Nothing of note ever happened in France, but everything was recorded in minute detail. Denis sat at the top of this heaping bureaucracy—a trophy to bland efficiency, for which he had beaten out hundreds of contenders. Grey never enjoyed a call from Denis, but he had expected someone else, so comparatively, it was a pleasant surprise.

"How much is a moment?" Grey asked.

"A car is on the way. They'll have coffee."

"I've already got an appointment today…"

"I called the clerk of courts and rescheduled you for next Monday."

"And what about—"

A loud honk shattered the dark morning and Grey had to fumble to catch the phone. He got it back to his ear in time to hear Denis say, "That must be your ride. See you shortly."

The line went dead. Grey looked at the phone: it had no further answers. He took it to the bathroom and tried to wipe the shaving cream off the earpiece. The white foam retreated deeper into the little holes. He dropped the whole thing in the trash can and wiped his face with a stiff towel.

*T*he sky was shrouded in orange and red, but the earth below was still painted in the cold blue of night. Grey sat in the back of a long Citroen that glided effortlessly down a wide avenue as if hovering over it. In the morning light, the car's tinted windows rendered the world dimensionless and the streets of Paris, unchanged for centuries, passed like an old black and white movie.

The car turned onto the plush streets of the Seventh Arrondissement, the most expensive neighborhood on the continent of Europe. The houses of the rich surrounded him, divided into two varieties: the artful ones, as pleasant to look at as they would be to live in, and the ungainly palaces, the crass temples of those that burned money just to show that they could.

There were too many of the latter outside, so Grey turned back to the electric razor on his lap. He turned it on for the fifteenth time and for the fifteenth time it shuddered pitifully and died. Electric razors were the tool of men in a hurry and it was a long time since Grey had been. So the batteries had run dry from disuse, leaving half of his face darkened by stubble. Denis was a stickler for appearance and wouldn't be able to resist a comment. Even his suit, his best black pin-stripe, would register as twenty years out of date and a little too square-cut for the Director's French sensibilities.

The car slowed. Up ahead, Grey saw yellow police tape stretched out from a building and around two trees in the sidewalk, forming a square courtyard. The tape, and the police cars parked around it, drew a suit-clad audience outfitted with briefcases, newspapers and coffee. So far, the show consisted of little more than a few officers milling around, but, for the gathering crowd, it held enough promise to justify being late for work.

The Citroen parked at the edge of the tape. A plainclothes agent hopped out of the driver's seat and went to announce their arrival. Grey leaned forward to inspect the building. It was three stories of dull granite. Faded gold letters—placed optimistically high for their size—announced that this was *La Banque de l'Orange*. The bank's face was pillared, tympanumed and adorned with every gaudy accent short of sequins, but the sides were flat and windowless, as if it had been sandwiched between two other buildings that had been since torn down. Thin parking lots on either side separated it from the far more tasteful structures that filled the block. Grey wondered how many generous offers on this property had been turned down; some very stubborn owner was dug in against the forces of time and money.

The driver returned and opened the door for him. Grey swung his legs out, ducked under the tape, and stood up. The crowd turned expectantly, hoping he might be the highlight of today's break-room story. Grey strolled to the building, careful not to make any memorable gestures. When he reached the front door, he dug a silver badge out of his coat and held it up for inspection.

The badge designated him as an attaché to the Parisian police—a wizard, as it was commonly called. He was supposed to be a forensics professor at the Universite Saint-Lazare who would, on occasion, lend his expertise to the professional sector. It was a thin cover, made thinner by his limited understanding of forensics, but it worked for the casual observer. The sad truth was, no cover was good enough to fool the people that he really wanted to.

Grey hadn't expected to recognize anyone outside, but found Jerard Venerdi, Denis's protégé, standing out front in a sharp blue Police Nationale captain's uniform. Jerard was thin, young, and everything else Grey vaguely remembered once being.

Jerard had risen fast in the ranks of the DST and it was jarring to see the captain's mien on someone so young. His success had a lot to do with his bright eyes and winning smile, and having brains enough to never offer his opinion. But his rank also bore the mark of Denis's hand. Success and beauty seemed to run hand in glove, but Grey wasn't one to judge. He worked for the CIA; the internal affairs of the DST were far beyond his bounds.

Door duty must have been humiliating for an up-and-comer like Jerard, but Grey took it as a sign. The three bars of a captain would outrank nearly any officer who might try to bull his way inside. Whatever was going on, Denis was keeping a tight lid on it.

"Sorry to interrupt your shave, sir," Jerard said, flashing white teeth. Jerard had the relaxed smile of a man to whom nothing bad had ever happened. It probably hadn't. But in Grey's world, it was too early for cheer. He squinted at Jerard with disapproval. The kid straightened to attention and pulled the door open. "He's down in the basement. The staircase is the third door on the left. Just follow the cable."

Grey nodded. A thick lime-green cable budded off of a generator truck and passed through the door by his feet. Grey followed it in.

The foyer of the bank must have been a glorious place back in the middle of the century, but had since fallen into disrepair. It was a big room, with walls of white stonework and wood panels. Time had warped and splintered the wood, and varnish had been liberally applied to cover the damage. An imposing crystal chandelier hung low in the center of the room, its trunk globbed with dull white paint. Its chain disappeared into the dark heights of an unseen ceiling, no doubt ready to collapse at a moment's notice.

Grey crossed the plush red carpet, following a path worn blond by years of use, to a wall of freshly-polished steel bars. Set in the middle was a gate that was so precisely milled it didn't so much as rattle when he tried to pull it open. A face stared at him through the bars, the bronze bust of a man unknown beyond these walls. There was a shiny spot on his forehead, at just the perfect height for resting someone to rest an arm.

Grey turned back and saw the hallway Jerard had mentioned. He followed the green cable through the furthest door, and downstairs to the basement.

At the base of the stairs, the cable blossomed into a forest of yellow floodlights. It was so bright Grey felt like he had just walked into high noon. He squinted and looked around.

The basement was dominated by two large heaters, new enough to still have tags and contrasting sharply with the decaying ductwork they fed into. Cheap vinyl tile covered the floor, and the walls were cinder block painted white. The air was tainted with the smell of bleach, making the room feel cleaner than it looked. Grey heard his name and turned to see Denis scurry up.

Denis was much shorter than Grey and so gaunt he made supermodels pine for thinner days. He wore a huge, thick, drab-olive overcoat that made him look like a young turtle playing in his father's shell, his only act of rebellion a bright blue tie.

"There you are," Denis said. His voice was a little too feminine, even for France. Looking at Grey, his face drooped with disapproval.

"This really isn't the best timing," Grey said. He was happy to skip his other appointment, but only if this situation was serious enough to provide a good excuse.

"Shut up," Denis said with ice that Grey wasn't used to. Then he smiled again, clamping a hand of leather over wood on Grey's forearm, and steered him into the room. "Right this way," he said. "There are some people you need to meet."

In the middle of the room, two men stood waiting, one as tall and thin as the other was short and fat.

"It's about time you got here," Denis said, chastising Grey for the benefit of the waiting men. "This is Dr. Peerson and Lt. Faison. Gentlemen, this is Professor Grey Stark, he's our local forensic expert."

The tall one was Faison. Grey already knew him—or, at least, had seen his face before. He was Grey's height but his mid-section was stretched unnaturally long, as if he were seen through a fun-house mirror. His pasty face was speckled with stubble, and his hair resisted all attempts at a comb-over; it floated like a black wave crashing on a smooth white rock. His jacket didn't match his pants, and his socks didn't match either them or each other. His look was somewhere between doctoral candidate and homeless.

Faison was the Directorate's detail man, called in when they needed someone to dust a warehouse with a toothbrush. Denis considered the man's brain a feather in his cap—he would brag that military intelligence called for Faison's help with the hard stuff—but the man himself was feeble and antisocial. He was also immune to promotion: though easily ten years Denis's senior, he was stuck with a lesser rank and pay scale than young Jerard at the front door.

"Monsieur Stark," he mumbled, his accent thick. His voice always had an undertone of suspicion, whether he was questioning a witness or ordering a crepe. Grey didn't guess Faison had many friends outside of the DST and he knew he didn't have any in it. Grey smiled at Faison and shook his hand like he meant it, his act of charity for the day.

Then Grey turned to the shorter man, whom he knew nothing about. From a distance, Dr. Peerson could easily be mistaken for an egg balanced atop a potato. His pointed head was a mountain of pink broken only by dried-pea eyes sunk deep in the folds of his face. What little hair he had was divided evenly between bushy caterpillar eyebrows and a raccoon's tail that wrapped from ear to ear. He wore a tan suit that looked off-the-rack and his jacket hung to either side of his expansive belly, with little hope of meeting in the middle.

What really set Dr. Peerson apart from Faison was his jolly demeanor. He greeted Grey in a jolly British accent, smiling a jolly smile that dug deep canals into his jolly fat face. He was so jolly that Grey expected him to whip a sack off his shoulders and offer him a present. This thought amused Grey, but Peerson spoiled it by offering him an NSC badge instead of a handshake.

NSC was short for the NATO Security Commission. It was a new organization, not even two years old. While NATO always had an intelligence bureau, until now it was only a minimal effort, a formal channel for NATO member countries to share information. The Commission, as the NSC was called, was a far more insidious undertaking.

They had their own staff, and a sizeable one at that. They ran their own operations, used paid mercenaries to execute pirates in the China Sea, and reportedly hired an assassin right off of Interpol's most wanted list to murder a Central American dictator. Their spies would tell them anything they wanted to hear, and their agents were loyal only to their paychecks.

The NSC's mission, so they asserted, was to target terrorists and the countries that harbored them. This was a broad claim, one that allowed for everything from gun-running to wiretapping politicians—especially those who had voted against their charter.

Their charter had been jointly submitted to NATO by the US President and the British PM, personally. Their support—along with that of the countries they were able to buy—made for a slim majority, and the moment it passed, every country that hadn't voted for the NSC lodged formal protests against it. But once the ball got rolling, it was impossible to stop. And the Commission had already become a powerful organization.

Back at Langley, any janitor with an NSC badge had access to more classified information than the Director's office. The Commission was taking private meetings with the President himself, and dictating foreign policy without so much as dropping the CIA a memo. The biggest offense, however, was their habit of commandeering established contacts. They isolated the CIA from its own spies, and what information they did share had key pieces filtered out. They didn't bother to hide this censorship. They didn't need to. The Commission was the golden child and the CIA was just a tired patriarch waiting for its own funeral.

That didn't explain what Peerson was doing in Paris, though. France had been the most vocal opponent to the Commission, and even threatened to pull out of NATO over it. After the NSC's prominent role in the Iraq debacle—when they asserted that the country had enough nuclear weapons to level every major city in Europe—the French PM declared that they had hijacked NATO's name to add legitimacy to their dubious claims. So it was a mystery how the Commission got a man here. Grey looked up at Peerson. The man was sweating merely from the effort of standing still. A bigger mystery, he thought, is why they would choose *this* man.

Grey handed the badge back. Peerson dabbed his bald pate with a handkerchief before taking it. He smiled at Grey, smug but kindly, as if to say that he would stay on the benevolent side of dictatorship. Grey tried to return the smile, but it came out with more sneer than he had planned.

"Gentlemen, how may I be of assistance?" Grey said, trying to sound professorial. That Denis had used his cover story to introduce him meant there was a fair chance the room was bugged.

No one said anything. Grey found himself squared off with Peerson, as if the next thirty seconds would determine alpha status for the entire investigation. Denis inserted himself between the two men.

"Grey has full clearance to work on cases such as this," he said. His words passed unheard, so he tried a different tactic. Squeezing Peerson's arm, he said, "Doctor, why don't you show Professor Stark the body."

"Quite right," Peerson exclaimed, sparking to life and waddling across the room. "The subject died early this morning, three-thirty-five to be exact. We have witnesses to the time of death, so we won't need an autopsy. That and every clock in the place stopped when the power went out."

Peerson waved his hand in the air, motioning everyone to follow. "The power died at three thirty-three. A peculiar time,

I should think." He led the group to a human form draped with a white cloth. Peerson motioned to the sheet but made no effort to remove it. Either he couldn't be bothered or he couldn't bend that far down without tipping over.

Grey crouched down and drew the sheet back. The man underneath had looked more human when he was covered. His neck was twisted a turn too far, passing around his back to reach the other side. A single vertebrae lay next to his head, one side coated in lead like a wad of chewing gum. The guard's face was expressionless, leaving no final thoughts for the world.

He was just a boy, Grey thought. His hair was well-trimmed, his guard uniform clean and pressed. A gold band on the guard's left hand meant that right now someone was awaiting his return. She would be warming up some breakfast. Or perhaps a bed.

"He came downstairs to check the fuse box," Denis said, cutting off Peerson, who had opened his mouth to speak. "He was shot from behind. Point blank, execution style. Two other guards arrived in time to see the assailant escape through that window there."

"The window is alarmed," Peerson chimed in, "so we know he didn't get in that way. He must have arrived earlier. We're still waiting to interview the evening shift." Peerson turned to Denis for confirmation, but the French Director of Operations returned a thin smile. Denis doesn't like Peerson either, Grey thought, if it was time to start counting his allies.

Still kneeling by the corpse, Grey ran his hand over the entry wound. Congealed blood collected on his finger tips, thick and red. He rubbed it against his thumb, feeling something gritty in it, like sand. He found similar grains embedded in the skin around the wound. He dropped flat on the ground and sniffed the corpse's neck. It had the sulfur smell of spent gunpowder.

Grey sat up again. The other men were staring at him and Peerson's mouth hung open. Grey ignored them and continued his inspection. There were powder burns in the jacket collar, and in the man's hair. All in all, it was a lot of powder, even for a close range shot. It was as if the man had been shot with an ancient flintlock. Or maybe a 'zip' gun, the sort junkies make out of plumbing parts. But no junky would be down here. And there wasn't much intrigue in a dead bank guard. Not enough to draw Denis into the action.

Grey's knees crackled as he rose, and he hoped the other men couldn't hear them. He accepted a handkerchief from Denis and wiped the blood from his hands. "You say the power went out?" Grey asked, folding the blood to the inside of the cloth and handing it back to Denis.

"Yes," Denis said, leading the group to an unusual-looking device in the middle of the floor.

The bulk of it was a copper tub, square, about two feet on a side and one deep. It was filled with a milky liquid. Six copper tubes rose from the liquid and fed into white bottles that were circled around the device. A copper shaft rose from the center, topped with a Pyrex jar—the sort used in laboratories. The jar was full of near-microscopic particles suspended in clear liquid. A spider's web of thin wires covered the whole device, converging into a solid aluminum box that was the size of a very complete dictionary. Grey wasn't much in the electronics department, but there was something in this device that felt familiar.

"What is it?" he asked.

"What do you think it is?" Peerson huffed with a level of derision that most people reserved for when they were out of earshot.

"It's a bomb," Faison chirped excitedly. "But it's entirely new. I've been studying it for an hour and I can't even figure out the simplest—"

"We'll have plenty of time for that later," Denis interrupted, gesturing at his ear. "Sorry," Faison said, shrinking backward. "I forgot…"

Grey knelt gingerly by the device. The liquid was the source of the bleach smell; it burned his nostrils. There was a second smell there, too, like decaying fish. He couldn't make anything of the liquid, so he moved to the aluminum box. It was welded on all sides, leaving no way to open it. Hundreds of thin wires went in through a hole on one side, and an inch-thick black cable emerged from the other. He got to his feet and followed the cable across the room.

As the wire neared the wall, its rubber coating blistered from heat damage, then grew brittle and cracked. Grey opened the fuse box and saw that the wire was clamped to an enormous fuse, likely the main for the whole building. The fuse had blown violently; it was puffed out and scarred. Grey reached for it, but changed his mind; he didn't know which end was still live.

He dug a fingernail into the cable, chipping away the brittle rubber and inspecting the twisted copper inside. This cable could carry a lot of electricity, but there was no indication of what it was used for.

Grey walked back to the device. From this angle, he noticed it was covered in small markings, what looked like Arabic letters. In a moment, he saw the pattern: there was a matching set of letters on each wire and the place where it clipped to the device. There were similar pairings on all the parts. They were assembly instructions. Grey looked up. Faison stood over him, tapping his nose knowingly.

This was what Denis had wanted Grey to see, and he sprung back to life. "There's only one more thing to see for now," he said, leading the group to a table by the stairs. "Then we'll have forensics brief us this afternoon, back at the police station." Denis didn't really mean the police station, what he meant was a conference room at the Directorate's headquarters—a bug-free location where they could talk openly. But out here, Denis was supposed to be a cop.

The table was crowded with evidence bags. Most of them held tools, individually wrapped and labeled. Grey picked up a screwdriver. There was a piece of yellow tape on the handle with a Persian word written on it. Or maybe it was a sentence, for all he knew about Persian. He grabbed a pair of pliers and noticed a similar coding. Whoever masterminded all this didn't put much faith in their man's intelligence.

Denis went right past the tools and held up a large clear bag. Grey knew it was improper to feel the elation that he did, but he had been sidelined in France for almost twenty years, doing nothing but waiting for something of note to happen. And now it finally had: inside the bag was a Muslim prayer rug, the kind they knelt on during daily prayer. Or right before a suicide attack.

Denis received nods from each of the three men. "Right," he said, dropping the rug and heading for the stairs. "If you'll excuse me gentlemen, I have a lot on my plate right now."

Grey didn't want to get stuck with the other men, so he hustled after Denis. "Catch a ride?" he asked.

Denis inspected Grey for ulterior motives, found none. "Certainly," he replied.

Grey bounded up the steps, excited. Bombing a bank wouldn't amount to much, as far as terrorist acts went, but it was the biggest thing to happen in France since the 1st Infantry felt the sand of Normandy underfoot. When Grey had been sent to Paris, it was because the CIA wanted him to disappear.

Ever since then, he'd attacked every dull assignment with vigor, hoping that every small success would remind Langley they were wasting one of their best agents on trivia. But now they had found a terrorist bomb in France. If anything was going to get him back into the game, this would be it.

Grey glanced fondly at Denis, forgiving him for all the interminable stakeouts of political mistresses and the late night surveillances of corrupt French agents trying to sell useless secrets to countries he could toss a baseball across. Denis scowled back.

"Really, Grey," he said, "it would have been better not to shave at all."

IV

Twenty-eight hundred miles away in Langley, Virginia, the sun was just rising on the large H-shaped building where the CIA kept its headquarters. Long shadows from the leafless trees in the surrounding forest crept up the cement walls. The building was dark but for a single window's light, which cut into the morning like a square searchlight.

Inside that window was Tom McGareth's office, an unexceptional room despite his high rank. Tom sat at his desk, bent over a thin report. It seemed to be pulling him down by the eyeballs. His wide shoulders slumped from fatigue and his elbows were propped on the desk, thick fingers digging into the silver hair of his military-issue flattop.

Tom had worn a flattop for over thirty years, ever since his first one from a barbershop in Saigon. Back then, America was still winning in Vietnam, his hair was still blond, and his body was the carved marble of a Marine heavy weapon specialist. His face was still square and lean, with wide flat muscles running down his jaw and meeting at a deep cleft in his chin, but a couple decades at a desk had softened his flesh. Dark eyebrows, thick and low, added just a dash of bookworm to an otherwise career-sergeant face.

It was odd to see such a powerful man run down by a wispy little report, a mere three pages of memo. But this report capped a day that, while not even seven hours old, had already beat him senseless.

Today had started just as yesterday was supposed to end. Shortly after midnight, Tom received an L5 from the French DST. An L5 was the highest priority message one intelligence agency could send another, reserved for matters on the scale of presidential assassination or governmental coups. They were rare in general, and all the more so from France. Europe had been Tom's jurisdiction for seven years, and the last time France sent an L5, it went to his predecessor.

Tom had been finishing some paperwork in bed when the CIA switchboard operator called—as the Director of Operations for Europe, Tom rated a direct line to Langley. The L5, despite the weight it carried, didn't have much to report. There had been a terrorist attack in Paris, it had failed, and details would be forthcoming. At the time, it didn't sound like anything to get worked up about. And, by sheer coincidence, he already had a senior man in Paris. He instructed the DST to contact Grey Stark directly. Tom told the CIA operator he wanted a call the moment more information came in, and he ordered a car to be sent over to his house. That done, he crawled back into bed. Things of this nature tended to develop slowly and drag on brutally. He would later appreciate any sleep he got now.

It was a little before three o'clock when Tom jolted back awake. Something was wrong, too much time had passed. He called Operations; there had been no further word from France. By now, there should have been. Tom hung up and peered out his front window. The Georgetown streets were dark and quiet. A black sedan idled patiently by his front door.

After a quick shower, Tom hurried to the car and directed the driver to Langley. He used the car's secure phone to see if anyone from his division was in their office. He started at the top and—after twenty-two voicemails—got a young woman named Jill Topper on the phone. Topper worked in the cartography division, interpreting satellite photos. Europe had once been a booming department, with a staff of dozens working around the clock. But after the Soviet Union broke up, the place was nothing more than a stop-over for new hires, a place to hone their skills while waiting for something more interesting to open up. Topper had only been with the Company a week, and was shocked to find the director of her division on the other end of the phone.

Unsurprisingly, she didn't know anything about the case file, the L5, or even that anything was happening in France at all. She enthusiastically promised to find out what she could, then hung up before Tom could stop her. She called back long minutes later and told him that the entire European section was abandoned, which he already knew, but that the area next door was buzzing with activity.

In an attempt to promote cooperation between NATO's Commission and America's CIA, half a floor in the north wing had been loaned to the Commission. Over there, Jill reported, a couple dozen people were in a heated meeting.

Tom hung up the phone and cursed at it. He tapped the glass partition between himself and the driver, then pointed upwards. The driver nodded and accelerated to eighty. Tom would ask him to go faster, but to do so the driver was required to turn on the car's hidden police lights; the only thing worse than showing up late is advertising it. He should have driven himself.

When they finally arrived at Langley, Tom dashed to the NSC conference room, finding nothing but half-eaten donuts and coffee burning in the pot. He searched the office, finding a solitary NSC staffer, who reported that everyone else had gone home. "Been up all night working on that terrorist bombing," the kid said, anxious get out the door himself. But Tom demanded a report from him, in writing. In America, the NSC still answered to the CIA. At least that's what it said on paper.

He waited almost two hours before it showed up. The envelope it came in weighed more than the report itself, which was carefully worded to give the appearance that it contained important information. It did not.

The French Directorate had found what they believed to be a bomb in Paris. Evidence suggested it was a failed terrorist attack. The Commission liked the word 'terrorist.' It was their cue to step in and take over.

The report stated that they, meaning the Commission, had been concerned for some time that this bomb would resurface. The report was vague about what that meant, but clear on what they felt Tom's role should be: "The CIA should dispatch no further operatives to France. They will be briefed through NATO channels." In other words, he was to do nothing.

Tom knew a power grab when he saw one. A bomb in Paris shouldn't raise this much fuss, at least not over here in the States. But obviously the NSC planned to make a big deal out of it. Hell, they'd probably insisted France send the L5 to begin with. They were going to make a mountain out of this molehill, and, when they did, they'd probably try to blame the mountain on him.

The Commission had been gunning for Europe for months now, ever since the President had been re-elected. They had been making odd requests, like asking for status reports of terrorist activities in France—of which there were none—and then filing formal complaints about his lack of information. And they hounded him with questions: Why wasn't he tracking illegal immigration from the Middle East to Europe? Marseille, in the south of France, was one of the most open ports on the Mediterranean; why didn't he have agents stationed there?

These questions were a trap, a Catch-22. None of our European allies wanted American agents poking around their country. To do so would be an insult to their internal intelligence. The French were especially touchy, seeing as how they didn't much care for Americans to start with.

There hadn't been an ongoing CIA operation in France for thirty years and this hadn't, up until now, caused any problems. So if Tom had tried to comply with the NSC's requests by putting additional manpower in France, he would have just been wasting money and offending their allies. Besides, the country had so little intrigue that agents of the cold war went there to retire. On the other hand, since Tom didn't staff up, the Commission had only to wait for the next big incident, then blame him for inaction.

According to the report in front of him, the latter was happening right now. The Commission had even managed to get an agent on the scene, a Dr. Peerson. Tom had never heard of him, but that was the case with a lot of these NATO operatives—the Commission seemed to prefer people who didn't have any ties with outside agencies.

Peerson had supposedly been tracking a member of the Iranian terrorist group Il Siyâh when they crossed over into France a few days ago. Despite the information sharing agreement the two agencies had, this was the first time they mentioned it to Tom. If he complained, no doubt they would only ask him why he didn't already know.

As for Grey, they wanted him to report to Peerson, to offer both his support and his local connections. It wasn't a request, it was an order with the word 'please' tacked at the front.

Tom's hands were tied. This was the kind of offense people were supposed to quit over, and he was certain that was their hope. But he didn't give up so easily. Politics were always a hazard of this occupation, and he had plenty of practice walking the fine line between doing his job and accommodating the special interest of the day. It was a harrowing path and, after twenty-eight years, he did it for only one reason alone: he loved his country.

It seemed corny—and was impossible to explain to his power-hungry coworkers—but it was true. Tom was one hundred percent Ohioan and he could trace his roots back to the American Revolution. His job took him all over the world, but he never found another place as beautiful, nor people he liked more than right here. Even a country as barely foreign as England made him feel out of sorts. To him, America was so much more than the revolving list of empty-headed, self-righteous politicians that he reported to and his job was to keep the CIA functioning no matter what half-assed schemes this year's government was pursuing.

If anything gave him an edge in this matter, it was Grey Stark. The man was far more capable than his dusty file would lead someone to believe. Tom knew him personally; he had worked with him in Berlin some years back. Actually, Tom reminded himself, he had worked *for* Grey, before his infamous fall from grace.

Back in the Cold War, Grey ran five different German spy networks all by himself. He had even placed three pigeons in the upper echelons of the German Communist Party. His information was so good, he knew what was happening in East Berlin before Mother Russia did. Grey knew how to pick good informants and he knew how to spin them over to our side. If it came to it, he could also kill them. The latter he was a little too good at, but Grey's past mistakes were a boon to Tom now.

While exiled in France, Grey had been a model agent: punctual, congenial, and quick to file his paperwork—all things he never bothered with back in Berlin. But Tom hadn't bothered to note this in his personnel file. Grey had been hung out to dry. After what he did, he was lucky they hadn't fed him to the Russians. The only way Grey would ever get out of France was to quit the Company. And maybe not even then.

So all Tom ever stuck in Grey's folder was his annual evaluation, which marked him "Satisfactory." Anyone who bothered to check it would predict Grey to be a washed-up alcoholic by now, his record protected by a supportive boss—a friend who was happy to cover up a few minor incidents for the sake of old times. Surely if the NSC suspected otherwise, they would have moved to incapacitate Grey as they had done to himself. Their oversight gave Tom the tool he needed to fight back.

He paged through the report one last time. He was well within his bounds to ignore the Commission's requests until he got confirmation from his own boss, the CIA's Deputy Director. He looked at his watch. It was closing in on seven and Tom's secretary would come in at nine o'clock. He picked up the phone and told her voicemail he needed a meeting with the Deputy Director as soon as possible. That bought him at least two hours. Next he called Operations and had them page Stark to the embassy for a video conference. It was a rather extreme way to communicate, especially as Grey was carrying a scrambled cell-phone, but a video feed was a much larger digital soup than an audio one, making it much harder for any potential eavesdroppers to decode their conversation. Besides, there was no rush. As long as he talked to Grey before the Deputy Director, he was under no obligation to pass on the Commission's instructions.

Or to even hint that those orders existed.

V

"*I* have three key pieces of information to share with you this afternoon," a man rasped in the darkness. "I'm going to work through them slowly so as not to lose anyone and I'd appreciate it if you'd let me finish before asking any questions. Chances are, if I'm not telling you something, it's because I don't know the answer."

There was a pause and then a slide projector clicked on, illuminating a ghoulish face that seemed to float above it. The face belonged to Henri Allanté, the Head of Analytics for France's external security division, the DGSE—the local equivalent to the CIA. Law barred the DGSE from operating directly in France, but it was common practice for them to offer their lab to the Directorate. After all, the DGSE had the best-equipped lab in France and maybe all of Europe. And, more importantly, they had Henri.

There was nothing in Henri's looks that would impress anyone. He had a squirrel's nest of hair, glasses so dirty they appeared to be frosted, and a tweed jacket that looked like the battlefield of some great moth war.

His attitude was nothing special, either. He was a clock-puncher for whom working late meant answering questions on the way out the door. If someone was lucky enough to catch him in his office, he'd put on his vulture's scowl and spend more time berating his inquisitor for stupidity than answering questions. Henri believed that every day and every person in it would turn out to be disappointing, if not outright irritating. But in spite of this attitude, he rose to the top of his field simply because he was good at his job.

His brilliant mind was uncanny in the way it sorted fact from theory, found the essential among the immaterial, and pontificated on biology, chemistry, and physics with the ease of a doctoral scholar. And he usually held his temper during a presentation, as long as everyone did what he was told and didn't interrupt him with useless questions.

Satisfied that this wasn't about to happen, Henri turned to his report, a typewritten document of no less than twenty pages which he had compiled since this morning's discovery. "Thanks to a match in the CIA's computer, we now know for sure that the device you discovered is a bomb. Unfortunately, the details of how the bomb works are either lost, or so extremely confidential that the CIA has chosen to lie about them being lost." Henri looked to Peerson for confirmation.

Grey looked as well, wondering why, if it was the CIA's files, the NSC was providing the information.

Peerson shuffled papers in his briefcase, either ignoring Henri or unaware he was being addressed. Sitting down had caused his neck to wad up into a pink life preserver, saving his head from the sea of flesh below.

Henri let himself be ignored for a few moments, then continued: "So until that information surfaces, I'm afraid I'll be doing a lot of extremely time-consuming and very likely redundant work. Let's start by reviewing the crime scene."

Henri clicked a button and the DSGE logo lit up the projection screen. The letters were made from curvy parallel lines that would have looked right at home on the back pocket of a pair of designer jeans. Only French intelligence, Grey thought, would be more concerned with style than legibility.

The faint smell of burning dust came off the projector, mixing with the sterile conditioned air of the conference room. Henri clicked again, replacing the logo with a slide of the bank's basement, taken this morning. He began to recite information that would fascinate any aspiring architect.

"The room is eight meters at its deepest point. Five and a half at its widest. The ceiling is generally four and a quarter meters tall, but duct work brings it down to as low as three in certain places…"

Grey rubbed the bridge of his nose, suppressing a yawn under the cover of his palm. Lack of sleep was catching up with him and Grey knew from experience that Henri would drag through every unnecessary detail before getting to the meat of his report. He looked around the room. It was oval in shape, split halfway up the wall and offset five feet, forming a counter on one end and a low cubby on the other. This kind of elegance wouldn't fly in America. Size was the determining factor there and a room that could fit twenty people was better than a room that could fit fifteen, period.

A large oval table filled the room. It had the appearance of solid walnut, but its thin veneer was chipped in several places, revealing cheap particle-board construction. Faison sat opposite Grey, scowling at the table and idly digging a bamboo-like finger into his nose. Peerson sat next to Faison, eyes riveted on Henri. He nodded enthusiastically at every word and made detailed notes on his yellow pad. The only other person in the room was Denis, sitting next to Henri, his face buried in a laptop computer. As Director of Operations for the French DST, this was his home turf; no doubt he had already been briefed and was only here to answer questions. Or deflect them.

Henri droned on about which quarry had produced the bank's stonework. The information was numbing and Henri's deep voice a lullaby. Grey flipped open his briefing folder, hoping to occupy his sluggish brain. It contained, almost verbatim, the information Henri was reciting. He flipped ahead. Words and pictures, but nothing engaging. Grey's mind wandered back to his briefing with Tom McGareth earlier this morning.

It had been odd from the start, his getting paged to go to the embassy. Tom wanted a video conference, which meant stopping at the pharmacy and shaving in the embassy's bathroom. Video calls were the latest luxury that government agencies spoiled themselves with, justifying their cost by claiming it saved on travel. And yet no one volunteered to cut their travel budget. Video transmission did, however, offer higher security. And it seemed to Grey there were a couple people right here in the room that Tom might want to keep a secret from.

It had been years since Grey had seen Tom and he was shocked by how much the man had aged. Grey had to remind himself that they were practically the same age, because the man on the screen could have easily passed as his father. Desk jobs did that to you, especially those that came with power.

"How's the frau?" Grey asked.

"She's with the kids in Munich."

"Again? Wasn't she just there six months ago?"

"Hasn't come back yet," Tom said.

"I'm sorry to hear that," Grey said, hoping he sounded sincere. He never knew what to say to news like that.

Katherine Gerburg—now Katherine McGareth—had been one of Grey's highest placed spies in Berlin during the Cold War, a secretary to the Council of Ministers with access to pretty much anything the government was doing. That is, until her cover was blown. Then they had to yank her out overnight.

Grey personally led the extraction. A small team crossed over to East Berlin and moved her to a safe apartment. They were doing a quick cut-and-dye job on her hair before sneaking her out to the countryside while Tom was on lookout in the street. Tom still smoked back then, and in the rush to put the operation together, made the mistake of bringing his own brand.

It was well after midnight when a couple of KGB dogs came upon him. Dogs were the lowest form of agent the KGB had: big, dumb and violent. Left to their own devices, they wandered around at night looking for trouble. As a deterrent, they were the best curfew Russia ever set.

One of the dogs noticed Tom smoking. They weren't looking for Katherine—American cigarettes drew big money on the black market those days. The dogs figured he would have a stash of them somewhere, and the situation turned ugly quick. Tom didn't dare signal Grey lest he give away the operation. It was sheer luck that Grey noticed when he did and by the time they had dealt with the dogs, Tom was in bad shape. Grey decided to send him along with Katherine to the countryside rather than risk sneaking a wounded man back across the border.

Katherine was impressed with what Tom did to protect her. She took on the role of head nurse and two months later, when Grey sent a team to extract them, they were already engaged. Tom took a job stateside and that was the last Grey heard of him until seven years ago, when he resurfaced as Grey's boss.

"Same old story," Tom said. "This job has never been easy on family. You know that as well as anyone."

"Not much to report yet," Grey said, changing the subject before Tom asked anything he didn't want to answer.

"Not much here, either. Henri sent over some photos and our lab thinks it's a chemical bomb. A senior clerk thought he recognized the design, but he can't find the file on it. You know how that goes."

Grey did. History will never know how many files the CIA has destroyed. Sometimes they did it to cover their mistakes, but mostly it was because the information was too hot to keep a record of. In this business, it wasn't a matter of if secrets were going to get stolen, but when.

"We'll poke around," Tom continued, "But I don't think we'll find anything. Unfortunately, that means it's possible the file was stolen, which means it's possible it was the blueprint for last night's bomb."

"That doesn't seem likely."

"No, it doesn't. We don't even know how much detail was in the file. It could have been anything from a single photo to the complete plans for its construction."

"Anything else?" Grey asked. What Tom had told him so far hardly justified a conference call. But what he said next did:

"We're not assigning any additional agents to the case."

"You're not?" Grey faltered. A case like this usually called for a dozen or more.

"You're our man in Paris," Tom said, adding "and I have complete confidence in you." It was as if Tom had forgotten *why* he was their man in Paris. "We'll be getting stiff competition from those NATO people. Seems they've sold this operation as a 'test case' to the French government, to convince them of the advantages of integrating their intel with the Commission's. How they got it all set up so fast is anyone's guess.

"It'll be a feather in their cap if they break this case first," Tom said, his underlying tone saying that what was good for the Commission would be bad for the CIA. Which just made it all the more surprising that Tom wasn't flooding France with agents. They must have clipped his wings somehow.

Tom told him that they were still pounding out the details of the CIA's role in the investigation and that he would get back in touch when he knew more. In the meantime, Grey was to launch his own investigation as if the NSC didn't exist.

Grey felt like a pawn in one of those irritating power games that happened when two intelligence organizations 'worked together.' The men at headquarters were like grand masters of chess, considering every move far into the future. Sure we were cooperating today, but it couldn't hurt if we got a little more of the credit than they did, or even if it looked like we pulled the whole operation off by ourselves. It was thinking like that which kept the agencies on guard, made them keep information from each other and hindered the investigation. As far as Grey was concerned, that sort of cooperation only played into the hands of the bad guys.

There was a time when Grey would have argued with Tom, but he needed this case. He doubted he would live long enough to see anything this big come through France again. He looked across the conference table over at Peerson, who nodded his head at everything Henri said and threw compliments to everyone in the room. Peerson might look more pomp than circumstance, but he would be one of the Commission's top agents. And he would have a plan.

The NSC's goal was simple: global domination of the intelligence community. They had enjoyed an auspicious start, and now had France in their sights. This promised to be an interesting case, but, as of yet, it wasn't. Not enough to offset the monotone of Henri's voice.

Without even realizing it, Grey fell asleep.

When Grey woke an hour later, Denis was still hard at work on his laptop, Faison was reshaping a paperclip and

Henri had progressed to the bomb itself. Peerson, the only newcomer to one of Henri's lectures, seemed at the end of his patience. He squirmed anxiously in his seat.

"All of the chemicals in the device are common," Henri explained. "The high-chlorine solution could be purchased from a hardware store or made by distilling household bleach. The copper bucket contained little more than salt and vinegar—"

"So what makes this a bomb?" Peerson interrupted. All eyes turned to Henri, who famously took any interruption as a chance to hone his invective tongue. But, to everyone's surprise, he smiled patiently. Grey wondered how deep the Commission had their hooks into France.

"Let me jump ahead," Henri said, advancing the slides rapidly—another unprecedented move. "We cut this metal plate out of one of the bottles. By all appearances, it's an electrode." Grey sat up: they were getting to the good stuff.

"With the naked eye," Henri continued, "It's just a piece of flat steel with a thin line scored down the center. But magnify it a hundred times and we see thousands of fine copper hairs rising off the surface. The hairs are uniform, mere nanometers in length. They'd be as difficult to manufacture as they would be to preserve; a foam peanut dropped from three inches would crack them off.

"And look at this," Henri blustered with rare excitement. "The central groove itself is anything but straight. It's curved, and the curves expand logarithmically, with the last one half the length of the entire plate."

"A particle accelerator," Faison blurted, reddening when everyone turned to look at him. Denis nodded approvingly and Peerson grasped his shoulder like a proud parent, feeding him a quiet compliment. Everyone was doing such a good job of pretending to get along, Grey half-expected them to join hands and break into song.

"That's exactly right," Henri said. "Unfortunately, we have no idea how it might work. There's no feed mechanism and sodium is, to say the least, an incredibly stable molecule."

"I don't understand," Grey said, his voice crusty from sleep.

"Neither do I. Most chemical bombs simply use electricity as the catalyst for the reaction. This seems tremendously complex if that's all they're after. The one thing I am certain of," Henri said, switching to the soft tone common to controversial statements, "is that this device is far too complicated to have been manufactured in Iran."

"Which suggests the involvement a third party," Peerson chimed in.

"That's one possibility," Henri responded politely.

"Who could this other party be?" Peerson pressed.

Henri shrugged.

"North Korea?" Peerson asked. As far as questions went, this was more of a statement.

"It's possible. You would need something along the lines of a microchip facility to build this and there are plenty of countries that have that. Russia, China. Maybe North Korea."

"But we have to think motive," Peerson said, circling his finger in the air like he was twirling a doughnut. "I'm assuming no country could build this device without knowing it was a bomb?"

"It is unlikely," Henri said, then chewed on it for a minute. "Basically impossible. Anyone who knew enough to make it would be able to discern what it did."

"And would therefore be a willful accomplice?"

"It would seem so."

Peerson liked this answer. He hunched over his yellow notepad and scribbled furiously. Grey still had unanswered questions:

"Why is Iran's involvement a foregone conclusion?" he asked.

"Mr. Stark. Have you been sitting there the whole time?" Henri wasn't letting him off the way he did Peerson.

"I must have come in late."

"Page thirteen," Henri sighed, "which we already detailed, describes how the dyes used in the prayer rug— the one found next to the bomb—are common to Iran and how the composition of the soil in the rug is consistent with samples that we've collected from Iran."

"So we know the rug was made in Iran. Does that make the bomb Iranian? For all we know, the rug was planted at the scene."

Henri's face soured with disdain. "I'll leave the more complicated theories to those more qualified," he said, not meaning a word of it. "Shall we press on? This last bit is by far the most intriguing—"

Henri advanced the slide, but Grey never saw it. Double doors swung open, bathing the room in light.

The silhouette of a woman stood in the doorway, bell-shaped hair atop an hour-glass sport jacket, and tight slacks painted on curves that a bullet would stop to admire. A woman like that didn't have to burst into a room to stop conversation.

A breathless policeman arrived behind her, looking apologetic. The woman surveyed the room until she found Grey.

"You son of a bitch—"

Denis was on his feet, moving quickly to intercept. "Please, Mrs. Stark, this is a classified meeting."

Leigh Stark stepped into the light of the projector. Her hair was raven-black, her eyebrows arched over a chiseled-thin face, which was twisted into a scowl that belonged on the roof of Notre Dame. Thin cracks in her forehead and at the corner of her black eyes hinted at an age that her body did not. She was French-born, but her temper betrayed Spanish blood. She stopped Denis with a look.

"The name is Ms. Fugate," Leigh said in a voice that forecasted snow. Henri slapped off the projector. Grey rose slowly, drawing Leigh's gaze.

"Something came up," he said, trying a disarming smile.

"My car is out front," she replied.

Grey shrugged. He gathered his briefing folder and walked to the door. Leigh motioned him ahead and followed tight on his heels.

VI

The afternoon sun blinded Grey as Leigh led him down the wide granite steps of the DST headquarters. Her blue Saab convertible was parked in the no parking zone at the base of the steps and her Police Nationale identification card was on the dash to ward off the meter maid. The card had expired three years ago, but cops got parking privileges for life. She also didn't have to worry about speeding tickets.

Grey was barely in his seat when Leigh gunned into the heavy afternoon traffic, slipping between two cars with only a few inches to spare. She sped down the road, dodging between lanes as if stitching a needle through the tightly knit traffic.

Grey was an uncomfortable passenger, especially when Leigh was driving. Her car was what she would call a classic—a swollen, mid-seventies sedan with bench seats the size of sofas. Grey, however, would just call it old, and he didn't put much stock in Leigh's sense of maintenance. The car's ride was soft—partly by design, but mostly because the shocks had worn out decades ago. The convertible top was down not, Grey suspected, because it was a nice day, but because it was still broken, as it had been since last winter.

It had never been Leigh's style to keep up with life's more routine issues. Bills went unpaid until utilities were cut off, her checks were no more likely to pay off than a lottery ticket, and she hadn't cooked at home since the first time the dishes got dirty. As for what condition the Saab's brakes were in, Grey would rather not wonder.

He looked out the side window and tried to relax. Tall buildings waltzed past like giant pieces of modern art. They were in La Defense, the financial district of Paris.

Far from the ancient world of carved stone and carriage-ways that Paris was renowned for, La Defense was modern France, with the same shining glass and steel found in any major city, though perhaps with a bit more flair. The men and women here didn't lounge in cafés, spin poetry, and paint bad watercolors. They dressed sharply, shaved daily, and dashed between buildings like ants late for a picnic. It was in La Defense that the gears of France's industry turned, and it was an economic power to rival England, Germany, and even America.

It was here, also, that Grey first met Leigh. She tried to arrest him for brandishing a weapon in public, then shot him when he pushed past her. It hadn't been the best moment in their relationship, but, unfortunately, it also wasn't their worst.

Over a decade had passed since that day and, by the looks of it, Leigh had weathered them better than Grey. What age took, she had replaced with style. Her black hair had thin streaks of red. The same red lined her full lips with the precision of a Renaissance painter. Her tan suit matched her mocha skin. Leigh's beauty was the second most deadly weapon in her handbag and, if anything, she looked better now than the first day he laid eyes on her.

The buildings scattered and the sun punched through; Grey wished he had sunglasses. Leigh donned hers, smiling at his discomfort. It was a wonder she didn't tie him to the hood. Grey chuckled, thinking about it. Leigh frowned, jerking around a corner and slapping him into the door.

"You taking us to court or to the morgue?" he asked.

"The next time you speak, it should be an apology and then a goodbye."

"I'm sorry. Goodbye." Grey mock-opened the door, but Leigh took a hard right and Grey had to grope for balance.

"After we're divorced." Leigh dropped a stack of papers on his lap. "You can start signing them now and they'll be ready when we get there."

Grey picked up the papers and pretended to browse them; he already knew them by heart. She was keeping the apartment, but it had been hers to start with. She didn't want any money and let him take whatever else he wanted. She even offered to buy what furniture he didn't have room for.

It seemed that the only thing she really wanted from him was his signature.

Grey stuffed the papers into a worn leather pouch sewn into the door. "We have plenty of time," he assured her.

Leigh took a sharp right, zigzagging on purpose, just to throw him around.

"Meaning what?" she spat.

"Meaning stop driving so fast. We're on our way to the courthouse. If we make it there alive, this will all be over soon enough." Grey's words warped in his throat as the car slid through a traffic circle, tires fluttering.

"There is no soon enough."

Grey made a fuss over adjusting his seatbelt. As he followed the shoulder strap back, he saw a black sedan scream out of the traffic circle behind them. It was a Mercedes, so new it didn't have plates yet. Its windows were tinted, the driver anonymous.

Grey stared at the sedan; he hadn't had a tail in nearly ten years. "There's someone following us," he said, adjusting the passenger-door mirror.

"You noticed that, did you?"

"You could have said something."

"I assumed it was one of yours. Someone to rush in with another last-minute excuse."

"Not mine," Grey said, watching the car in the mirror.

"If they're not here to save you, why aren't you signing the papers?"

"Because I haven't had a chance to read them."

"You've had a copy for months."

"I've been busy." The Mercedes switched lanes, sped up. It was making its move. "They're coming," he pointed out.

"It's all very scary," Leigh said, mocking him.

Grey gave her his most convincing look, but she just gave it back. He glanced in the mirror: the car was nearly on top of them. He reached for the papers. "Alright, I'll sign, but at least *try* to get away."

Leigh shook her head.

"Now!" he growled. His urgency hit a nerve and she accelerated from sheer reflex. She grimaced at Grey, suspicious. "I'll keep our distance. You sign."

Grey read the top page of the thick stack.

"Page three," Leigh prompted him, pulling a pen from her breast pocket. They locked eyes as he took it from her. Grey flipped to the third page and signed where it said, "Defendant." The title felt unfair.

"And on page nine."

Grey flipped forward and signed. It took him three tries; Leigh weaved through traffic with violent flicks of the steering wheel and the car's soft suspension rolled like a boat on the high seas.

"This guy is good," she said.

Grey looked in the mirror. "How do you know it's a guy?"

"On page fourteen," Leigh continued, "there are four places to initial." Grey did as he was told. "And then on the final page, you just sign and date and we're done."

Grey flipped to the final page. His pen stopped an inch from the paper. She deserves this divorce, he told himself. I've been a terrible husband. The pen touched the paper. Grey looked to Leigh for a reprieve. She was not smiling, not triumphant. She had the grim determination of a soldier doing what had to be done. And then she jerked forward.

"What the hell?" Leigh exclaimed. The Saab slid down the road, twisting to the left as the Mercedes locked onto the edge of its bumper. Leigh cranked the wheel to the right, compensating. The car straightened and Leigh downshifted hard, not wasting time on the clutch. The transmission crunched and the engine howled, but they pulled loose.

"This isn't a friend of yours," Leigh said, convinced.

"You noticed that, did you?" Grey replied. But before he could sneer, they jolted from another impact.

VII

"Right this way, please," Denis said, gesturing Dr. Peerson off the elevator and into the upstairs lobby of the Directorate's headquarters. The room was cavernous, its walls covered by tremendous sheets of rough-hewn black marble that were bolted up by giant stainless-steel wing nuts. It was so quiet that every footfall on the granite floor echoed overhead. Peerson thought he could hear himself breathing.

The room was empty save for an oval-shaped security desk against the far wall, raised such that the two uniformed guards seated behind it were eye-level. Denis presented his identification to the guards and placed his hand on a biometric pad. The guard slid the ID card into a reader and inspected the results on his computer.

"Bonjour, monsieur," he said.

"Bonjour, Anton," Denis replied. "Un visiteur. Le monsieur est anglais."

The guard nodded and produced a blank white badge, which Denis filled out. "If you would, please, sir," the guard said to Peerson in a heavy accent, gesturing toward the biometric pad. Peerson stepped up and put his hand on it, feeling a slight tingle. It was the most advanced reader available, recording everything from his handprint to his blood pressure.

Peerson had been unimpressed with the security downstairs, especially with Stark's wife barging into the conference room, but he could see now that they hadn't yet entered the part of the building that mattered. There would be no one bulling their way through the thick steel door beside the guard's desk—it looked like it could withstand a rocket launcher.

So the DST wasn't as clueless as they first appeared. Not surprising, but perhaps disappointing. As much as he intended to work with them where he could, he would be wise to think of them as an opponents. This investigation had to be handled in a very public way and the Directorate's track record suggested they would do everything they could to stifle information and downplay the importance of this morning's discovery.

He would need someone from their own staff on his side, a malcontent who was ready to push the boundaries of authority for the sake of personal gain. Almost on its own accord, his eye fell on Faison, who shadowed them like a younger brother. Peerson had read the man's file. They didn't get much more malcontent than him.

— — —

Faison stood back from the other two men, not entirely sure why he was there. It wasn't like Denis to include him in an investigation like this. It wasn't like Denis to notice he existed. Denis focused on his precious operatives, those glamorous men who worked in the field. He ignored the men who did the real work around here, the invaluable cogs at the heart of the machine. Men like himself, who once spent eighty-three straight hours hand-decrypting the emails of a suspected hijacker, who dug through fifteen-thousand fabric samples to locate a murderer's tailor from a few threads that were snagged on a broken mirror.

It was possible Denis was finally amending past negligence, but unlikely. And it was too late for that, anyway. More likely, Faison was just here to baby-sit this NATO man. That was exactly how little Denis thought of him.

Still, he thought, there might be an opportunity here. He needed to stay in the middle of this investigation and this flaccid doctor didn't seem the sort to get stuck on the sideline. He'd have to keep an open mind about it.

That decided, Faison occupied himself by estimating how many kilos of marble were hanging on the wall. He had done this before, but forgotten to account for the holes used to secure them. It was a pleasant enough way to pass the time.

The guard handed Peerson a white plastic badge with the DST logo across the top. His name was written on a sticker, along with a warning that, by the end of the day, the sticker would turn red and invalidate the badge. Orange letters read, "Only with escort." He hadn't expected to get the run of the place, but this was downright insulting. Cooperation, it seemed, wasn't high on Denis's list either.

"So I'll get a new badge everyday?" Peerson asked, trying to sound pleasant in face of such obvious adversity.

"For security reasons, you'll have to check in every time you enter the building," Denis replied. "As you requested, Faison here will be your permanent contact."

"That wasn't exactly what I meant."

"Just be sure you have his extension, because they won't look it up for you."

Peerson gave him a cheerful smile—no point in fighting the small battles—and clipped the badge on his jacket.

Faison stepped forward and identified himself, then the steel door slid smoothly to the side. The three men stepped into a short hallway with walls of frosted glass. No doubt the walls hid a battery of detectors, from thermal imagers to backscatter devices that could see right through their clothing. At the moment, Peerson wasn't armed. He wondered if they would care if he was.

The steel door closed behind them, and a few moments later one in the opposite wall opened, leading to a small, unassuming room. A bay window was cut into the far wall and Peerson strolled over to take a peek. He grabbed at the wall as vertigo gripped him.

Three stories below, a stadium-sized room buzzed with a level of activity that would rival Wall Street. The room was packed with maybe three hundred people, doing everything from making phone calls to manning terminals. Groups gathered in several spots, pouring over reports or engaging in heated arguments. Two walls were lined with clocks and televisions that broadcasted news from all over the planet. The people on the floor had headsets, and could dial into anything that caught their interest.

The far wall was covered by an IMAX-size projection of France that dominated the room like the false idol of a science fiction movie. Orange lines outlined the individual counties and major French cities were mapped out down the side. Color-coded dots and numbers flashed over the map in a pandemonium of data; to understand them all, one would need a key the size of the Bible.

Among the world's intelligence agencies, the French Directorate might come in a leisurely fifth in terms of size, but they certainly spent their money in a dramatic fashion. It would take dozens of projectors to run a wall like that and this one room alone would have cost tens of millions. It cost enough, Peerson thought, to show it off by putting a window in the front entrance.

"That's the main control room," Denis said unnecessarily. "We'll take a proper tour some other day." He led Peerson down a hallway lined with offices. "If you don't mind my asking," he said, "how did you manage to get to France so quickly?"

"What do you mean?"

"I got word you were at the airport not an hour after I first learned about the bomb."

"I was in London and took a helicopter over. We have an arrangement to be notified immediately of incidents like this."

"I have such an arrangement with MI6 and the CIA," Denis said, emphasizing that Peerson was neither.

"And we have an arrangement with them."

"I had yet to contact either of them when I heard from you."

"Then you were errant in your duties and that's why I arrived first."

Denis grimaced. He wasn't going to get any straight answer from this man. An hour-long flight from London was pushing the limits of credibility. It was more likely that Peerson was already in the country. Hell, he probably didn't even ride in the helicopter, but just met it at the landing pad. But Peerson would never admit as much. For him to be operating in France without declaring himself broke more treaties that Denis could count. But agencies did that to each other all the time and, if Peerson were to come clean, Denis would forgive him out of custom.

What bothered Denis was how quickly Peerson knew about the bomb. The leak wasn't necessarily inside the DST—there were plenty of other departments in the know—but it might be, and that meant Denis would have to play his cards close to his chest.

Furthermore, he was alarmed that the Commission was taking such an interest in this; in the past they'd shown no notice whatsoever of France's internal affairs. He was also worried they knew more about the bomb than they were letting on.

As they turned a corner, Denis spun on his heel and asked, "Is it a coincidence that your forte is Iran?"

Peerson had to stop quickly to prevent his bulk from smashing into Denis.

Denis had hoped that by throwing Peerson off balance, he would also throw him off guard and make him betray something he didn't mean to—in his expression, if not in his words. But Faison bumped Peerson from behind, spoiling the moment. Faison mumbled an apology, which Peerson accepted loudly before turning back to Denis. "You're well informed."

"On some things." Denis said, walking again. "How could the Commission know Iran was involved before seeing the evidence?"

"It was more of what you'd call an educated guess. We'd gotten information that Iran was up to something. It seemed a safe bet this was it."

It was a reasonable answer, Denis admitted. He stopped at a small door with the brass number '168b' tacked on it. He smiled in anticipation, opened the door and motioned Peerson inside. He had to motion again to Faison, who was reluctant to enter.

It was a small office, to say the least. A metal desk—the type popular in the fifties—bisected the room and easily consumed a third of its floor space. A black coffee mug sat on the desk, holding two cheap ballpoint pens. A Michelin map of France was pinned to the lemon-yellow walls. The desk chair looked like it had been abandoned by retreating Germans.

Denis didn't enter. "This office is yours. I've been ordered to give you my complete cooperation, and you may depend on it." He turned to leave.

"Speaking of cooperation," Peerson said. "We seem to have lost our CIA representative."

"Yes." Denis looked around as if Grey might be hidden behind the door or under the desk. "I take it you don't know Mr. Stark very well, then? He's a bit of a loner, seems to work better that way. You'll get used to it."

Peerson opened his mouth, but Denis cut him off. "Stark is not my agent, but Lt. Faison will be assigned to this full time. You will find him very reliable."

"What about operators?"

"For what?" Denis countered.

"There is always a need."

Denis frowned. The last thing he wanted was to give Peerson his own agents. But it was too early to dig in his heels. Better to feed out the line and see what Peerson did with it. "I'll assign you Jerard Venerdi as well. He's very talented, the youngest captain in the history of the Directorate. I'll make more agents available as the need arises."

That works, Denis thought. Jerard was another way he could keep track of Peerson and besides, working on an international task force would pad out his résumé.

Faison rankled visibly at Jerard's name, dreading the thought of working side-by-side with Denis's pet. But Denis didn't really care what Faison thought. After a certain age, failure becomes self-evident, and—in Denis's mind—Faison's low rank said it all.

"Anything else," Denis asked. Peerson shrugged and Denis shut the door before another word could be spoken.

Peerson looked about the room, almost surprised to discover Faison was still standing there. The man had an uncanny knack of blending into the walls. He sighed, suddenly tired. "Listen," he said, pulling several thick folders from his briefcase, "These are the files they gave me back in London. I haven't had a chance to get into them, so we might as well divide them up and see if there's anything interesting." Peerson casually peeled off the top of the stack and held it out.

Faison took the proffered files, happy for the excuse to leave. Peerson watched him struggle with the door and skulk down the hallway. That one, he thought, was going to be a challenge.

As for Denis, Peerson thought, the French are notoriously conservative. He could count on the Directorate to wait for overwhelming evidence before they took any action at all. He could work around that, but it was nothing to look forward to. He had hoped Grey Stark, with his reputation for action, would be of some assistance. But Stark had vanished like he had the gift of foresight.

With some effort, Peerson squeezed around the desk and dropped into the creaky chair. He wondered if this was really an office at all, or if they had gone so far as to fix up a closet for him. At least he knew where he stood with Denis.

Peerson leaned back in his chair—feeling his work done for the moment—and took a nap.

VIII

*L*eigh pressed the gas pedal so hard that her toes tingled, trying to squeeze the last bit of horsepower from the old Saab's engine. But her car was hopelessly outclassed and the dark Mercedes rammed them at its leisure, bashing the rear bumper to tinfoil.

Since there was no chance of outrunning their assailant, Leigh could only hope for a more artful escape. Up on the right, she saw her chance: a thin alley joined the road at a sharp angle—a fork in the road for cars traveling in the other direction.

The Mercedes dropped back half a block, then accelerated to strike them again. The Saab reached the alley. Leigh cranked the steering wheel hard, yanking the handbrake to lock the rear wheels. The car spun, pressing her against the door and choking Grey on his seatbelt. When they were facing the alley, she straightened the wheel and stabbed the accelerator. The Saab, still in third gear, bucked and stalled out. They slid to a halt.

The Mercedes roared, targeting the soft metal of the passenger's door and doubling its speed. Grey unbuckled, slipping his hand into his coat and pulling out a small Berretta automatic. The gun's barrel was so short that it looked like he had dipped his thumb in black paint.

Leigh turned the key, the starter whined but the engine wouldn't catch. Grey jerked the barrel back, loading a nine-millimeter bullet into the chamber—ridiculously large for such a small gun. He aimed at the approaching Mercedes, trying to draw a bead on the driver. Sunlight reflected off the dark windshield, obscuring everything inside. The sedan was coming fast and nothing was going to stop it. Grey slipped his finger off the trigger and braced for impact.

The Saab sputtered to life, jerking forward as Leigh shoved the gearshift into first. The Mercedes smashed into the rear fender, missing the door by inches. It drove the Saab sideways, popping it onto the sidewalk and into a lamppost, which wilted over them.

This close, Grey could see their assailant's shadow through their windshield. He raised his gun, but the Mercedes retreated, its reverse gear whirring. Someone slapped Grey's back.

"Get off me!" Leigh screamed. Grey had been thrown into the driver's seat and she was pinned under him. He rolled back to his seat and Leigh jammed down on the gearshift. It ground fiercely, but didn't engage.

The Mercedes stopped fifty yards back, tilted forward, and spun its tires. It launched at them, the round hood ornament bearing down like the crosshairs of a rifle. Leigh got the Saab into gear, but the car didn't move—it only shuddered. The rear fender was bent into the tire, holding it fast.

Grey leveled the Beretta, guessing where the driver's head was behind the dark glass. He squeezed off three shots. The gun recoiled in his hand and the shots went wide. The best one punctured the hood, the other two didn't even hit the car.

The Mercedes descended, the silver teeth of its front grill coming right at him. Grey raised his hand, as if to hold the car back. Just as he felt the hood slap against his palm, the Mercedes slipped off to his right—the Saab had wrenched free, its engine screaming.

The Mercedes clipped the back of the Saab, tearing off the rear bumper. The Saab shot into a narrow alley, bouncing over cobblestones as it rose up a steep hill.

Grey leaned over, trying to find their assailant in the side mirror. With a crunch, the mirror was gone and a stone wall hurled by an inch from his face. He recoiled into his seat. They were in an old section of Paris, the alley barely wide enough for two horses to pass. Leigh squeezed the Saab through with only inches to spare.

Thick blue smoke rose off the Saab's rear tire. Grey got on his knees and leaned over the back. The bent fender was shredding the tire.

He stood up to get a better look, but was yanked down by his belt. A stone archway passed low overhead. Grey decided to stay inside the car. He looked at Leigh, who was intent on the road.

"Thanks."

"How bad is it?" She meant the tire.

"Bad," Grey replied. Leigh shrugged.

Behind them, the Mercedes screeched through the archway. It was wider than the Saab and scraped on both sides, throwing off sparks like a sword on a grindstone. The anonymous driver held steady and the car came through with only superficial damage. And it was gaining on them.

The road ahead forked. Leigh didn't know this area; she turned to the right, downhill. The car shot off a tall step, soaring into the air and killing any delusions that they were still on a road. Every fifteen feet there was another step and the car sea-sawed downhill. Grey grabbed the bottom of his seat to keep from being thrown out, but it was breaking loose from the floorboard.

The Mercedes stayed on their tail, floating with the ease of a pianist running his hand down a keyboard.

The alley snaked downward. Leigh wasn't driving anymore; the car just ricocheted between buildings like a pinball heading to the gutter. They tumbled through a shopping district, passing small boutiques that through some miracle weren't open. Chunks of the Saab flew off with every impact, shattering store windows as they passed. The hood was pounded into the shape of an arrowhead. The car was dissolving.

Glimpses of salvation appeared over the bouncing hood: the stairway ended in a 'T,' meeting a small level road. The road was barely one lane; it was going to take a perfect turn.

"Hold on," Leigh said, pulling the wheel to the right and working the parking brake. The car started to turn, but the alley was too tight: it hit a wall and was knocked back straight. Leigh tried turning in the other direction and the tattered rear tire blew, its rim folding under the car. The axel snapped in half and a thick metal shaft littered onto the road. The car struck the jutting corner of a jewelry shop and was knocked into a spin. It skated off the final step and rolled up onto its side.

Outside Grey's window, the road was sliding by. He grabbed Leigh's headrest, pulling himself away from the rasping pavement.

The Saab slid across the road and drove into the stone wall on the other side, spilling Grey onto the pavement. The car pivoted, swinging around to swat him against the wall. He tucked into a ball and braced himself. The trunk pressed into his back, sweeping him along the road. The top of the windshield hit the wall and the car stopped. He was sand-wiched in, with just enough room to stand.

Grey shot to his feet, drawing a long slender knife from his boot, its blade cross-hatched from meticulous sharpening. Leigh hung from her seatbelt, conscious but disoriented. He wrapped his arm around her and cut her loose. She hugged his chest and he lowered her to the ground, letting go immediately. He felt unsteady holding her that close, and he didn't like it.

The two of them stood in the narrow gap between the car and the wall, the only noise was the squeak of a wheel as it spun in the air. The wheel turned slower and slower without seeming to stop.

"What do you think?" Grey whispered.

"Let's go," Leigh replied. She rotated her spine, stretching. Grey slipped the knife back into his boot and drew his gun.

"You'd better let me," Leigh said, reaching for the Berretta. Grey jerked it away, giving her a snarl. Her eyes narrowed to angry slits.

Grey put his foot on the passenger's seat and climbed up the inside of the car. He got under the driver's door—now their roof—and pushed up with his shoulder. The hinges were broken and the whole door rolled off, clanging to the street.

Grey listened for any sign of their assailant. He heard nothing. He raised his gun, then peered over the door sill. The Mercedes was perched on the final step of the alley, aimed right at him. Its engine roared and its wheels smoked. It rocketed off the step, hurling forward.

"Duck," was all Grey managed, letting go and tumbling down into the car. Leigh hopped into the back seat just as the Mercedes struck with a deafening clang. The Saab's windshield folded and the car flattened against the wall.

Grey hung in the air, suspended by his right hand, which was pinned to the wall by the headrest. His shoulder was twisted like a rope, bulging where the joint had come out of its socket. He tried to pull his hand free, but it didn't budge.

He grabbed the door sill with his good arm, taking his weight, and rolled his legs up. He set a foot next to his wrist and pushed. The joint in his shoulder stretched and pain rippled through his body. He pulled harder and his hand popped loose. Unsupported, he tumbled down through the car, landing on the passenger door.

Grey lay on his back, staring up through the open doorway at the clear blue sky. The tendons in his shoulder contracted and his arm pulled back into its socket with the deliberate pace of a rubber toy in winter. He tried his hand, it barely moved.

"Who the hell is that guy?" he asked.

"Someone from your charming past?" Leigh's face appeared between the two head rests; she was trapped in the back seat.

Grey shook his head, "No. Not in France. Those things don't happen here."

The Mercedes slammed into the car, pounding a bumper-shaped dent in the floor. White veins appeared in the metal: it was tearing apart. Leigh was knocked into the stone wall, barely getting her hands up to protect her head. They heard a whine as the Mercedes reversed, backing up for another run.

"It's happening now," she said.

"Enough of this." Grey grabbed the gun in his left hand; the hand was uncoordinated, and it took concentration just to get his finger on the trigger. Leigh was dumfounded:

"You can't be serious," she said.

"I got it," Grey replied.

"T'es une putain de tete de mule…"

Grey ignored her, struggling up to the open doorway. The unsteady car rocked under his weight. He perched on the driver's seat, braced his feet on the steering wheel, and popped his head up. The Mercedes bore down at him. He fired at the dark window, his untrained hand trembling. The bullet bounced off the front bumper.

He steadied the gun on the door sill and fired again, missing the car completely. The Mercedes slammed into them, flipping the Saab onto its hood. Leigh was scooped up by the back seat and Grey was tossed halfway out the open doorway. The gun flew from his hand and clattered onto the Mercedes' hood.

The Mercedes held the other car's weight for a moment, then its front tires blew and it sunk to the ground. The Saab angled down on top of it.

Hooking his foot through the steering wheel, Grey stretched his whole body out from the car, reaching for his gun. The sticky smell of antifreeze filled his nose as the Mercedes' engine sputtered out.

The driver's door of the Mercedes flew open and a man in a white turban leapt out, dashing behind the car. Grey got his finger on the gun's trigger and fired. The bullet struck asphalt. He fired again, with no better result. His hand was shaking so much he couldn't even see the gun's sights.

A long-barreled revolver rose from the far side of the Mercedes. It fired blindly and Grey heard the bullet whip past his ear. He coiled his legs up, pulling back into the Saab like an eel into its hole. A second bullet ripped through his hair as he dropped behind the doorway. The car leaned away from the wall now, making it easier to move inside. Leigh leaned up from the back seat.

"What are you doing?" she demanded.

"He's trying to kill us."

"So why don't you shoot him?"

"You think this is easy?

"Give me the gun." Leigh reached for it, but just then two bullets plunked against the bottom of the car. She threw herself back as a third one ripped through the metal not an inch from her thigh.

Grey was bothered by the sound of the other gun: It wasn't the clean pop of a modern weapon, but the dirty blat of a revolution-era musket. There was something to that, but he would have to figure it out later. He popped up through the doorway and fired two more shots, hitting nothing. The Beretta's barrel jutted forward; the gun was empty.

A bullet thumped into the underside of the car, punching a cone-shaped dent right where Grey's heart was. He lost his footing and slipped, catching himself on the driver's seat but dropping the gun.

Grey heard the hollow click of a firing pin, followed by the tinkle of empty cartridges on the pavement—their opponent was reloading. Grey dropped to the ground and looked for his gun. He found it in Leigh's hand. He motioned for it, but she held out her empty hand.

"Clip," she said.

Grey wanted to argue, but couldn't waste the time. He drew the spare clip from his holster and tossed it to her. She caught it and released the old one, which clattered to the ground. She drove the new clip into the handle and the barrel snapped into place, loading the first round. Grey winced at the rough treatment of his equipment. She motioned him to the top of the car as she crawled over the trunk to the back.

On Leigh's cue, Grey poked his head up. Shots rang out from behind the Mercedes' trunk, but he dropped back down as quickly as he had gone up. While he distracted the gunman, Leigh stepped out from the side of the Saab, holding the gun straight in front of her like a fencer's saber. She marched forward, firing. Her bullets punched a neat row of welts, boring into the trunk but lacking the power to go all the way through; they ricocheted inside like swarming bees.

Leigh's target popped up: a thick-bearded Arab, wide-eyed and bewildered by this new assault. Leigh fired her remaining two rounds. She was fifteen feet away, but her aim was so tight that the bullets only left one hole. It would have been a deadly shot if not for the man's turban which, in the split second before she fired, Leigh had mistaken for his head. The bullets passed through the cloth and the man lived.

The Beretta was empty but Leigh pressed it to the Arab's forehead, hoping he wouldn't notice. Their eyes locked, hers black on black, his impenetrable brown. Leigh motioned for him to stand. He rose slowly, leaving the revolver on the ground.

He was several inches shorter than Leigh, who wasn't that tall herself. His skin was dark except his forehead, which had a large pink scar. His beard added years, but Leigh could see he was young. Very young.

The man noticed the open breach of Leigh's gun. He lunged for his revolver, scooping it up. Grey came up behind him, knife in hand. The Arab rolled backwards and away—coming to his feet in a full sprint—and took off down the road. Leigh raised the pistol before remembering it was empty.

"Clip!" she yelled.

"That's it," Grey replied.

"What do you mean, that's it?"

"I don't have another clip."

The Arab was almost out of range. Leigh turned to Grey, eyes tight. "You only carry one clip?"

Grey didn't reply. He watched the Arab turn a corner and disappear.

"Who the hell only carries one clip?" Leigh asked.

"It helps if you only fire one bullet at a time."

Leigh looked at the gun. It was so small the clip stuck out from the polymer handgrip. "Tu te fous de moi? Only seven bullets and it can't even punch through sheet metal."

"That happens to be a Berretta Tomcat. Extremely compact."

"Compact is the first thing I look for in a gun. Do you keep a derringer in your garter?"

"Some of us have to be discrete," Grey said. "I can't just hang a cannon from my hip the way you cops do."

"Former cop," Leigh said, tossing the gun at him. Grey tried to catch it, but it bounced out of his uncoordinated left hand, scraping across the pavement. Leigh crossed her arms and tilted her head back, her favorite stance for an argument.

Distant sirens broke the mood. A group of kids gathered on the walkway—the vanguard of what would quickly become a crowd.

"We'd better get out of here," Grey said.

"We're just going to leave the crime scene?"

"Yes," Grey said, unable to think of an explanation that she would accept. "I have people who will take care of this."

"That must be nice."

Grey looked at the two cars piled up, smoke rising in the air and fluids pouring onto the road. "Stay if you like," he said.

A retort popped to Leigh's mind, but she let it go. She didn't want to stay either. She leaned into what was left of her car, retrieving her handbag and the divorce papers. She looked at Grey and said, "There's a hole in your hair," then strolled down the road.

Grey collected his gun off the pavement and rubbed his thumb over a wide scratch. He noticed a piece of paper on the Mercedes' front seat. He unfolded it and saw his own face: a photocopy of his passport. One of them, anyway. Below the photo was scribbled *60 Jardin de Valmy*—the address of the Directorate's headquarters. He flipped the paper over; there was nothing else.

Grey stuck the paper in his pocket and hustled after

Leigh. He had no idea what this was all about, but it was certainly bigger than some homemade bomb in a run-down bank in the Seventh Arrondissement. And he wasn't even sure where to start looking.

BOOK TWO

1

The Hotel Ségur is perhaps the most luxurious hotel in Paris's Right Bank. It rises several stories above the neighboring buildings and, for those who can afford it, offers west-facing suites with an entire wall of glass. These rooms provide a view that would make a postcard blush: the rooftops of old Paris, framed by the wide curving Seine River, and capped with the sparking Eiffel Tower. By coincidence, these windows also face the Seventh Arrondissement and, with a decent pair of binoculars, one could see the small bank so recently thrown into the spotlight when a bomb was discovered inside.

Such binoculars were provided complimentary with each suite, and the sole occupant of one suite had used his a number of times for this very purpose. His name was Richard Charles Fiddich.

The activity at the bank ceased hours ago and Richard had shifted to matters of appearance. He was in the bathroom, leaning over a convex mirror and carefully inspecting his thick beard—magnified to the size of a porcupine's quills.

His beard was blond and straight as raw silk, but he was hunting down the few stubborn hairs that rebuffed the touch of chemicals, remaining black and tightly curled. Convinced that he had removed all offenders, Richard set down his tweezers and looked at himself in the mirror over the sink.

Every hair in Richard's head was so shockingly blond that it seemed he would glow in the dark. It was a harsh contrast to his skin that, in spite of a heavy chemical peel, was still the dark hue of cured leather. Even more unsettling were his eyes, iridescent blue from contacts thick enough to blot out the dark brown underneath.

Richard smiled and enjoyed seeing himself smile. His new look brought him a lot of pleasure; he could spend the whole day at the mirror without the slightest decline in ardor. But just then the TV in the front room caught his attention. The large plasma screen was tuned to Globecast, a twenty-four hour news channel out of Great Britain. The report he had been waiting for was beginning.

"Early this morning, a Paris security guard thwarted a bombing attempt at the cost of his life," a well-sunned newsman said with enthusiasm. A graphic over his shoulder depicted a cartoon explosion with dollar-sign shrapnel. The man took an officious tone and began his report:

"The Banque de l'Orange is a quiet bank in a quiet neighborhood. But this morning, it drew the world's focus when police uncovered a bomb hidden in the basement. An unidentified man was seconds from exploding the device when he was discovered by the bank's security guards. The perpetrator escaped after a brief firefight which left one security guard dead. Police are still unclear what the motivation behind the attack is. The French DST has been called in to assist on the case and Director Denis Rousseau briefed reporters personally this afternoon."

Richard moved into the front room and gave the TV his full attention. Denis was framed by two stout policemen who made him look smaller than he already was. But he looked relaxed, ready to smile if only the situation weren't so serious. He spoke directly at one reporter, answering his question.

"No, I can't say we're ruling terrorism out at this time. Of course, we're also not ruling out greed." A polite laugh filled the room. He pointed into the audience, "Yes?"

"What of the American assertion of Iranian involvement?"

The question caught Denis off guard. Flashbulbs popped, catching his sour look. He found his smile again, dismissing the question: "I haven't heard anything about that," he said, pointing to someone else. The TV cut back to the anchorman.

"While the DST were hesitant to acknowledge terrorism as a motive, the Americans are convinced it could be nothing but. The President himself addressed the subject during a scheduled speech in America's Midwest."

The President stood at a podium in front of a barn-sized flag. His audience sat in a grassy field decorated with tractors. He was a young president—better known for his charisma than his intellect—but nonetheless a gifted speaker. He wore a powersuit, an outfit more befitting a CEO than a politician, and had a stern look on his face.

"This is not just a man who died in the line of his duties," he said, "but the latest victim in our long and difficult war on terror. And he's a hero, too. A man who gave freely his life to save so many others. As I speak to you here, we are working with our colleagues in France. We have good leads, and we're following them. When we find the culprits, we will bring them to justice."

The anchorman came back: "And while the American President stopped short of naming suspects, it's no secret that this morning they re-deployed the 3rd Infantry and the 1st Armored Divisions from Baghdad to an American base outside of Basra, putting them six miles from the Iraq-Iran border. Also, in the port of Umm Qasr, a number of American naval ships are making preparations to sail, including the flagship aircraft carrier, *The USS Eisenhower*.

"The United States traditionally uses air power at the start of any conflict, but the Eisenhower, which carries seventy-five fighter planes, hasn't been called up since the liberation of Kuwait in the early nineties. With us today is retired British General John Hackett, who will tell us how this ship could be significant if the Americans are indeed planning to invade Iran."

A thick man with a thicker mustache explained, in great detail, how he would use an aircraft carrier against Iran should anyone better armed than a television reporter ask him to. Richard returned to his grooming.

So the French weren't ruling out terrorism yet, Richard sneered. What kind of ignorance was that? There was plenty of evidence. Were they expecting a letter of confession?

Richard squeezed gel from a metal tube and worked it into his hair. He shouldn't worry over what the French thought, his part of the operation was over. Tomorrow he would get his money and be set for life, free to do as he pleased.

He glanced at the TV again. Globecast had covered the bomb continuously since early this afternoon, despite having nothing new to add to their initial story. They just kept rotating through different reporters and experts, hoping to make the story feel fresh. The next reporter up was a starved woman whose chemical-blonde hair puffed up like a giant marshmallow. She stared at the teleprompter and prattled about foreign affairs, not understanding a word of it. Her real assets started below the neckline: plump golden breasts, exposed through the open collar of her Oxford button-down. This woman was used for reporting the news the way candy was used to coat medicine.

Richard stared at the woman, at her hair, her makeup, her breasts. Of all the wonders the West had to offer, women were by far the most enticing. And how he ached to get his hands on a creature like that!

Ever since his arrival in France, he had been stunned by the behavior of the women. Just by walking around, he was exposed to the most carnal displays of women attacking men with frantic, unquenchable lust. These women required only the most minimal commitment, called dating, before they would surrender their body. More than once, he had seen them settle for the price of a few drinks.

Richard, however, didn't have much luck, at least not at first. While some foreigners were considered exotic, he was looked down upon. Women didn't notice him, and his attempts at conversation were immediately shot down. He'd even suffered the humiliation of having his drinks sent back.

Richard didn't give up. Instead, he moved to the back of the bar and quietly watched. From there, he learned that Western women were lured in by the simple powers of wealth and good looks. So he set out to acquire both.

He honed his French. He created his New Zealand ancestry, a far more alluring heritage than his own, with the added benefit of being obscure and therefore covering any slip-ups he made. And he prepared a battery of anecdotes—his pick-up lines, as they said. He took his best war stories and recast them for the Western ear as hunting tales, while promoting himself to protagonist.

Richard had always been a good storyteller; he was too thin to get by on muscle, and the world he grew up in was brutal. He earned his keep by being entertaining. And he was pleased to learn that, here in the West, a quick wit was far more valued than a strong arm. And, now that he knew the rules to the game, women were starting to notice him. He felt their stares, their lust, where before there was only scorn.

Richard's transformation was almost complete: he didn't just look like a Westerner, he had become the gentleman that every Western man dreamed of being. And his fortune was secure as well; in just a few days, he'd be getting his payoff—riches that would embarrass a sheik. But it was hard to be patient, Richard thought, transfixed by the television. Women like that made him hungry.

He was jarred from his thoughts by a knock on the door; he wasn't expecting anyone. He switched off the TV and walked to the bureau in the bedroom. He fingered the top drawer, which held a number of handguns, and waited. Another knock came, harder and faster.

"One moment," he called out. He left the bureau unopened, checked his face in the mirror one last time, and walked to the front door, pulling on a white jacket that matched his pants. He swung the door open without checking the peephole and was shocked to see Amin standing there.

There were a number of ways that this afternoon's events could have turned out, and none of them involved Amin coming to his door. But here he was, his clothing stained and his face glistening with oily sweat. The man would have looked entirely at home in a dusty Tehran marketplace, but in Paris he stood out like a fly in the buttermilk; anyone could have followed him here. Richard glared at Amin, hating him for his incompetence, and for jeopardizing the cover he had worked so hard to create—a cover he intended to keep a lot longer than this operation. But he calmed himself when he saw the wild look in the Arab's eyes; the man's hands were shaking.

"Come in, brother," Richard said, wrapping his arm across Amin's back, pulling him into the room.

The stranger's hands sent a chill down Amin's back. He knew that his brother stood before him, but his eyes found nothing familiar. Even the voice, heavy with foreign accent, bore no trace of Thoaab'a el Fassid. Amin averted his eyes from the aberration and gave his report.

"I have failed," he said. "The saboteur lives." The stranger nodded, then looked at his forehead.

"You've been shot," he said, reaching out with an unnaturally pale hand. Amin backed away, fingering the hole in his turban. Red coated his finger. He had forgotten about the wound.

"There was a woman with him," Amin said. "She is skilled, much more so than he."

"Come," the stranger gestured. "Sit."

"It is not bad," Amin protested, but he allowed himself to be pulled into a chair. The blond man took off his coat and walked behind him, unwrapping his turban. Amin touched the old scar on his forehead, self-conscious.

Another mess to clean up, Richard thought. Like the van this morning; the idiot had left it in hourly parking at the *airport*, the one place where an abandoned van would draw attention. But no great matter. He had fixed that and he would fix this, too. But his first priority was to get his brother under control. Amin was a man of extreme discipline, but when shaken up, he became unpredictable and dangerous.

The red patch in the turban widened as he unwound it, but when the last wrap came off, it wasn't the nick on his forehead that made Richard's blood run cold. It was the giant scar that covered the entire left side of Amin's head, its baby-pink flesh wrinkled unnaturally.

He had seen the scar many times, but it had been years. Amin wore his turban religiously, covering all but the part he couldn't, the circle that crept down to his forehead. Fully exposed, as it was now, his brother's mutilated head was sickening. Worse still, it reminded Richard of the day it had happened. They were so young then; the scar on the surface was nothing compared to those inside.

Richard buried those thoughts. "It's not bad," he heard himself say, testing the small bullet wound with his finger. He fetched a bottle of peroxide and a stack of white towels from the bathroom. He cleared his throat and dug out his old voice, the one he had before all the lessons. That was the voice his brother knew. "We'll fix it up in no time. Now tell me what happened. Where's the American?"

"I lost them, Thoaab'a. And the car is destroyed."

Richard rankled at the sound of his old name, but he was careful not to show it. Amin trusted him because of the blood they shared, and that trust was essential to Richard's next move, whatever it was going to be.

"Never mind the car," Richard said. "I am glad you're all right." He wrapped a towel around Amin's shoulders and pulled it tight as a hug. "I'll call our brothers tonight; they'll know what to do. But let us take a moment for your injuries."

The towel was warm and comfortable, and Amin was tired. The stranger was out of sight and his brother's soothing voice was nearby. Thoaab'a was the older, the smarter and the wiser. Thoaab'a had cared for him since their parents had died. For fifteen years, Thoaab'a had led them down the path of vengeance. Today vengeance had been thwarted, but Allah had not abandoned them.

Amin would get the man who sabotaged the bomb, who robbed him of his martyrdom—delayed it, he corrected himself. As Thoaab'a had said this morning, this was just a small setback. Il Siyâh had promised another bomb and another chance. But before they could send it, he must eliminate the saboteur Grey Stark. And the woman who protected him.

His brother was right: he must be patient. He must rest and heal, and wait for the new orders. He knew about the woman now, and there would be no surprises next time.

And next time he wouldn't fail.

II

*D*enis tapped two red capsules onto his desk, capped the bottle and dropped it into his desk drawer. His fingers idled over the flask of brandy stashed there, then decided against it. It was still early, and it was going to be a long night. He chased the pills with clammy black coffee from a stained paper cup. He rubbed his temples and turned back to the letter on his desk.

The letter was a formal statement, prepared by an American bureaucrat whom he'd never heard of, formally declaring that the enclosed evidence was sufficient proof of Iranian involvement with the attempted bombing. The Americans didn't know anything more than the French did, but were far more willing to take the NATO Commission's insinuations as facts, and to glue together unrelated events. This work of substantiated fiction had been sent to him for his signature, and for the Directorate's concurrence on these findings. It was the third letter he'd received from the

Americans this afternoon asking him to sign off on the Iran theory. It was no more convincing than the others.

This was typical of American problem-solving: first decide what the answer is, then bend the facts to fit. Denis's trouble was, with the Americans so sure of themselves, he was under a lot of pressure to produce a reasonable alternative. But it had barely been sixteen hours since they discovered the bomb, and it was absurd to think that a proper investigation could bear fruit so quickly.

It didn't help that France's own press was taking the American's side, decrying Iran and campaigning for the French military to join the American effort. Denis found it odd that the United States was so anxious to go to war over a bomb planted in someone else's country—a country they otherwise didn't seem to care much about.

There was a knock at his door. Denis slid the letter aside and pressed a button under his desk, unlocking the door. Like most modern organizations, the DST had done away with secretaries, but Denis was often in conference and needed a locked door to maintain his privacy. He also had a proximity sensor that chimed if someone stood by his door for more than a few seconds.

When the door opened, Denis was relieved to see it was Faison—a welcome alternative to Dr. Peerson, who had already made a number of uninvited visits today. Peerson was especially irritating because, already firm about Iran's involvement, he was busy mounting a case against North Korea. He was convinced they had supplied the bomb's technology and his assumptions along that line were the most imaginative yet.

Faison hugged a thick folder to his chest. Denis motioned him to a chair.

"For me?" Denis asked.

"It's from Peerson," Faison replied, nodding. Denis darkened.

"He's sending you now?"

"No." Faison mistook Denis's irritation for confusion. "It came from Peerson's files, but he hasn't read it yet."

Faison dug through the folder and pulled out several pages, passing them across the desk. They were photocopies of an old operation file, speckled by generations of re-duplication. Odd shading and distortion hinted that some of the duplication was done under less than ideal conditions, such as with a miniature camera in the dead of night. The resulting document was difficult to read.

The first page was the cover. The CIA logo was clear enough, as was the title, *Summation of Events, Operation Deadfall.* During the cold war, the CIA was obsessed with code names. Everything they did had one. Operation Pygmalion, Operation Red Poison, Operation Commie-Be-Gone, Operation Taking a Pee Break. After a while, they used up all the relevant phrases and the code names became more obscure and confusing, until they dropped them for all but the better-publicized operations. Since Denis had never heard of Operation Deadfall, he could assume it occurred no later than the mid-eighties.

There were more words at the bottom, but they were lost in a crease from a previous photocopy. Denis flipped the page and saw a photograph that, while blurry, was undoubtedly the same device that was found in the bank this morning.

Denis found the photo disturbing; the photo corroborated everything they knew so far and suddenly made the bomb much more real to him. The photo also gave it a name: the caption labeled it, "The Deadfall Device."

The operation's summation began on the next page. It was eye-opening, to say the least. The bomb had been developed by the Americans, which was no surprise, as it was no surprise that the Americans weren't claiming it. Not when it had turned up under the current circumstances. What was striking, though, was they were apparently so disturbed by what they had created, that they cancelled the project immediately upon its completion and tried to bury all evidence that it had even existed.

This had backfired. The more desperate they were to erase it, the more anxious Moscow was to get their hands on it. After several failures, the KGB convinced a 'radical student' to steal the plans.

Project Deadfall had been a joint effort between the government and an unnamed university. Back in the eighties, there were still a few students left with communist leanings. Or who at least felt that a level playing field between the two major superpowers was the best deterrent for global warfare. Whatever motivated this student, he got the plans as far as Berlin before their absence was noticed. What followed was a horrifying free-for-all.

West Berlin already was—for both the CIA and the KGB—the single most active region on the planet. But things really kicked into high gear when the Deadfall plans hit town. Both sides mobilized, each stepping up their efforts to match the other's.

Denis skimmed through the next few pages, which cataloged innumerable incidents between the two agencies. By the sounds of it, the whole city was a blood-bath. The CIA had the home-team advantage and the KGB got slaughtered, losing three agents for every American one. Three long days later, the Americans reported they had destroyed the final copy of the plans. Project Deadfall was contained and the team that had developed it was debriefed and disbanded. End of story.

Denis was overwhelmed by this new information, but when he looked up to Faison, the lieutenant anxiously motioned for him to continue.

The next and last page was an eight-by-ten color photo-copy captioned, "Final Copy Recovered." It showed a canvas diplomatic bag leaning against a car's tire, with a black silk-screen of the Russian flag. Next to it was a binder of tobacco-colored leather, *Project Deadfall* spelled across the cover in gold lettering. There was a red handprint on the cover, the color of fresh blood. The photograph was credited to Agent Grey Stark, CIA. Small world.

"So Grey is somehow linked to the bomb?" Denis asked. He was oblique on purpose, prompting Faison to give an opinion before offering his own. By way of reply, Faison took out a loupe—the small magnifying glass that photographers use to inspect negatives—and positioned it on the photograph.

Denis leaned over to look with growing apprehension. At the bottom of the leather cover, there were words, small and hard to read. After several attempts, he was able to make out: *Technical Schematics for the Deadfall Device, a Low-Reaction Nuclear Ordinance.*

*L*eigh sat at a marble-topped table, nestled under the brown awning of a café along the edge of a stone-covered plaza. The afternoon was coming to a close and people and pigeons bustled around, getting their last few errands in. The scene was idyllic—precisely the experience that drew so many tourists from all around the globe to Paris. But it went unappreciated by Leigh, who had lived there all her life. The only thing she noticed was that the October sun arced low across the sky, blinding her every time she looked up from the table.

Earlier, Leigh had taken a few minutes to brush her hair and reapply make-up. She still looked a bit harried, but could have as easily spent the afternoon shopping as destroying her car in a high-speed chase. She had the contents of Grey's folder spread around the table, held down against the light evening breeze with bottles and shakers. The report was long on technical explanations, like how electrical filaments could excite saline, and short on why anyone would care if it did.

She gave up on it just as Grey strode into the far side of the courtyard.

He had gone off to find a pharmacy, and now his injured hand was wrapped in white gauze. Leigh also figured that he bought some pain killers, but he would have taken them already, not wanting her to see. Grey was halfway into his chair when he saw what Leigh was reading.

"That's top secret," he spat.

Leigh shrugged. "I won't tell anyone."

Grey gathered the papers with his good hand. "No, I'm serious. You can't read that." Leigh pressed down on the papers in front of her, clamping them to the table. Grey tried to tug them free, but could not.

"I think I've earned the right," she said.

"I don't get to make those decisions."

"Obviously."

Grey let go of the papers. He looked around the courtyard, debating if he should just storm off now and be done with her.

Leigh motioned for a waiter. "Sit down, I'll buy you a coffee. How's the hand?"

"Shitty."

"Do you think it's terrorism?" Leigh asked, tapping a picture of the bomb. Grey ignored her. "What about the Iranians?" she tried. He turned to her, so angry he could explode. "Looks like it's the Iranians," she said, giving him a knowing smile. Grey was too tired to maintain his anger. He deflated.

"Yes, I think it's terrorism," he said, dropping into his seat. "But maybe not Iranian. I have conflicting information."

"This seems pretty damning—"

"Everything about this case," Stark cut in, "indicates a level of technological sophistication that Iran doesn't have."

"Hence the North Korean connection."

"You sound like Doctor Peerson."

"Who's that?"

"I can't tell you, but it's not a compliment."

"Let me help you practice for him. North Korea?"

"Too simple. There's no known connection between the two countries, so why would they suddenly collaborate?"

"In police work, we like simple answers. We get more sleep."

"In police work, you get simple answers. Bank robbers don't spend millions of dollars planting misleading information. Governments do."

Leigh didn't agree, but there was no point in arguing. Grey had a cold war mentality, but countries like Iran didn't have the budget for that level of deception. "So you think someone set it up to look like Iran was working with Korea?"

The waiter arrived with two coffees, laying them out with the care of an artist. Grey waited for him to leave before answering: "I think it's rather neat that our two most outspoken enemies are implicated in this."

"Wouldn't it make sense that your two most outspoken enemies would move against you?"

"Move against America, maybe, but not France."

"I'm not sure they can tell the difference."

"We have better accents."

"Or you might, if you bothered with a second language."

"I speak fluent German."

"And does that mean you used to work in Germany?"

"I can't—"

"—tell me that, yes. You've mentioned that a few hundred thousand times already. You're like a child's toy with a string hanging out the back. But I already knew you spoke German. It's one of the three facts about your life that isn't a government secret. I should point out that this is France, and even those of you with the weakest grasp of history know that speaking German is not an asset."

Grey didn't reply. Her quick wit was one of the things that had attracted him to Leigh, but, after seven years of marriage, it had lost its charm. It was the voice of the past, of the good days, reminding him that they were long gone.

"If not Iran, then who?" Leigh pressed. "An evil genius out to destroy the world?"

"It happens," Grey replied. Leigh was dubious. "It does," he insisted. "Not to destroy the world, but to make money. Or to grab power."

"We'll skip that for now. Who would plant evidence against Iran?"

"The United States, likely."

"By which you mean the CIA." Grey conveniently distanced his agency from the ills wrought by America.

"No, there's someone new," he replied. Leigh waited for more, but Grey changed tack: "And why would someone attack me? I haven't even found anything yet."

"Attack us," Leigh corrected. "Are you sure it's related?"

"I think so. I keep thinking about the gun the Arab was using. It sounded loud and dirty, like the barrel was worn out."

"So?"

"So the guard in the bank was shot with a very messy gun."

"You think it's the same one."

"And therefore the same guy."

Leigh nodded. "It would be a stretch to call that a coincidence. Maybe you've already discovered something and just haven't realized it yet."

"I haven't. I didn't even get through the briefing, if you remember."

"You had a prior engagement, if you remember."

Grey didn't want to talk about it. He took great interest in his coffee, made a production out of taking a sip. Leigh considered smacking the cup into his face, but thought better of it.

"Okay," she said. "So what do you make of the bomb self-destructing?"

Grey choked on his coffee—it splattered down his shirt and onto the table. "What?"

"Right here," Leigh said, rescuing the report from the spill. She thumbed forward and read: "'…and the most confusing thing is a capacitor that appears to have been added as an afterthought. It has a separate timer set to go off seconds before the bomb exploded, drawing a massive amount of electricity and causing the building's power to short out. Thus the bomb failed. Surely the designer of such an intricate device would have known that this capacitor exceeded the tolerance of both the available power and the device itself.'"

"It was sabotaged."

"Long before it got to the bank."

Grey grabbed the paper from Leigh's hand and read the words for himself. There was a picture of the sealed aluminum box—the one attached to the device—cut open. Taped to the inner wall, the capacitor was as obvious as a TV strapped to a donkey. Whoever sealed the box knew it was in there.

Someone on the inside, Grey thought, disarmed the bomb before it even got to France.

IV

*D*enis blinked several times, testing his eyes, and again looked through the loupe. The words were still there, exactly as before. The Deadfall Device was a nuclear bomb. "Que Dieu nous protège," he whispered.

"Comment?" Faison said, cupping a hand to his ear.

Denis shook his head. He slid open his desk drawer and pulled out the flask of brandy, along with two glasses. He poured a tall one for himself and a short one for Faison, whom he knew didn't drink.

It was a brandy of rare taste, but Denis didn't bother. He flipped the liquor down his throat like tossing it into a sink. He refilled his glass and re-emptied it. A nuclear bomb had been smuggled into Paris and he hadn't so much as noticed. All of their safeguards, all the time and money they spent on intelligence, and nothing. This wasn't just his own failure, but the failure of the entire Western intelligence community that such a weapon could be brought to France without detection. Who could sleep knowing such a thing was possible? He poured himself a third drink, but shoved the glass aside. Getting drunk wouldn't fix anything.

Faison regarded his brandy with curiosity, sniffing it suspiciously and wetting his lips. More of it evaporated than went into his mouth.

"How did you come across this?" Denis asked, pointing at the report. He listened while Faison related how Peerson had given him the files, then asked: "So Dr. Peerson hasn't seen these yet?"

"Not that I know of."

"And he doesn't know we're dealing with a nuclear bomb?"

"He hasn't said anything."

"Yes, well. Someone will tell him, but it won't be us. There's more at stake here than just agency pride." Denis tapped the report with emphasis, then slid it into his desk drawer. As an afterthought, he pulled a ring of keys from his pocket and locked the desk. "Speaking of which, any word from Mr. Stark?"

Faison shook his head. Denis picked up his phone and said, "Get me Tom McGareth at CIA headquarters in Langley," then hung up. "Not a word to anyone about this," he told Faison. "But we might want to get you some additional—"

Denis was going to say 'man power,' but he stopped short. Certainly Faison did a good job by bringing in this report, but right now he regretted having assigned him to

Peerson. He wished he had a more capable man working with the Commission, but if he replaced Faison or added more people to the team, it would raise Peerson's suspicions. "Just let me know if Peerson gets wind of this," Denis said, hoping he didn't sound patronizing. "Or if you come across anything else interesting."

Faison nodded and stood up. He regarded his drink again, wondering if it would be rude to take the glass with him. He decided not to risk it.

Denis's phone rang. He waited until Faison was out of the room before answering.

"Mr. Rousseau," Tom's voice said over the phone. "How can I help you today?"

Denis knew Tom well—he had frequently briefed him on any French issue that the CIA took interest in—so he immediately caught the mistrust in the American's tone. Denis wondered if he was playing this wrong, but he didn't have an abundance of options. He needed to know more about the bomb and the CIA had the files.

"Hello, Tom. I have some information that might interest you."

"And what would that be."

"Do you remember a huge operation in Berlin in the mid-eighties, Operation Deadfall."

"That was a little after my time."

"But not Grey Stark's."

Tom considered that for a moment, then spoke with genuine interest, "What do you have?"

Denis summarized what he knew. When he finished, Tom let out an appreciative groan.

"So that's what it's all about," Tom said.

"The trick is, it appears that NATO's Commission hasn't learned about this yet. Particularly how Grey's background ties in. I remember that he was Head of Operations in Berlin at the time."

"He was, and that gives us a leg up." Tom caught himself: "I didn't mean to imply—"

"No," Denis cut in. "I see it the same way."

"So neither of us is particularly fond of the NSC?"

"Not in the slightest. And we need to move quickly. They're setting up shop over here."

"Tell me about it. What's the plan?"

"We'll want to talk to Stark first. The trouble is, he's gone missing."

"I can get a message to him, but…" Tom trailed off.

"But what?"

"Nothing. I'll take care of it. And I'll see what else I can dig up on Operation Deadfall."

"I wouldn't dig too much, you might lead the Commission right to this."

"Point taken. Let's keep in touch."

— — —

Tom placed the phone in its cradle, gripping it like the muzzle of an angry dog. Black thoughts tore through his mind. This was a real crisis and instead of charging forward, he was stuck tap-dancing around inter-agency politics.

The CIA'S Deputy Director had confirmed the NSC's authority this morning, so if he were to contact Stark with anything besides instructions to report to Dr. Peerson, it would be borderline treason. But if he put Grey in the Commission's hands, he'd be handing them all the cards. When word got out that the bomb was nuclear, it would be Iraq all over again and Tom would be powerless to stop it.

Outside his window, Tom saw a small fluffy cloud floating in the blue sky. It was carefree, too high up for earthly troubles. Tom watched it for several minutes, then forced himself to accept the decision he had already made.

He owed Grey his life, but that was a long time ago. Tom had burned agents before, on far less important matters. It was unpleasant, but it was his job. He shouldn't hesitate now, not if the end justified the means. Hell, if Grey knew what Tom knew, he'd volunteer for it.

Tom turned to his desk and started an AES-256 encrypted message. He had to word it carefully, as it would be logged by the computer. If this blew up—as it most certainly would—he had to look as blameless as possible.

V

The store windows were made opaque by dozens of colorful posters, all of them advertising cheap international calls, mostly to Africa and the Middle East. There was no order to the posters; they created a jumble of prices that repeated and contradicted each other, and were nearly impossible to sort through.

A store like this would be offensive in any other part of the city, but this was northern Paris, a city within the city, and it belonged to the immigrants. Half the population was black, half was Arab, and all were Muslim.

Here, they remade the world from which they had come, filling the streets with a reckless mix of stores and street vendors that sold anything they could put their hands on, from knock-off handbags to mysterious meats cooked on makeshift grills. Jobless locals flooded the marketplace, bargaining for things they couldn't afford, practicing for the day they had money in their pocket. Take away the paved streets and cobblestone sidewalks and it could be any third world country. Or, more accurately, all of them at once.

Here it was the European who stood out, but there were enough around—either passing through or just curious— that Grey was disregarded as he weaved down the crowded sidewalk. Pushing open the door to the poster-clad store, he stepped inside.

Inside was a long dim room. Patchwork paint outlined where booths and signs had been removed and Grey guessed the place was once a diner. A small cluster of desks held ancient computers that were labeled 'internet' in rainbow letters. Opposite was a row of mismatched phone booths, their doors replaced with curtains. In between them was a table too small for the family of four that dined at it.

An Arab man in his mid-forties rose from the table and hustled over to meet Grey. He seemed to shrink as he approached, until he was chest-height to the low cash register at the door. His family was in native garb—his wife in a dark dress with a kerchief to guard the modesty of her hair, and his children wearing long linen t-shirts—but the man had adopted a western outfit, a collared shirt and tie beneath a blue v-neck sweater, as simple as it was old-fashioned.

"Hello, my friend," he said, forcing a smile. As the owner and the operator of the place, he would be working fourteen-hour days, seven days a week—his *real* friends would have the good taste not to show up at dinnertime, no doubt one of his few opportunities to see his children awake.

Grey asked for a phone and the man sent him to booth six, the one furthest back. The man was wearing a heavy gold ring: a stylized circular rendering of the word "Allah." It was the Iranian coat of arms. This was a lucky man, Grey thought. For every Arab family that moved to Europe, there were tens of thousands more trying. And if the next few days went badly, the Iranian border would close up tight.

Grey walked to the booth, smiling at the children as he passed. They ignored him, fighting over a toy dinosaur. He slipped behind the curtain and pulled out his cell phone. It was designed to look cheap, and was delivered to him pre-worn, so that it wouldn't draw attention. He had been paged, and he dialed that number into the landline. An electronic voice announced that he had reached Grapevine Temporary Services. Grey dialed a four-digit extension and another voice told him to leave a message. He thumbed zero twice and the phone rang. A man answered:

"Operator, how may I help you?"

"I need a babysitter for tonight."

Grey heard some paper shuffle and the man said, "I have Julian available."

"Julian with a J?"

"Yes, sir."

"Let me talk to him."

Stark slid a catch on the side of his cell phone and unfolded it like a small laptop, a miniature keyboard on the bottom and a touch-screen at the top. Resting it on his bandaged hand, he clicked the "Phone Services" icon.

He drew a thin cord from his coat pocket. One end plugged into the cell, the other clipped around the landline's cord. An LED flashed orange, then settled to green as it sorted out the phone's wires. The cell phone said, "Enter Encryption Code." Grey typed in 'JU.'

On the other end of the line, the operator pulled out a red plastic box labeled 'JUlian.' He sliced the safety tape with his thumbnail, removed a small microchip and plugged it into a slot by his phone. A screen above the chip said, "Negotiating."

Stark muffled the landline's microphone with the palm of his hand and put a wireless headset in one ear, first hearing a screech like a fax machine, then silence. His cell phone displayed, 'Line Secure.'

"Boot" The man on the other end said, beginning the final authentication.

"Pencil," Stark replied, pulling the word from memory.

"Fireplace."

"Chalkboard."

"Apple."

"Stain."

That was it. No clever pass-phrases, just simple, unrelated words pulled from a dictionary.

"I have a download for you," the operator said.

Stark pulled out his wallet and raised the driver's license flap. Below it were three colored memory sticks; he selected the yellow one and slid it into his cell phone. "Go ahead."

The headset went dead. A graphic on the phone showed the download progress. When it was done, the operator came back. "Anything else?"

"Nothing on my end," Grey replied.

"Have a nice day," the man said and hung up. Grey unclipped everything and cradled the receiver. He walked straight out, so as not to give the clerk an unnecessary second look at his face, dropping a two-Euro coin on the counter as he passed.

Outside, Grey crossed the street and turned down a sidewalk lined on both sides with blue-tarped stands. Vendors sold everything from fresh meat to bootleg DVDs. The air stank of sweat and shea butter. He pushed past aggressive merchants and customers alike, keeping his head below the tarps so no one could track him. After a few blocks, he emerged at the Gare du Nord train station.

Gare du Nord had a cavernous arced roof five stories tall and wide enough to park twelve trains side-by-side. The platform at the end was the size of a small soccer field and was lorded over by a massive mechanical board that listed outgoing train destinations across Europe and Asia. Travelers milled through kiosks, buying fresh fruit, coffee, and meals to go. After the outdoor market, the air felt fresh and dry, and the building was startlingly clean. Grey could have shaved in his reflection on the marble floor. The Parisians, he thought, had more in common with their German neighbors than they liked to admit.

He bought an evening paper and walked upstairs to the station's café. He sat at a table in the back corner, ordered a coffee and pretended to read. For having lived in France nearly two decades, Grey's inability to read the language was an embarrassment. He knew enough to find his way around town and sort through most menus, but he didn't know nearly enough to read the paper. He had never bothered with the language because, at no point in the two decades that he had lived here, had he intended to stay much longer than he already had. Nevertheless, between the pictures and the few words he did know, he saw that the two main topics were the bomb and America's subsequent troop build-up along Iran's border. It seemed that the population of France was, on the whole, split evenly on the topic of joining the war on Iran.

Grey's coffee arrived and, expecting no further interruptions, he propped the paper up as a cover and unfolded his cell phone. He clicked a few buttons to bring up the message. On the small screen, it spanned four pages.

The first page simply said:

```
TO: GREY STARK
FROM: TOM MCGARETH
***EYES ONLY***
```

Grey clicked to the next page:

```
ON RECEIPT OF THIS MESSAGE,
YOU ARE TO REPORT TO DR.
PEERSON IMMEDIATELY FOR
ORDERS. YOU ARE TO ASSUME A
SUBORDINATE POSITION TO HIM
FOR THE REMAINDER OF THE
INVESTIGATION.
```

The word "subordinate" rankled Grey, and he wondered if it was meant to. He clicked forward:

```
PRESENT DR. PEERSON WITH THE
FOLLOWING INFORMATION AT YOUR
DISCRETION: THE BOMB WAS U.S.
DEVELOPED, UNDER THE TITLE
PROJECT DEADFALL. I SUSPECT
YOU ARE FAMILIAR WITH THE
OPERATION SURROUNDING IT.
```

Grey felt his heart skip. He was more than familiar. It had been the bloodiest op in CIA history, and he had been calling the shots.

The Russians had stolen some new piece of nuclear technology and were trying to get it over the wall. Grey never learned the details, but he knew the weapon was hot. Every agent in Berlin was mobilized and more were flown in from all over Europe. The Deputy Director himself came over from Washington to supervise. The operation was put together overnight; they didn't even have time to name it. Not that it needed a name—it couldn't get confused with any other operation because every other operation had been put on hold.

The directive was simple: stop the bomb's plans from getting across the border at all costs. That was easier said than done. While the plans had been printed on paper meant to resist photographing or reproduction, somehow there were at least a dozen copies floating around the city. Every time they thought they had captured the last one, reports of another would pop up.

The KGB wanted the plans badly and threw every agent they had at the job. They set up endless feints and distractions, hoping to overwhelm Grey's team and have him chasing the wrong lead while they moved the plans into East Berlin. This sort of horseplay was common, and something Grey had never taken personally; this was a game where thinking counted and rash behavior cost everything. Unfortunately, his boss saw it a different way. Every time Grey moved on the Russians, the Deputy Director gave him the same order: kill everyone, no matter if the plans were there or not.

It didn't take the KGB long to figure out that the rules had changed. They started to return fire, shooting anyone they recognized as CIA—or thought they did. Grey had no idea how many innocents were killed just for being in the wrong place. He made it a point not to find out.

At the height of the operation, the death reports came so frequently as to overlap each other. And the Russians weren't the only ones killing civilians. Grey was given a standing order to kill anyone who caught so much as a glimpse of the document. He would have gladly abandoned the operation if his boss hadn't been looking over his shoulder.

The whole thing only lasted three days, but the body count ran to seventy-four operatives, fifty-three on the Soviet side and twenty-one American. Such numbers were unheard of in intelligence work. Even World War II had nothing to match it. In the final days, Grey had so few agents left that he was out on the streets himself.

The Russians made one last-ditch effort to get the plans across, using an agent as beloved to the CIA as she was to the KGB. She was a charming woman who worked at a local bank. Her real job, however, was to distribute money to Soviet agents, and then obscure all records of the transaction.

No attempt had been made to conceal her identity and, from a CIA point of view, she was too small to worry about. In fact, Grey and several other agents had opened accounts at her bank, using it as excuse to tease her. One of his men had even asked her to marry him.

It was inconceivable that the Russians would involve her in this. The woman had no more training as an operative than

Grey did as a taxidermist. Maybe they had hoped to throw him off with their sheer audacity. Maybe they had simply run out of options. Either way, she led a good chase—better than anyone would have expected—getting to within fifty yards of the Brandenburg Gate with only a bicycle. Grey caught up with her in no-man's land, the open field that separated East and West Berlin. Lacking a more subtle alternative, he mowed her down with his car.

One hit wasn't enough. She got to her feet and hobbled east on a broken leg. The Russian border guards opened fire on Grey, forcing him to run her over a second time. It was the most unpleasant thing he'd done in his life. At the time.

That was the only moment when he had held an actual copy of the plans, sitting in the middle of a field of rubble with machine guns from both superpowers trained on him. The plans were bound in ornate leather, but felt thin, no more than a hundred pages for all the carnage that surrounded them.

By now, he was less worried about the Russians getting their hands on the plans than some uppity West German border guard trying to confiscate them. He didn't dare look inside, so he photographed the cover as proof that they had been recovered, and burned them right there.

It took eight hours to negotiate his peaceful removal from the neutral zone. During that time, he was pinned down behind his car, the Russians taking pot-shots at him and his only company the broken body of the woman he had playfully called, "Katia the Cash Machine." It was only there, squatting on the broken cement, that Grey realized he had never known her real name.

The operation ended there. At some later point, the brass in Washington retroactively named it Operation Deadfall, but for those who had seen the horror, it was bitterly referred to as 'The Operation.' If it was mentioned at all.

The KGB's attempt to steal the plans for Project Deadfall had cost them their entire German operation, so they brought a talented military general in to take over Berlin. He was known simply as "The Major," and he was a ruthless man destined to be Grey's downfall.

The throaty blare of a train horn echoed through the station, pulling Grey back to the present. He clicked to the final page of the message:

> I DON'T HAVE TO TELL YOU HOW
> CRITICAL THIS ASSIGNMENT IS,
> NOR THAT THE WORLD WILL BE
> WATCHING YOUR EVERY MOVE. YOU
> MUST REPORT TO PEERSON AS
> QUICKLY AS YOU DEEM POSSIBLE,
> AND PROVIDE HIM WITH ANY
> INFORMATION ABOUT DEADFALL
> YOU DEEM USEFUL. YOU HAVE MY
> COMPLETE CONFIDENCE IN THIS
> MATTER.

Christ, Grey thought, clamping the phone shut, Tom doesn't want me to report to Peerson at all. All the double-talk in the message, the way he kept saying, 'deem.' That wasn't Tom's style at all; he meant for Grey to go it alone.

Of course, it didn't take much insight to see why: the CIA was in a political battle with the NSC, and if their only agent in France was reporting to the other side, then they might as well just give up. But Tom wouldn't dare tell Grey outright that he shouldn't to report NSC; that would be a terminal career move. He could only imply it in the vaguest of terms, lest he find the Military Police knocking on his office door. This was where Grey had the advantage: as long as he stayed on the move, they would have a hard time shutting him down—even after they learned he was disobeying his orders. Meanwhile, Tom could cover for him, and protect him if he got into trouble. Not that Tom could offer much protection these days; the CIA's power was flagging.

The real question was, did Tom want him to go rogue for his own political gains, or simply because it was the right thing to do? The Deadfall Device was a nuclear weapon, so if that's what they had found last night, it certainly raised the stakes. If the bomb had detonated, it would have killed millions and rendered one of the world's most beloved cities a smoking crater. And the retaliation would have been even worse; they would have sown salt into the ruins of Iran.

But it hadn't detonated. Someone had stopped it, someone on the inside. It could be that the bomb was just a message, Il Siyâh warning the West of its newfound power. Or

VI

"Third time's a charm," Grey muttered, stepping out of the cab onto the crowded sidewalk of the Odeon district. He had been on the hunt now for hours and the pink twilight had given way to darkness, leaving the sky a roof of hazy orange; the glow of the city lights blocked out the stars. This was the third neighborhood on his list and his feet were starting to hurt.

Grey passed eight Euros to the cab driver on a bill of six-twenty; a good tip, but not enough to get him remembered. Across the street, Leigh got out of a cab of her own, no doubt over-tipping since she had Grey's money in her purse.

Leigh had insisted on changing before they went out, which meant going to her apartment—Grey had been unable to convince her of the danger of such a trip. To make matters worse, she had insisted on a long shower and then spent a half-hour picking out her outfit. She chose an ankle-length heather coat that shrunk her waist and swelled her curves to cartoonish proportions, opening wide at her chest like a fruit basket. She wrapped a maroon scarf around her neck and dug out matching shoes.

Grey had skipped the shower, not that she had offered, and hadn't dared go near his own apartment. The piece of paper from the Mercedes stuck in his mind: if they knew that much, they would know a lot more. So instead he stopped at an off-the-rack clothing store, bought a new outfit and changed in the dressing room. He wore tan pants and a blue pin-stripped shirt under a camel-hair Mackintosh. It didn't fit his taste, but he blended with the other Parisians just off work. And with Leigh strutting around in that outfit, his best friend wouldn't notice him.

Grey walked toward the blinking lights of a movie theater marquee. There was a tangle of people out front, as many pushing to get inside as were shoving to get out, and more still just standing around smoking and chatting. The confusion made for the perfect cover, and sure enough, right in the middle of it, old Vladimir was doing his drunken hobo routine.

He had a long sheep's face, with dingy sideburns and matted silver hair down to his shoulders. His tweed jacket was worn through at the elbows and his green pants barely covered his calves. He looked like one of those 'dress up the homeless' campaigns gone bad, and smelled like he hadn't seen a shower in weeks.

He walked up the sidewalk, pushing against the crowd whenever he could, one hand crinkling a can of cheap beer while the other obsessively flicked a lighter. He plowed through the mass of people, loudly proclaiming his need for money and cigarettes. But he wasn't here for the handouts. His eyes were sharp, scanning the crowd for an easy mark.

Grey backed out of the crowd and surveyed the area. There was only one escape route, a thin alley alongside the theater. He caught Leigh's eye, motioning first at Vladimir, then to the alley. She nodded and started down a cross-street. Grey walked to a phone booth and pretended to make a call.

Vladimir turned onto the crosswalk, targeting a college-age man with the stiff grim canter of a German and weighted down by a backpack so full it looked inflated. Germans were the perfect prey because their country was basically crime-free; they knew the outside world was dangerous, but had no practice in recognizing the danger. Sadder still, when someone robbed them, they were more prone to ponder the thief's motivation than call for help.

The kid was mesmerized by the Paris night, reading the theater marquee as he crossed the street. Vladimir body slammed him, knocking him back a foot. Before the kid got his balance, Vladimir was in his face, screaming that he should watch where he was going, and bathing the poor guy in the horror of his breath. And meanwhile, Vladimir dug his hand into the kid's front pocket.

Vladimir had the roughest hands in the business and needed this screaming routine to distract his victims. Half of them noticed anyway, but he came out of nowhere, moved fast, and confounded them with wild-eyed theatrics. Before his victims could process what happened, he'd be down the sidewalk, lighting someone's cigarette as if they were the oldest of friends. And moments later, he was gone entirely.

If Vladimir scores a wallet, Grey thought, he'll make a break for the alley. If not, he'll circle around and try someone else. He would usually make three or four hits a night, each in a different part of the city. Afterward, he returned home, cleaned up, and hit the town in attire more befitting the former proprietor of the largest KGB safehouse in Western Europe.

Vladimir got lucky with the German. Grey gave him a few seconds' lead, then followed him down the dark alley. Backlit by the street, Grey had no way to enter unseen, but the alley was empty. Worried he had waited too long, Grey dashed to where the alley crossed another and peered around the corner. To his left, he saw nothing. To his right, two shadows faced off like wrestlers in a ring. He crept toward them.

Leigh pressed a high-caliber chromed automatic against the bridge of Vladimir's nose. The gun was the massive sort that cops carried more for effect than function. She must have grabbed it from her apartment when Grey wasn't looking. He doubted she still had a permit for it.

Vladimir, for his part, held a knife at Leigh's throat and pretended it was a standoff. It might have been; Vladimir was good with a knife.

Grey stole up behind the Russian and cleared his throat. Vladimir jumped, then stepped back, waving his knife at both his adversaries. Grey held out his empty hands, his right one useless in its gauze wrapping. Vladimir flinched at the sight of them, retreating another step.

"Are we fighting about this?" Grey asked.

"No, Grey. Not with you." Vladimir was fluent in all the European languages and when he spoke English, his accent could have been from anywhere on the continent. He dropped his arm and folded the knife into his sleeve.

"It's good to see you again," Grey said in a soothing tone. Vladimir relaxed: Grey wanted something. The Russian's over-confidence emerged.

"And you, too, my old friend. Playing Bonnie and Clyde these days, are we?" He leered at Leigh provocatively, but as a former cop, her skin was too thick. She yawned at him, keeping her gun on his forehead. "I heard you had retired," he continued. "You're not here to kill me, are you?"

Grey nodded to Leigh and she pushed the gun into a holster under her arm; it was so big she had to raise her arm over her head to get it in.

If Vladimir was going to try something, it would be now. Leigh was distracted and Grey unarmed. But he was content to ogle Leigh's breasts as they shifted beneath her tight dress—they rose and fell as she put the gun away. When she pulled her jacket closed, Vladimir smiled appreciatively at Grey.

His mouth was an abstract mosaic of porcelain and metal that should have been ashamed of itself. There was a dark hole in the side large enough to hold a cigar. Grey had removed those teeth himself, many years back. Vladimir hadn't learned any manners in the interim: "Did you bring her just to show off," the Russian asked, "or is she part of the bargain?"

Grey's temper cracked. In one fluid motion, his knife was in his hand, the point of it denting the skin on Vladimir's neck. "Before you push your luck," Grey hissed, "you might want to be sure you've got any."

Vladimir looked defiant at first, but it melted away. "I am sorry," he said. "Old habits die hard." He turned to Leigh. "I apologize for any offense."

Leigh nodded and Grey's knife disappeared.

"Are you up on current events?" Grey asked.

"Only locally. There's something you'd like to know?"

"If you've got a minute."

"I have, but this is hardly the place."

"I'm in a hurry," Grey said.

"You always are, my friend. Why don't we meet at Le Salon Rouge in an hour?"

"There are plenty of places to drink right here." Grey pointed down the alley. Vladimir frowned distastefully.

"No, it wouldn't do at all," he said. "The drinks won't cost you nearly enough. Besides, I need a shower." Vladimir started to walk away, but Grey's knife came back to his hand, blocking the way. Vladimir was amused.

"Come off that, now," he said. "If I'm not there, you can always come back and kill me tomorrow." Grey lowered the knife. Vladimir strolled to the street and dissolved into the crowd.

A giant man was perched on a stool by the entrance to Le Salon Rouge, his log-thick arms hanging almost to the pavement. He looked like a thug, but Grey knew better. This man had a long and distinguished career. He had garnered the Order of Lenin during the invasion of Afghanistan, then did a brief stint with the GRU—Russia's military intelligence—before retiring to the Moscow police. Last Grey heard he was a Captain, though he didn't have the brains for the part.

Grey was surprised to see him here. He remembered him as both honest and proud, two things that were hard to cram into the polyester doorman's suit of this thief's den. But with mother Russia in economic shambles, being a doorman in Paris paid better than a Siberian oil well.

As Grey and Leigh approached, recognition flickered in the giant's eyes. He dropped from his stool and slung up a hand that was large enough to hide a coconut and strong enough to crush it. "This is no place for trouble," he grunted.

Grey had to crane his neck to see the man's face. His features were as bold as a caveman's, his swollen forehead casting a shadow over his eyes. "Of course not," Grey said, hoping he sounded casual. "We're here on Vladimir's invitation."

The giant processed this for a while, then nodded. "No weapons," he grunted.

"No weapons," Grey said, raising his hands for a pat-down. It didn't come. The giant, having exhausted his English, waved them in and sat back on his stool.

Its wooden legs bowed under his weight.

Le Salon Rouge was a leather and wood affair reminiscent of the banker's clubs of days past. But it was dark, the only lighting hidden behind the thick red velvet drapes that hung down the walls. The red light diffused through the room, denying the eyes focus and depth. The people floated in the room as if cut out of a magazine.

A row of women lined the brass-topped bar, mannequin-perfect. They were prostitutes, the highest grade of the former Soviet Republic's most profitable export. Their fees would make a surgeon blush, but for most of the clientele, they were provided gratis.

When the Iron Curtain fell, every general and statesman who was able cashed in on their position and escaped to Paris before the dust settled. For the Russian mafia, this bar was one-stop shopping for information and connections. Their investment in women kept useful contacts both happy and available.

Grey's eyes traveled up the bar and back down again, unable to look away. These women were beautiful and elegantly dressed, trying for the illusion of romance—something that was far more tempting than sex alone.

Rich laughter filled the room. "See anything you like?" It was Vladimir.

Vladimir was transformed by a tailored Armani suit, his long hair combed and oiled. In just an hour, he had gone from rotting hobo to ennobled statesman. He still had the bad teeth, but he was Russian—that was practically a tradition.

"Come over here, my friend," he said loudly. Meeting with the CIA was good for his reputation and he wanted everyone to notice. It made him seem like he was still important, and importance was a commodity in this place.

Grey led Leigh through a maze of red sofas. It was early, so the men were still talking with other men. After a few drinks garnished with familiar war stories, they would lose interest in each other and head to the bar for softer company.

When they arrived at Vladimir's table, a waiter was unloading three vodka martinis. Vladimir knew Grey didn't like vodka; spies knew these things about each other.

The waiter stood patiently until Grey realized he was supposed to pay. He over-tipped him for their host's benefit while Vladimir pawed Leigh with the excuse of helping her out of her coat. Underneath, she was wearing a backless cream-colored dress that draped down her chest from an inch-thick collar, then tightened into a skirt at her waist. It ran out of fabric halfway down her thighs, leaving the rest of her legs bare. Grey wondered where she had stashed her gun.

They settled in opposite the Russian, the drinks on a low table in between.

"So, what do you need to know from Vladimir?"

Grey pulled out a photo of the bomb. Vladimir set his drink down, immediately excited.

"I feel I am looking at something classified, am I not?"

Grey spread his hands in a gesture that could mean anything. The picture was classified, but admitting that was admitting to treason. Not the sort of thing he wanted to announce.

Vladimir pulled low-slung eyeglasses from his jacket and settled them on the tip of his nose. He tilted his head back, inspecting the picture with a studious expression he had probably learned from a movie. He made a series of inquisitive noises and capped them off with, "Very interesting. Very interesting indeed."

"You know what it is?" Grey asked.

"Are you testing my memory?" The question didn't seem to want an answer, so Grey didn't give one. Vladimir continued: "This is the Deadfall Device, a wonderfully

THE DEADFALL PROJECT

destructive weapon. It has been rumored," he said, shooting Leigh a glance, "that even the plans themselves can kill you."

"So you've seen it before?" Grey asked.

Vladimir nodded modestly, "I've seen a photo, yes. And the plans."

"But we destroyed the plans."

"So proud and sure, you CIA."

"You're telling me that the KGB got the plans after all?"

"I'm not telling you anything, actually, except that your tone is irritating."

"Maybe we should step outside," Grey said, rising to his feet, "and discuss this privately." Vladimir rose also, accepting the challenge. In this room, he had to be brave, even if that meant being stupid as well.

"I have a question," Leigh said. Both men looked over and she turned it on for Vladimir. She started with her eyes, opened wide with innocent curiosity. Men liked to have answers for pretty women. Before she spoke, she leaned forward and grabbed her knees, using her arms to plump her breasts and to reveal their every detail through the thin fabric of her dress. "You say you've seen the plans?" she asked.

Vladimir thumbed his mouth thoughtfully, but his eyes were dumbly fixed on her chest. He dropped back into his seat. "I can't say for sure. I saw something like it."

"But you recognized the bomb, so you remember it? You must have gotten more than just a passing glance."

"Those plans made quite a fuss. I wouldn't forget."

"This was in Berlin?" Leigh spread her legs, keeping the show going.

"Where else? It was many years back."

"West Berlin, or East?"

"I really don't remember."

Grey didn't enjoy watching Leigh show off, but admired how effective she was. Anyone could accomplish beauty in her youth, but the beauty of the aged was reserved for a select few. Men lusted for girls, but women were captivating. And Leigh didn't hesitate to use it whereas most girls didn't even know how. Unfortunately, she wasn't getting any further than Grey had. Either Vladimir had already told them all he knew or was holding out for something more concrete than a woman's promises. "Maybe I can jog your memory?" Grey asked, reaching for his wallet.

Vladimir shook his head, not answering as much as breaking free of Leigh's spell. He set the photo between them and tapped it with a skeletal finger. "Where did you find it?"

"You know I can't tell you that."

"But here in Paris, huh?"

Grey nodded.

"In the Seventh Arrondissement." Vladimir asserted, making the connection. "I saw it on the news. That is a very compelling place for a nuclear weapon. You're getting a lot of pressure over this, no?"

Grey didn't respond. He had already said too much.

"Tell me," Vladimir continued, "was it really made by the Iranians?"

Grey couldn't cover his surprise.

"You see," Vladimir said, "I do keep up on things. Apparently better than you do." He drained his glass and stood up. Grey seized his wrist.

"I need to know if the KGB got the plans over the Berlin wall."

Vladimir glared at Grey's hand until he released him.

"I'm afraid I'm not the right person to ask," Vladimir said. "I never heard that the plans made it to Russia, but I wouldn't have. There's only one person in all of Europe who could tell you for sure."

"And who would that be?"

"You know who I'm talking about."

Grey did know, and he didn't like it. "Where can I find him?"

"You must ask Jacques. Only he can set up a meeting. You might say Jacques is the secretary general." Vladimir gave Leigh a knowing smile. Her face was blank.

"Who are we talking about?" she asked.

"We are talking, my dear, about the Major. A man who would really, really relish the opportunity to kill your husband."

"He's not the only one," Grey injected, hoping to divert the conversation.

"I would relish watching you die, true, but that's an entirely different proposition. To kill you myself, well… you're not worth giving up all of this." Vladimir gestured around the room, ending with the ladies at the bar. He was already moving toward them as he said, "Now, if you'll excuse me."

Vladimir walked to the bar and sidled up next to a beautiful, empty-faced brunette. He ordered a top shelf martini and graciously offered one to the girl.

"You're spending big tonight, vova," the woman said, flicking on the charm.

"Yes, detka," Vladimir replied, glancing back at Grey and Leigh. "I believe I have just come into a great deal of money."

VIII

"We have concluded our investigations. We have gathered the facts, and the conclusion is undeniable." The President hesitated, his hands tightening on the edge of the official White House podium.

A regular viewer would think the President was bracing his courage, but to a trained eye like Peerson's, it was just part of his perfect delivery. The President, like all of the best politicians, would never show genuine emotion on camera. His feelings were kept on a tight rein, used only to evoke sentiment in the audience. •

Peerson sat in his closet-sized lemon-yellow office and bent over the screen of his laptop computer, watching the President's speech on the Globecast website. The speech had been given in Washington at nine o'clock last night—3:00 A.M. in France—so Peerson hadn't bothered with it until the morning. The speech wasn't pressing; he'd already been briefed on what would be said.

"What we now know," the President continued, "is that the bomb was a nuclear weapon capable of leveling the entire city of Paris and of killing millions." The President paused, letting the news sink in. The room was so quiet that Peerson heard a reporter gasp.

"It is by the grace of God that we were spared the most appalling disaster of this millennium," the President continued, "but it will be by the actions of the American people that the terrorists won't get another chance. This nuclear bomb could have been planted in any city, in any country, and if we do not treat this like an attack on our own soil, we can depend on being the next victim." Peerson nodded in appreciation.

"We know this bomb was the work of Il Siyâh agents that operate out of Iran. The Iranian government gives these nuclear terrorists safe harbor, allows them to train and plan, and even provides them with money and weapons. A few hours ago, I issued a mandate to the Iranian government, demanding they stop harboring these criminals and immediately turn over those responsible for the Paris bomb. On these two requests, we will accept no negotiation." The President neatened some papers on the podium, then looked out at the small audience of reporters. Hands shot into the air. "Yes, Greg?"

"Mr. President, does this mean that Iran is now a nuclear power?"

Peerson chuckled gleefully. All of the reporter's questions were pre-approved, some were even fed to them, allowing the President to give intelligent, well-researched answers seemingly off the top of his head. And better still—as with this question—he let the reporter make the insinuation. Greg's question put the idea of Iran as a nuclear power in the world's mind, but the President didn't say it himself, so no one could accuse him of misleading the public.

"That's a good question," the President said, "I don't have an answer yet, but we know there is another party working in conjunction with the Iranian Il Siyâh, supplying them with the technology, if not the weapons themselves."

"So you believe there are more of these nuclear bombs out there?"

"It would be foolish to think otherwise." The President selected another reporter in the crowd. "Mr. Taylor?"

"Mr. President, American troops have been mobilized in Iraq…" The reporter hesitated, realizing that the chief executive had never personally confirmed this.

"Yes, they have," the President replied, drawing an easy laugh from the room.

"Of course," the reporter continued, embarrassed. "The question is, does this mean you've ruled out a diplomatic solution?"

"A diplomatic solution is always preferable. We've been talking to Iran from day one. I can't predict how successful or unsuccessful we'll be, but I've instructed the Secretary of State to make it her highest priority. Even as I left her a few minutes ago, she was on the horn with our ambassador over there, discussing the alternatives."

"Alternatives to war?"

"Alternatives to war, yes. But let me finish my earlier answer." The President tightened his lips, mentally preparing, then thrust his chin out as if he were a cocky young boxer—one who never had humility mashed into him. "We won't repeat our mistakes of the past. We'll take time for negotiation, yes, but we won't allow the terrorists to slip away or give them another chance to strike at freedom.

"We have chased these same criminals from Afghanistan to Iraq and now to Iran. But that's where it stops. We're building a tight net around Iran, quarantining it from the world, leaving no path for the terrorists to flee." The President gazed into the room, listening to his voice echo in the silence. When the last echo faded, he pointed to another reporter. "Yes, Jim?"

"Mr. President, what about a joint action with the French?"

"The battle against terrorism is everyone's battle, but no one has a bigger stake in this fight than France. I'd love to have them with us."

"But France has spoken against military action in Iran."

"The Prime Minister has expressed his doubts," the President smiled cryptically, "but the French people don't seem to share his opinion."

"So you think public pressure will change his mind?"

"France is a free country. Their government is elected by the people, same as we do here. I doubt the P.M. would stay in office long if he didn't act in his people's best interests."

The video cut back to the Globecast anchorman for commentary and Peerson closed his laptop computer. Unfortunately, he thought, the majority of the French people still *did* share the Prime Minister's opinion. Maybe if the bomb had actually exploded these people would wake up from their little rose-tinted world. Peerson shook his head distastefully, as if the French were sitting across the desk from him.

He flipped through the morning's mail. It was mostly memos; everyone wanted to get their support of the war on the record. And now that the President had gone public about it being a nuclear bomb… well, things should progress rapidly.

Peerson noticed a wide brown envelope in the stack. It was hand-addressed, the writing slanted and tight. He recognized the handwriting. There was no stamp or return address, so it must have been dropped off at the front desk. Taking such a risk implied that the contents were urgent. Peerson stuffed a sausage finger under the flap and tore it open.

He pulled out a thin stack of photographs which showed Grey Stark and his wife walking into a bar. Peerson didn't understand why he should care, until he reached the last one, shot from a distance, and showing the name of the club: Le Salon Rouge.

He stared at the photograph. His hand found the phone and dialed an extension without looking. It rang twice.

"Oui?"

"Faison? Peerson here. I've got something you'll want to see. What's our operative's name again? Jerard? Bring him along as well. It looks like we've got work for him."

Faison said he would come right up and Peerson hung up the phone. He set the photograph on his desk and laughed.

"Missing agent found cavorting with old enemies," he said aloud, shaking his head, "Mr. Stark, what are you thinking?"

IX

*A*min smoothed the white towel, pressing it against a floor as warped as a topographic map. He was in a small room in a run-down hotel. The plaster walls had worn down to the slats, the mattress was stained, and the air smelled of cheap cleaning products. The bathroom floor had rotted away, and he didn't dare use it for fear that it couldn't hold his weight. Amin didn't mind, though. The place was reasonably priced in an expensive city, and they let him pay cash and put any name he cared to in the register.

For all its decay, Amin felt more comfortable here than in the depraved palace where Il Siyâh was keeping his brother. Of course, Thoaab'a had made many sacrifices in order to blend among the decadent Westerners.

He knelt, the loose floorboards bending under his weight. He regretted the loss of his prayer rug—the towel was a poor substitute, a sour reminder of his failure. He decided to double his prayers, to assure Allah he would not fail again.

Amin looked at his watch. It was one past eight in the morning, time to begin. He stretched his arms out, bowing and rising as he recited the Prophet's Prayer. He had barely begun when he felt footsteps coming up the stairs, shaking the floor beneath him.

Amin was on the forth story, the top one. He was the only person staying on the whole floor, and the maid had already been up today. He looked to his gun, sitting on the table, wrapped in the greasy towel he had used to clean it.

He reached for it, but the floor creaked under his weight. He froze, arm outstretched, watching the door and hoping for some hint of who was on the other side. The shadow of feet shuffled under the door. He held his breath, gauging the distance between his hand and the gun.

The door handle tilted, moved by an unseen hand. It rattled against the lock and then straightened again. Amin knew he should say something. He searched his mind for the words, but they didn't come. Long ago, the brotherhood had given him French lessons—in case his boat was stopped by the harbor patrol. But he hadn't learned much, and remembered even less. Now, under pressure, his mind was a complete blank. He didn't have the skill for languages that his brother did. He wished Thoaab'a was here now.

Then there was a faint knock and a whisper in his native tongue: "Open up, brother."

Amin rose to his feet, leaving the gun on the table, and opened the door. Thoaab'a was wearing a dark overcoat with a raked fedora, like a fictional detective. He slipped inside and pulled the door shut behind him.

"Is everything okay?" Amin asked, alarmed at his brother's timing.

"Yes, but there is much we should discuss."

"So pressing? It's time for Fajr."

"Is it?" Thoaab'a looked at his watch, a bit confused. Amin wondered incredulously if his brother could have forgotten second prayer, but Thoaab'a slapped his wrist and said, "My watch must be off, I finished mine before I came over."

"Or my watch is," Amin said with relief. "You will wait for me?"

"Of course," Thoaab'a replied. "Allah before all things."

"I have another towel," Amin said hopefully. It had been a long time since he had company in prayer.

"No," Thoaab'a said. "I have… things I must think through."

"I understand." Amin was embarrassed by his poor offer; Thoaab'a would prefer his rug. He dropped to his knees and began his prayers anew. As he chanted, he felt Allah come to him and lift his burdens, freeing him of the pain that mercilessly burned his skin day and night. Prayers were the best part of his day, his communion with God and a small taste of the Garden of Paradise.

— — —

I should have just prayed, Richard thought. It would comfort his brother and be better than just watching. But he had tried praying several times over the past week and couldn't find the words. It was ironic that, even though he had disavowed Allah, he felt like a heretic when he spoke his name. He shouldn't care, and he didn't, but he was still afraid to pray in front of his brother. Amin's vigorous faith made him feel exposed, like his brother could sense his dissent. Besides, there was something sick about a man so desperate for God's comfort that he would pray on a towel.

Richard slipped off his fedora and raked his fingers through his hair. He loved how soft it felt. This whole country was soft. To a man like Richard, hardened by a life the West couldn't possibly imagine, France laid its bounty out for the taking.

Richard couldn't understand why Amin didn't see it, why he clung to humility when so much was possible here. But his brother had always been odd. Especially since that day, over a dozen years back, when he got that terrible scar on his head.

Back then, they had been a middle class Iraqi family with a modest house, a car and two parrots. Their father was an oil technician, specializing in drilling. After the occupation of Kuwait, the Iraqi government asked him to help inspect the captured oil rigs. It was one of those requests a man didn't say no to.

Richard was ten at the time, and Amin only seven. To them, it seemed like a great adventure. They moved to a large house in Khasman, and were given many toys and more food than Richard had seen in his entire life. It was the perfect life, until the American jets started bombing.

They were moved to a dark basement, which they had to share with three other families. The bombing continued for weeks, but Father had explained there was nothing to worry about, that the Americans were only bombing the Iraqi army. "Matters of the military," he said, "have nothing to do with this family."

Father always left before dawn. A car would collect him and the other fathers, and take them to wherever that day's work was. It had happened one such morning, when all of the families were outside saying goodbye.

Richard had eaten too much breakfast that morning and didn't feel well. Father hugged him in the doorway, then led Mother and Amin to the car. They were all hugging goodbye when Richard heard the scream of a falling bomb. The sound was so clear—both then and in a thousand nightmares that followed—but no one else heard it. His memory of his family was that moment, standing like a photo, then disappearing in a burst of light. Richard was thrown backwards by a blast of hot air. His head struck something hard and he blacked out.

He woke up covered with dirt. The world smelled of charred flesh and burning oil. He stepped outside. The wind whistled as it cleared the smoke. There was no sign of the car, no sign of anything until he saw Amin. His brother stood in a daze, still holding Father's hand. But the hand was all that was left of Father. Or Mother. And half of Amin's head was burnt to ash like the tip of a spent match.

Richard scooped Amin up and ran until he found a hospital. It was a military hospital, in what was once a schoolhouse. The doctor said there was nothing he could do, that his brother would die. They bandaged him and gave him a bed, doing what they could to make him comfortable.

The wounded soldiers avoided him at first, unable to face the sight of a dying child. But, despite his diagnosis, Amin lived on. The soldiers began to consider him a miracle, a sign from Allah. They took him not as a child victim, but as a noble fighter in the war with the Americans.

Any other child would have burst from the attention— Richard would have, if anyone had so much as noticed him. But Amin seemed oblivious to the fuss, oblivious to everything. He would occasionally talk, but only to Richard. Mostly, he just stared into space, his gaze as blank as an empty room.

When the ground war started, it brought chaos and panic. The Americans advanced rapidly and all of the able soldiers fled the hospital to avoid capture. One of them, a burly tank commander from the Red Guard, insisted Amin go with him. "Allah has big plans for you, little one," he said.

Amin wouldn't leave without Richard, so the commander put them both on the back of a truck and they drove off the map.

The commander linked up with other men, rebels who hid during the day and struck at night. They crossed over to Iraq and joined up with the resistance group Il Siyâh, which back then was just a couple dozen men with a hijacked truck full of American weapons. The group had more words than means, and the frustrated tank commander soon left them to re-join the Iraqi army. But Richard and Amin were to live with Il Siyâh for the next eight years. It was here that Amin became the center of attention, and not just as a mystical symbol.

Amin took an interest in guns and the men amused themselves by teaching him to shoot. He caught on quickly, and all were surprised at his accuracy. At the tender age of nine, his tiny hand barely able to grasp a pistol, there wasn't a man on the mountain who could outshoot him. He became the centerpiece of Il Siyâh's propaganda and men traveled great distances just to see him shoot.

Richard, too, found his place. His famous brother remained tight-lipped, so Richard filled the gap. He related the story of Amin's scar to their visitors, embellishing it with every telling. He had a flare for drama, and was soon called upon to recount all of Il Sayâh's heroic deeds. "Thoaab'a's re-telling," one man quipped, "is better than being there yourself."

And so the two brothers rose to prominence within the fledgling resistance. And while it hadn't been Richard's idea to raise funds by smuggling heroin, his verbal skills made him the obvious choice to be their contact in the West. Amin had grown too old for his child-savant reputation, so took charge of security on the cargo boats. The two brothers still saw each other occasionally, but their lives moved in very different directions.

Amin remained a singular tool of hate and revenge, honing himself constantly in marksmanship, fighting and gymnastics. He never cared for much else. Indeed, for all the shipments Amin guarded, he never learned to pilot a boat and could barely swim.

On the other hand, Richard grew to love the West. At first, it was the simple things: solid walls, air conditioning and a thick bed with clean white sheets. France was so completely opposite of his dusty guerilla lifestyle that it felt like he had found the escape hatch to Paradise. He learned that very few people here had supported the Gulf War, and he grew to understand that, with democracy, one could no more blame a man for the actions of his government than blame a spider for being poisonous.

Heroin smuggling made a lot of money for Il Siyâh, and Richard didn't do badly himself. His contacts in Marseille showed him how to take his own cut and introduced him to the wonderful things that money would buy. Soon, he was spending less time at his Spartan apartment off the coast and more time in the clubs and bars of Marseille. It became a chore just to go back to meet the ship.

He remembered feeling that he had more than any man could ever want. It's funny, he thought, how appetites grow. And now, of course, he had a far more affluent sponsor than Il Siyâh.

Amin rolled the towel up and set it on the shelf with the same reverence he would give his own rug. The prayer had cleared his mind and gave him the strength to look at his pasty, frosted brother without showing the repulsion he felt. Amin regretted his feelings; he deeply respected Thoaab'a for what he did, dressing like the Devil so he could sneak around inside of Hell. And without his brother's work, Amin couldn't do his own.

There were no chairs in the room, so Amin sat on the bed by his brother. He sat close, not wanting Thoaab'a to feel self-conscious about his appearance. Amin didn't know what nightmares beset his brother, living as he did, but Thoaab'a's face was thick below the eyes and it was obvious that he had not slept well last night.

"Did you find the saboteur?" Amin asked.

"I did."

"And?"

Thoaab'a shook his head. "There were too many people around. I have to be careful, I don't have the skill with a gun that you do."

Amin put his hand reassuringly on his brother's knee. "It is better that you leave them to me. We wouldn't want to risk your position." His brother nodded and seemed assured by his words. But Amin had always found it hard to tell what Thoaab'a was thinking.

"Was the woman still with him?" Amin asked.

"Yes," Thoaab'a replied, his eyebrows rising appreciatively. "She is impressive."

Amin nodded; he had seen her shoot. Unlike the Americans, neither of them relished the thought of killing a woman. But sometimes it was necessary. The biggest offense was that the Westerners would arm their women and teach them to fight.

"She will be a big challenge," Amin said, "and not just morally. But she protects the saboteur, so it must be done."

"You can take her?"

"She is a good shot, and clever. She caught me off guard last time, but next time I will be ready. More importantly, she is an infidel. She flaunts her hair and dyes it. Allah will guide my hand against hers."

"That is good," Thoaab'a nodded. He drew a breath and hesitated, a measured performance for the sake of his brother, and spoke apologetically: "I'm afraid we have to put off our hunt for the saboteur. We've received new orders."

Amin flared with anger. "I won't..." he started, but his brother laid a hand on his arm and assured him that their revenge would come. It had amazed and puzzled Amin how quickly his brother had learned the name of the man who sabotaged the bomb. How Il Siyâh learned, he corrected himself. His brother had been his only contact with the brotherhood since he arrived in Paris, and he had begun to think of them as one and the same.

"The resistance is sending another bomb," Thoaab'a said. "We are to pave the way for it." Amin felt his smile stretch the skin on his face. Excitement welled up inside him and he hopped to his feet. He paced the room, then moved to the window. It was early, but already two drunks shouted at each other in the alley below. You could sit at this window, Amin thought, and watch the West decay before your eyes. Someone needed to pull the trigger; it was a mercy kill. Amin turned back to his brother.

"Tell me what I must do."

X

"*I*f we're stealing a car, there are literally hundreds of them just sitting on the street."

"We're not stealing a car," Grey replied.

"So what are the bolt-cutters for?" Leigh asked impatiently. Grey was being tight-lipped about his plans, which meant that he knew she wouldn't like them. She didn't care much for the neighborhood, either.

As a cop, her first beat was the slums of Paris. Though barely a twenty minute walk from the city center, it could have been the other side of the world. Violence was a way of life in these quarters, with roving gangs killing each other over everything from women to territory. Leigh had even seen a homeless man brain another one, just to get his shopping cart. And far too often, she'd be called in to rescue some innocent who just didn't know better than to be walking around here. Fortunately, it was still early, and low-rent criminals liked to sleep in.

The morning was pale white, somewhere between fog and rain, and cold—Leigh's breath puffed into the air. She was shivering, having only a thin coat to wear over the same thin outfit from last night.

Grey had spooked when they left the Le Salon Rouge, certain they were being followed, and insisted they take a couple of rooms at a hotel rather than return to their apartments. Leigh hadn't noticed anything, but she trusted his instincts. Or at least she had last night.

This morning, his actions weren't speaking too highly of his judgment. First he declared his hand healed and threw away the gauze. Then he purchased bolt cutters, deciding it was unsafe to get his keys from his apartment—he didn't say what the keys were for. And now he led them to one of the worse sections in town, navigating with more guesswork than sense of direction.

They turned onto a dead-end street, one side a crumbling cement wall and the other a row of arched green doors. Grey, pleased with himself, strode down the block, stopping at a double-door with the number "5" tacked up with a bent nail.

Grey slipped the bolt cutter's jaws over the thick padlock that hung from the wrought-iron hasp. He squeezed the handle together and winced. Nothing happened.

He shifted one handle to the inside of his thigh, pulling the other to it with his good hand. The beveled jaw pinched through the shackle. He flipped open the hasp and tugged on the handle. The door shuddered open, sagging against the pavement.

Inside, dust swirled in the air. Light fell on the outline of a car, draped over with a thick canvas cover. Grey leaned the bolt cutters against the doorway and peeled the cloth back, revealing the dark jade of a late model MG convertible.

It was an impressive roadster, a modern two-seater that bulged up at the hood and out at the wheels. Foot-wide rubber-band tires were stretched onto aluminum-cast rims and the convertible top was ruddy leather with thick stitchwork at the seams. Grey leaned in the open window and turned the key that was already in the ignition. The engine fired instantly, purring like a tiger. A very fast tiger.

"Mid-life crisis?" Leigh asked.

"A car like this is useful in my line of work."

"The agency didn't buy you this."

"They don't even know I have it."

"That doesn't seem likely."

"Three years ago, I worked a human-trafficking case down in Lyon. Some Russian Mafioso was moving women to Israeli brothels. He smelled us coming and slipped away. In his rush to pack, he left behind the number to a modest Swiss bank account."

"Which you happened to find."

"Wadded up in his trashcan. I emptied the account to hobble him. You can't buy prostitutes without cash."

"Very noble. And then you bought this for your retirement."

"For my work. Untraceable plates, counterfeit papers. I work for the government, so I know which counterfeiters talk and which don't."

"And you didn't report any of it? Some would consider that stealing."

"The secrets you keep, keep you. I've noticed that most intelligence agencies have the bad habit of abandoning their agents just when they most need them."

Leigh shook her head. It was typical of Grey to over-justify barely justifiable actions. But then she saw another angle to what he was saying: "Is that what's happening? Are you being burned by the CIA?"

Grey shook his head. "Not the CIA. But…" Grey didn't have an answer. "I'd at least like to know what it is I'm supposed to know that makes me worth killing."

Leigh nodded. She opened the passenger door and slid into the seat, half expecting Grey to object. There was enough leather inside for a cattle ranch. Grey shoved open the other garage door and got in beside her. He familiarized himself with the dials and switches. When he ran out of things to fiddle with, he said:

"Your best play is I drop you off in some remote village and you sit this out."

"Agreed."

"But that's not happening?"

"No."

"You have nothing at stake here."

Leigh shrugged. "Your job is kind of fun."

"Getting shot at is not fun."

"Watching you get shot at is fun."

Grey scowled. "You're treating this too lightly."

"No, you're treating me too lightly. I used to be a police officer and I know how to use a gun, which is more than I can say about you. The guy who is after you is good. You wouldn't stand a chance alone."

"You're going to be my bodyguard?"

"Someone's got to. What you're working on is important, isn't it? The paper this morning said it was a nuclear bomb that the police found."

Grey nodded.

"This is my country, not yours."

"This could all be a wild goose chase—"

"You know any better geese to chase?" Leigh asked.

Grey choked back a retort. He didn't want her along, but that was for personal reasons. It would be foolish of him to turn down her help—to turn down any help. He wasn't going to get a lot of offers. Besides, she was right: this was her country. She had a better motivation than he did.

He dropped the MG into gear and eased it through the tight archway. It had been a long time since he had driven this car and he forgot how much he liked it. The bucket seats cradled him, the angled gearshift molded to his hand, and the thick steering wheel gripped his fingers, sparing him the work. Driving this car was like sprouting wheels from his body.

He drove through a maze of alleys, then pulled onto a busy avenue, joining the morning traffic as it crawled to the freeway. Grey was preoccupied with where he was going and what to do when he got there, and took no notice of the blue Citroen that pulled out from the curb when he passed.

It followed them at a distance.

XI

"**I**'ve been searching my desk for your report and I haven't found it anywhere."

"My report?" Faison asked. He knew he was being toyed with, but since Denis was the boss, he had no choice but to play flunkey.

"Your report," Denis replied. "The one that informs me that you've sent one of our agents out of town."

Faison glanced at Peerson, who stood at the doorway, almost too large to squeeze through. Denis had only called Faison, but both had showed up. These two had become inseparable—the Laurel and Hardy of intelligence. Peerson gave Faison a shrug, disowning the problem. Faison grimaced and turned back to Denis, "I'm not sure I know what you mean," he said.

"What I mean is Jerard. I went to look for him, only to learn from his ID beacon that he's somewhere south of Orleans."

"He is?"

"He is. But what is he doing there?" Denis asked.

"I don't know exactly." Faison formed his words carefully, as if cross-checking them with an internal dictionary. "I believe he's operating on a lead."

"Oh?" Denis shifted his attention to Peerson. "I wasn't aware we had any leads worth operating on."

Peerson looked at his feet, hoping Denis wouldn't press him about this. When it became obvious he would, Peerson clicked his smile on and said: "The bad news is we might have one."

"What does that mean?"

"Honestly, we didn't know Jerard was out of town. I wasn't even aware you had a way to track them. Your own agents, I mean. They have some sort of GPS signature?"

"Who is he following?" Denis said, irritated by Peerson's digression.

"Grey Stark."

Denis looked at Peerson like the man had lost his head, then glared at Faison like he wanted to rip his off. Finally he just sank into his seat and rubbed his eyes. He really was very tired.

For two days now, Denis had been dealing with a battery of politicians that could have stormed Versailles. Word had spread fast that the Paris bomb was a nuke, with dire results. Spontaneous riots were breaking out. Surly crowds were looting and destroying Muslim-run stores. Arabs were being attacked in the streets. There had been several deaths and one reported gang rape. France was in chaos. People wanted facts, but not nearly as much as they wanted blood. And damned be the politician who couldn't give them both.

The politicians were coming to Denis for answers, but he didn't have any. These things take time, he told them, and he had the entire DST working around the clock. But his constant reassurances were sounding hollow even to himself, like a goose that could only honk one note.

Ninety-five percent of all the decisions people make are emotional ones, requiring almost no factual support. The Americans steadfastly blamed Iran for the bomb and their dogmatism was defining it as the truth. Certainly it had become an uphill battle to convince anyone otherwise.

So it wasn't just the hours that were wearing Denis out, but the stress. And to top it off, he had to deal with these two clowns. Still, he needed to be more careful. Peerson wasn't here to assist with the investigation; NATO, or whomever it was that really ran the NSC, sent him here to take it over. Denis should be working Peerson over, not broadcasting his own weaknesses.

"Okay," Denis said in a softer tone. "Tell me why Jerard is following Grey Stark."

Peerson crossed to the desk and laid a photo down. Denis thought of a dozen possible responses, but didn't voice any of them. Peerson was here to play his hand and Denis was going to let him play it.

"It seems odd," Peerson said, "that an American agent would take his wife to a club full of retired KGB agents."

"So you stuck a tail on him?"

"He's supposed to be working for me."

"Who says he's not?"

"I didn't ask him to go there. He hasn't even checked in since yesterday. He's in direct violation of his orders." Peerson flushed, lofting a fist to strike at the desk.

Denis raised his hand. "I didn't mean to be antagonistic. I understand your concern. It's just that I have a lot on my plate and it would make my life easier if you kept me informed."

Peerson's anger vaporized—too easily to have been real. He accepted the apology with a nod. "Of course," Peerson said. "I know you have a special interest in Jerard."

"He's the pride of the department," Denis replied, but he could see Peerson knew better. "Sit down and tell me what you're thinking," Denis invited, gesturing to the chair opposite.

Peerson took the seat gingerly, as if his corpulent body remembered the failures of chairs past. He asked: "What if there was some connection between Grey's work in Germany and this bomb?"

Denis covered his surprise by scratching his forehead. Peerson had hit dangerously close to the truth. "How so?"

"It's just a thought. But the timing is right."

"So there is no proof?"

"Proof? You don't wait for proof to start an investigation. The point of an investigation is to dig up the proof."

Denis flicked his hand, batting Peerson's argument away. "I didn't mean to challenge you, it was just a question. You think that Grey is pursuing this connection without telling you about it?"

"I think that Grey is…" Peerson stopped short. "Yes, I suppose he could be pursuing such a connection."

"What else could it be?" Denis knew what Peerson wanted to say; he wondered if he would say it.

"It might be nothing," Peerson said, backing down. "But he somehow knows something we don't."

"He often does. He's a clever one."

"You trust him?"

"Completely," Denis said.

"And he trusts you. Has he told you anything?"

"He hasn't," Denis replied. He wondering how much Peerson already knew. The Americans knew the bomb was a nuke, so they probably had the same document Faison had taken from Peerson. Denis couldn't shake the feeling that he was the one being spun, not the other way around. But paranoia fed on stress and sleep deprivation, and he had had plenty of both.

"Your point is well made," he continued, "and I have no problem allowing Jerard to continue to track Grey Stark. I do expect to be the first to know what he learns." Denis directed the last comment at Faison, knowing his words were wasted on Peerson. Faison nodded agreeably, happy to survive what had started as such bleak circumstances.

"We'll need Jerard's GPS code," Peerson said.

"I can't give you his code."

"You're supposed to give me full cooperation," Peerson pressed. Not angry, calculated.

"For this case only," Denis responded. "Personal GPS beacons are permanent and confidential. Not for sharing."

"You could give it to him." Peerson directed a finger at Faison.

"I'll think about it. In the meantime, do let me know if either of *you* decide to leave town."

Peerson frowned. He didn't like this abrupt end to the meeting, but in Denis's office, Denis was in charge. For now. "Of course," he said, rising to his feet. He motioned Faison ahead, but Denis said:

"Faison, I wonder if I might have a word with you." Faison froze, looking at the door as if to make a break for it. After Peerson was gone, Denis gestured him to a seat.

"You never were an operative, were you?" Denis knew the answer, but waited for Faison to confirm it before he continued: "It's different out there in the field. It's dangerous."

"Yes, I know."

"Do you?" Denis snapped. "Bad guys carry guns, and they know how to use them. Out there, our people are on their own. They can't trust the local police, so the further they get from Paris, the further they get from help. Too many times we've dug up missing agents in the hospital. Or the morgue."

Denis was laying it on thick, but Faison knew why: Denis and Jerard shared a special relationship. It hadn't been just talent that got Jerard where he was. Well, Faison thought, not that kind of talent. Denis was overdue for a rude awakening about his precious operatives, but this wasn't the time or the place.

Over the next five minutes, Faison counted twenty-six different pens in a coffee mug on the desk. He estimated there were eighty-two remaining pages in the legal-sized notepad next to the mug and that there was just shy of three hundred pieces of wrapped mints in the large glass jar.

During all of this, Denis lectured like a school teacher— punctuating his points with pedantic questions. Faison absorbed nothing more than what he needed to articulate responses.

At the end of his speech, Denis scribbled a long hexadecimal number on a piece of paper, folded it and handed it to Faison. It was Jerard's personal ID code, the GPS signature that would allow Faison to determine, at any point, where Jerard was standing to within six centimeters.

"Take care of him," Denis said with threatening finality. Faison nodded one last time and escaped Denis's clutches.

Peerson was waiting for Faison in the hall. He took a fat glance at the paper in Faison's hand and gave him a proud smile. Faison shoved the paper into his pocket.

"In light of Mr. Stark skipping town," Peerson said, "I think it's time to bring you up to speed on a couple of things. Why don't we go down to my office?"

Peerson had been both a boon and a burden to Faison, but the man always had good information. Faison nodded and Peerson motioned him ahead.

XII

"Here it is five decades later and we're still calling on the Americans do our dirty work."

"Why is this *our* dirty work?"

The first man let out a snort so derisive that it would have led to a fist-fight, were it anywhere but on the 'edgy' talk show that boomed from the MG's radio. "Wake up!" the man said, "They didn't find the bomb in New York!"

"There's no link between the bomb and Iran, so why should we help—"

"Our government says there is. Just this morning, fourteen more senators recommended that we join the invasion of Iran. That makes one hundred and thirty-eight total."

"Not a majority."

"It will be soon. And look at the National Assembly: they're even closer. Our government is ready to defend—"

Grey pressed a button on the steering wheel and the radio fell silent. He couldn't help but think that the French were talking tough considering they hadn't won a war since the Revolution of 1848. And they only won that because they owned both teams.

The morning's mist had thickened to a downpour and rain beat on the car's leather roof like mallets on a timpani. The tires hissed, cutting wide grooves in the water that coated the E-11 freeway. They were heading south.

Grey flipped on the heater and the cold damp air warmed to a humid jungle. He ran the AC to dry the air, but it didn't have much effect. Even the most modern of convertibles made poor shelter when the weather turned bad. As the car heated up, Leigh unbuttoned her jacket and pulled it open to her shoulders.

"So where are we headed?" she asked.

"Marseille."

"I should have packed some shorts." It was a lame joke, but it at least deserved a polite smile. Grey didn't give her one. He was in one of his dark moods, his teeth clenched, staring down the road to that mythical point where the painted lines converged. Over the last few years, Grey had become so chronically distant that Leigh found silence the hardest thing to share with him. Especially now, with their life together over but for the paperwork. She said the first thing that came to mind:

"They gave it a code name."

"Who gave what a code name?" Grey scoffed. Leigh couldn't tell if his irritation was directed at her, or some unnamed annoyance that stewed in his gut. The latter was fairly common—Grey would drop into a funk and stay there for days without ever telling her why. She had long ago decided to simply ignore any angst that he didn't bother to discuss.

"The Americans. They're calling it *Operation Eternal Freedom*. I saw it in the morning paper."

Grey gave her no more than a grunt, but she was committed to the conversation: "Isn't that the stupidest name you've ever heard?"

"It might be the scariest."

"You don't believe the Iranians are behind this, do you?"

Grey had a lot on his mind and didn't want to chit-chat with his soon to be ex-wife. During their years together, Leigh had honed her instinct, learning the best times to irritate him with her prattle. He turned to her, intent on lashing out with the most sarcastic comment he could think of. But she looked tired and miserable, and her fancy dress was ruined from sleeping in it. She smiled at him, her make-up smudged and her lipstick worn off, and somehow was as beautiful as she had ever been. He turned back to the road; that woman, he thought, could charm the knife off a mugger.

"I'm not as confident," he finally said, "as some of my counterparts."

"And you're enjoying the chance to play spy again."

Grey thought about it and smiled. "Yes. I think I am."

That was the wrong answer; it was Leigh's turn to be irritated. "Care to tell me about this 'Major' that Vladimir mentioned?"

"I can't."

"Va. Te faire. Foutre."

"It's classified information."

"Of course it is. That's too incredibly fucking convenient an answer for it not to be."

"What?"

"You have the perfect excuse. If you don't want to tell me something, you just say, 'I can't tell you that, it's classified.' What happened to your face? 'It's classified.' You look tired, rough day? 'Classified day.' How's the casserole? Which dress do you prefer? 'Classified!'" She was screaming now.

"Leigh—"

"Don't even try. Do you have any idea how completely isolating it is to be with a man who won't even tell you what he ate for lunch? And what makes it really pathetic is that you're not even a real secret agent anymore. You *were* a secret agent, in some mysterious former life of yours, but now you're just a wanna-be secret agent who is stuck in France."

Leigh's face burned with anger, but her eyes had melted. Water dripped onto her dress, darkening it with round shadows. "I quit my job for you. I cleared my life out to make room for you and you put nothing…"

She trailed off. Grey reached a hand to her shoulder. She jerked away as if it were a poisonous snake.

"You put nothing back in," Leigh said, finding new venom. "You gave everything to a job that didn't want you, and you left me empty." She looked down at the floorboards, whispering from the strain. "You were supposed to be on my side."

Grey put his hand back on the steering wheel. The wipers slapped against the windshield, rain pounded the car. Finally he said, "Major General Nicolae Dragos."

"What?"

"That's who Vladimir told me to see."

"And he lives in Marseille?"

Grey shook his head. "Not personally, but the only man who can set up a meeting with him does." Grey drove on for a minute, then volunteered: "There's also another man there that I'd like to talk to. He might be able to tell me about the bomb so that I won't have to see the Major."

Leigh nodded, "Why does the Major want to kill you?"

Grey shrugged.

"Can't tell me, huh?"

Grey looked at Leigh. Her eyes were shiny, but the tears had stopped. "I wouldn't want to," he said. "It's nothing I'm proud of."

Leigh wiped her cheeks with her thumb. "Okay," she said. "Thank you for being honest."

Grey nodded. Five miles passed before he added, "It's long overdue."

Leigh pointed at a green road sign for Bourges. "Take this exit."

"Change your mind?"

"No. But I'm dressed for the ballroom and you look like you live with your mother."

"We don't have time to shop."

"That attitude alone," Leigh said, "necessitates my presence on this outing." She gave Grey a crafty smile.

He tapped the blinker and turned down the exit ramp.

_F_aison was hunched over a thick folder labeled: *Stark, Grey - Service Record*. He held an unsharpened pencil between his teeth the way a dog carries a stick, gnawing it thoughtfully and dribbling yellow flakes onto the desk. He chewed when he was thinking, and more than once had gotten a mouthful of ink. So now he kept a jar stuffed with pencils on his desk and stuck one in his mouth whenever he was working on something difficult. There were already several in the trashcan.

Also on his desk was the evening paper, with a picture of the American President and a two-inch headline that read: "We're going in!" The President pointed at the camera like he was posing for an army recruitment poster. By now, America's war was old news. More interesting was the sidebar article that detailed a pro-war protest in the First Arrondissement.

A half million French citizens gathered in Place Vendome, demanding their country take action against Iran. In the photo, two college-age kids held up posters. One said, "Rise up!" and the other said, "Fight our own fights!" Neither kid looked like he could tell a gun from a broom and one of them had a flower behind his ear. If France did join the war, chances were these two would be back tomorrow to protest against it.

Peerson arrived noiselessly at the open doorway. He watched Faison read for a moment, then knocked on the frame. Faison motioned him in.

"What do you think?" Peerson asked.

"This is a lot of information. How did you get it all?"

"He is one of ours."

"One of the CIA's, you mean."

Peerson shook his head paternally. "You've got to stop thinking of us as separate entities. We're all one big happy family." Faison looked unconvinced, so Peerson added: "Or will be soon enough."

"So you have access to the CIA's files?" Faison pressed.

"I don't know where this stuff comes from," Peerson shrugged. "I request someone's file and they give it to me."

"Ah," Faison said, looking back at Grey's file. It was fifty-odd pages of freshly-printed monochrome. For decades now, records were kept by simply entering everything into a computer, allowing them to be accessed from anywhere and printed out anytime. It was an efficient way to handle information, but not his favorite.

Faison preferred a more traditional approach to research. Here at the Directorate, he could walk down to the Records

Hall and view the original documents. Their files tended to be a disorganized mess of clippings and reports, but they were real. When reports were filed by hand, he could recognize the handwriting and feel the age of the paper. A computer record just didn't feel as authentic. Something that happened twelve years ago could have been updated yesterday. Even the photos were easy to manipulate.

Not that he suspected the report's contents had been tampered with. They just lacked the gravity of the original documents. Perhaps that was why Faison wasn't convinced.

"So Agent Stark did horrible things twenty years ago and you think that ties him into this?"

"You don't? It would explain a lot."

"It would explain everything, but it feels like a stretch."

Peerson was surprised by Faison's attitude. Frankly, he was surprised to see him show any attitude at all. "How so?"

"I think we're short on suspects," Faison said, "so we're making a big deal out of the one that we have."

"Do you like Stark?" Peerson asked. "I mean, personally."

"I don't dislike him."

"Fair enough."

"Do you?"

"I don't really feel that we've been properly introduced." Peerson gave a half-hearted laugh, then drooped into thought. "I guess I'm offended by his behavior. But that's not clouding my judgment."

"As far as you know."

Peerson leaned in as if to share a secret. "Let me tell you what I *do* know. There's a distinct connection between Grey Stark and this bomb. Denis trusts Stark to a fault, and it would take overwhelming evidence to convince him otherwise. Stark may very well be counting on this trust to keep the DST off his back while he runs around doing who knows what."

Faison nodded his head. He didn't agree with Peerson, he just wanted him to back away. His breath smelled of sour milk.

"However you slice it," Peerson concluded, "we have no excuse to not follow every lead we have. Our job is to be unbiased, and your own people are demanding answers."

Faison saw the gears turn behind the small green eyes, but he wasn't sure what to make of it. Peerson had already proved useful, and throwing suspicion on Grey certainly fit into his own plan. But his plan was delicate; involving Peerson was risky. So, unfortunately, was excluding him. He'd have to tread carefully.

"Okay," Faison said. "What do you want from me?"

"For starters, Jerard's GPS ID."

"Impossible. I've been given a direct order not to share it."

"Ah," Peerson said, and lapsed into silence. He never doubted Faison had such orders, the only question was, if properly motivated, would he disobey them. Peerson could promise all sorts of rewards, but in the end it came down to the strength of Faison's loyalty to the Directorate.

"It's really only a matter of time before France joins the Commission," Peerson said, as if it were an unrelated thought. "We're going to have to staff up quite a bit here."

"Are you trying to bribe me?"

"No, no." Peerson said with thin innocence. "But let me assure you that at the NSC we don't make our promotions based on sexual preference."

It was a bribe, Faison thought. But also a threat.

Peerson pushed to his feet and waddled to the door. Faison watched him go, wondering how much the man really did know. Denis was too obvious about Jerard, certainly, and their affair had been going on far too long. Interdepartmental romances were strictly forbidden, but Denis was too influential to suffer from either his sexual preference or from having an affair with one of his employees. It would, however, forestall Jerard's career and put his unmerited promotions under scrutiny. And these days, Denis took no greater pleasure than adding to his young lover's success. If Peerson leveraged their indiscretion—and that would certainly be his next move—he might be able to push Denis to give him what he wanted. And while Faison didn't want to help Peerson, it was better himself than Denis.

"Dr. Peerson?"

"Yes," Peerson replied, rotating back to Faison. Faison rose from his seat, dug his hand into his coat pocket and pulled out the paper Denis had given him earlier. He unfolded it onto his desk, quickly memorized the number, and joined Peerson at the door.

"I'm going to get a cup of coffee, would you care to join me?"

"No, thank you," Peerson replied, eyeing the paper like it was a half-naked schoolgirl. "I've got to go and file a report."

"Very well. Perhaps I'll see you later." Faison walked out, leaving Peerson alone in his office.

BOOK
THREE

1

*G*rey was down on his knees, gently probing underneath the trunk of his car. His fingers examined every bump and bolt until—halfway up the side of his gas tank—they discovered something that wasn't supposed to be there. He gave the object a tug; a magnet popped free and the back of his hand scraped against the leaf spring. He let out a grunt that echoed through the empty parking deck.

The garage was cool and musty, its smooth cement trapping moisture from the nearby Mediterranean Sea. Grey carried the object over to a cement pillar, where a triangle of sunlight cut through the structure. The device was the size of a small pager, smooth black plastic with no markings.

There was a battery cover on the back, inside of which would be written the device's transmission frequency. But if the battery came loose, it would stop transmitting and alert its owner that he had found it. Besides, Grey already knew what it was: a tracking device, manufactured here in France, for the exclusive use of the Directorate. Right now, Grey would be a red dot on the big map in DST headquarters. And, Grey thought, that meant it would be a DST agent who was tailing him.

Grey hadn't noticed the tail until this morning. After leaving the hotel's garage, he circled the block—a precautionary maneuver drilled so deeply into his head that he felt odd if he didn't. Noticing the blue Citroen gave him a moment of panic—his last tail had been less interested in following him than killing him. And that man was still out there somewhere.

So Grey felt relief to know it was the DST on his tail, but couldn't decide if he had been stupid to think he had kept the MG a secret or if he should be impressed that Denis knew about it. Of course, his tail and this tracking device might not be related. It would be wise to make sure.

He walked back to the MG and popped the trunk. He lifted the carpet up and pulled up the spare tire. He flipped it over and peeled off a Mylar bag taped to the rim—camouflaged against the brushed aluminum. Inside was a well-worn wallet that had once belonged to a German national named Max Heiss.

Heiss was in the coffee trade and routinely traveled to France, Spain, and Italy on business. Besides his native German, he was fluent in English and spoke limited French and Spanish. Face-to-face, the man looked nothing like Grey, but his physical characteristics matched, so when Grey put his own photo on Heiss's passport and driver's license, it was a perfect cover.

Grey flipped through the wallet, inspecting the cards inside. Besides the photo IDs, the identity included credit and bank cards, along with some random items, like a gym membership, a shopping list, and fifteen hundred German-minted Euros. The CIA had provided Grey with a number of alternate identities, but this was one he'd acquired through less orthodox methods. And he could only hope it was a better-kept secret than the car was.

He traded his wallet and passport with Max's, sealing his own inside the Mylar bag and taping it back into place. He put the trunk back together and was about to close it when he had another thought. He removed a black velvet bag from the side compartment. Inside were two spare clips for the Beretta and a pair of compact binoculars. Grey reloaded his pistol, stashing the spare clip in his holster, and slid the binoculars into his jacket pocket. He closed the trunk and replaced the tracking device under the car.

Grey emerged from the parking garage, squinting in the sunlight and patting every pocket before finding his sunglasses. He cleaned them methodically with a small cloth, giving his tail plenty of time to notice that he was standing there. Of course, the way Leigh had dressed him, it would be hard not to.

His black suit was French-cut: narrow at the shoulders and low-slung at the hips. It was tight in all the wrong places, making him feel stiff and unbalanced. His shirt was bright white in the way that only brand-new shirts are, and the green tie matched his archaic plaid overcoat—a style that, Leigh insisted, had risen Phoenix-like back to the height of fashion. He slipped on his sunglasses and strolled across the busy street, cutting through traffic and earning a few honks.

The outside air was baked dry and smelled like the garbage collectors were on strike. The streets of downtown Marseille were so dirty that a man felt sorry for his own shoes—and there were plenty of people who didn't even have any.

Marseille's waterfront was lined by wealthy estates, but the inner city was smeared with the most desperate of immigrants. They came from Africa and the Middle East, crossing over from Morocco in rowboats, rafts, or cramped cargo holds. They brought little except hope, of either finding a better life or escaping a past crime. For many, a squalid flop-house in Marseille was such a vast improvement on their lives that they had little ambition beyond their next meal.

This city had been a magnet for desperados since the late sixties, when it was the largest refiner of heroin in the world. Turkish opium, arriving by way of Lebanon, was traded openly in the marketplaces. France eventually shut the factories down, but by then the Mafia was well-established; they found other uses for Europe's least-regulated port. The city was the fertile bed for corruption, filled with criminals from every walk of life, be it the well-bred internationals, the mobster ruffians, or the desperate beggars who'd come at their victim with a butter knife they'd sharpened on the edge of the sidewalk. Life in Marseille was a bargain and there was little fifty dollars wouldn't buy.

Grey walked downhill, instinctively drawn toward the fresh air rising from the sea. Marseille hadn't been treated with the reverence—or the money—that Paris had and most of the historical buildings had either fallen down or were some-where in the process. The few that remained were scattered among cheaply-made already-decaying fabrications that had been thrown up in the last fifty years. After a few blocks, Grey turned into a glass-covered office building that looked like a six-story mirror.

The air in the faux-marble lobby was cool on his skin and Grey realized he had broken a sweat on his short walk. He scanned the pegboard occupant list and selected a dentist on the top floor as his intended destination. He presented Max's driver's license to the desk guard and stepped into the elevator.

The sixth floor was a white-walled hallway with mustard carpet, lined with wooden doors, labeled with engraved plastic plates. Grey walked down the hall to a large window and casually leaned against the sill. There was a sand-filled ashtray, so Grey slipped a cigarette out and lit it. He hadn't smoked in years, but they were the perfect excuse for loitering. He puffed it several times to get it burning, then balanced it on the rim of the ashtray. He slipped the binoculars out and scanned the streets below.

After a few minutes of watching the crowd move around, he honed in on a pair of legs sticking out below an awning across the street. The legs shifted anxiously, but held their ground, waiting. It looked like a man, but Grey would need a lower angle to be sure.

Grey stuck the cigarette butt into the sand and walked back to elevator. He selected the fourth floor and the door opened to a small reception. A well-polished woman smiled at him from across a wooden desk. Grey returned the smile, adding in a touch of confusion, and pressed the next button down. They smiled at each other sincerely until the closing doors relieved them of the burden.

The third floor looked like the sixth and Grey walked to the window. He had the binoculars in hand, but didn't need them: it was Jerard. He seemed to be staring right at him. Grey jerked back before remembering that the reflective windows blocked the view inside. He walked back and found the stairs.

He should have guessed it was Jerard. The young captain was smart enough to find Grey's car, but inexperienced enough to give himself away. Denis had been too quick to promote

Jerard, but the kid had potential. Given another five years—and a little real-world experience—he would be a top-drawer agent.

The steps bottomed out at a door with *Sortie de Secours* painted in red letters. The latch was wired to an alarm. Grey pulled a small multi-tool from his pocket and flipped out the Phillips-head screwdriver. He angled it into the doorjamb, unscrewing the latch-plate. A minute later, the plate tinkled to the floor and the door swung open. Grey stepped into the alley behind the building and propped the door shut with a brick.

He walked in long strides that made his new pants chirp. Jerard would wait out front for at least the next two hours, because that was what the manual said to do. That gave Grey plenty of time for his meeting, and he could even swing back afterwards to pick Jerard up again. If no one checked too closely, they would think he was just getting a cavity filled.

He stuck to the alleyways for several blocks before cutting back to the main street. He put Jerard out of his mind and focused on what came next. He only had this one chance to get what he needed without going to the Major. It would be a delicate situation and he had to be ready, no matter what happened.

II

*T*he late morning sun cooked Grey inside his suit as he crossed a crowded plaza, the air thick with dust and sweat. Streams of people pushed through each other while trolley drivers dogmatically clanged their bells, forcing their cars through the oblivious crowd. There was an angry tension in the plaza, so Grey skirted the edge then headed up a mountainous hill that was steep enough to have stairs instead of a sidewalk.

He climbed quickly, drawn upward by the cooler, cleaner air. As he gained altitude, the apartment buildings around him became houses and the houses became mansions. Exotic plants lined the path and flowers drooled from window boxes, their exotic scents filling the air. Grey was out of shape. Halfway up the hill his heart was pounding so hard he felt it in his teeth. His legs were thick and stiff, as if cast from heavy rubber. He was glad Leigh wasn't here to see him.

He had convinced her it was best if he went alone, that she would only complicate his negotiations. It was true, but he was more afraid of putting her at risk; this was going to be a dangerous meeting. Leigh was plenty tough, but in this case, her police training was a disservice. Cops are trained to walk among the citizens they serve, to be a moral beacon for the community. Grey's world was a shadow, hidden from the public eye, and the people he dealt with had no morals, no rules, and no hesitations. Unlike common criminals, professional killers didn't need to work themselves into a frenzy just to kill someone; they just did it, without losing so much as a wink of sleep. There was nothing in Leigh's experience to prepare her for that. The more Grey thought about it, the more he realized this whole mission was far too dangerous for her. He wished that she would just abandon him and jump a train back to Paris.

The road leveled off at the hilltop and he saw his destination: Marseille's Notre Dame. Every city in France had a Notre Dame, as they had an Arc de Triomphe. Most of them paled against their Parisian counterparts, but this building was the exception, if only for its location. It was a marble building perched atop the tallest hill in the city—three times higher than any other—and offered postcard-views of the coastline and outlying islands.

Grey entered the stone-tiled courtyard and leaned against the rail to catch his breath. From this high up, Marseille looked like a model of itself. Its earthy clay buildings were white in the sun and the red tile roofs glowed. Round hills swelled below the city floor, fading to green outside the city limits, and fading from view as they traveled toward the French Alps and, eventually, Switzerland.

To the south, the deep blue Mediterranean—startlingly flat against the craggy coastline—drew a lazy arc across the horizon. The square harbor was jammed with tiny ships, and the people along its edge were no more than the grain in a motion picture. Two decaying forts guarded over the narrow passage to the sea and, outside their high walls, two islands loomed off the coast like the stepping-stones of a giant.

The larger one, Frioul, had been two separate islands until they were joined by a barrier wall which created a harbor on the landward coast. The island's forests had been leveled centuries back to provide wood for warships, and the topsoil washed away, leaving nothing but bare rock, layered sheets of stone that vaulted into the air.

A day hike on Frioul was like touring a museum. Forts from every war since the Bronze Age littered the island, though it was abandoned now except for a short bank of hotels that lined the ferry dock.

The other island, D'if, was smaller in size but larger in reputation. Its twenty-foot sea-cliffs transformed seamlessly into a low stone wall, the outer barrier of a castle that covered the entire island. D'if drew a small tourist trade because Dumas had re-imagined it as a prison in his novel,

The Count of Monte Cristo. But Grey was fond of a different story from the island's past.

Back when Marseille was still just a fishing town and D'if a barren rock, the King of Portugal ordered his subjects in India to send the Pope the gift of a rhinoceros which, at the time, was one of the most exotic animals on the planet. But the cargo ship suffered some mechanical trouble and the rhino was abandoned on D'if, perhaps with the hope of fetching it later.

Fishermen working in the shallows of the island discovered the rhino there—very few Frenchmen had even heard of a rhino, and it must have seemed a terrible creature to them. Nevertheless, they adopted it, bringing it food and sowing grass on the island.

The Rhino's fame spread fast and far. Soon there was no fishing in Marseille because all of the boats were used to ferry tourists out to the island, the most famous of which was King François the First, all the way from Paris. His interest in the rhino was mild, but the island itself, he pontificated, was an excellent defensive location for his ongoing war in Italy.

The warm-blooded rhino passed away as winter took grip, but the castle built by François became a lightning rod for war. Attempts to storm the castle brought death and destruction to peaceful Marseille until the city itself became a fortress and its residents purveyors of war's rough trade. If there was one thing that the centuries hadn't changed, Grey thought, it's that the whims of the powerful change the face of the world.

Even in October, the Mediterranean felt like summer and Grey's sweat dried quickly in the breeze. He turned to the church. The building was both narrow and tall, built to capitalize on its steep surroundings. Its footprint was no larger than a basketball court, but it thrust its shiny gold statue of the Virgin Mary a hundred feet into the air. She could be seen glimmering from any part of the city, day or night, holding her baby up so that he could enjoy the view. Standing this close, the wispy clouds streaming behind her gave Grey vertigo.

The chapel, true to Marseille's violent past, was protected by a deep square moat. Grey crossed over the thick-plank drawbridge and under an arched entrance. The dark stone hallway felt like cold water, but quickly opened into a sanctuary warm and waxy, lit by a hundred candles on an iron rack. The room was spacious but not huge, a cathedral built on the quarter scale. High-set windows cast shadowy light on thick marble pillars and heavy wooden pews.

Hundreds of boats were strung around the room like beads, each a carefully crafted model of every ship that was ever launched from the harbor below. The models were brought here for blessing. They were pagan charms, but even the stringent Catholics had to accommodate the endless superstitions of seamen.

The walls were jammed with so many paintings that they might have been wallpaper. At the podium, a twisted, tormented vision of the Savior on his cross was rendered in plaster, then painted bright colors to compensate for its cheap construction. The whole room felt like an antique bazaar.

There were only two people in the sanctuary. One was an old lady, kneeling at the altar and making her daily peace with God. The other was Demyan Ermolov, for whom it was certain God would offer no forgiveness.

Demyan was a little short and was dressed in the humble canvas clothing of an Amish farmer. His brown hair was sun-bleached, and his face earnest and unscarred. He looked like he'd never had a mean thought his entire life, which couldn't be further from the truth.

In his previous life, Demyan was an 'information extractor' for the KGB. Anyone else would call it torture. For twenty years, he made his living snipping, shocking, and gouging people, many of whom were fellow Soviet citizens. There were few people that didn't fear him and even his closest associates considered him a monster.

When Gorbachev announced Glasnost, barely a half-hour passed before Demyan was on a private jet to France. He tapped his well-tended Swiss bank account and got his face fixed, learned the local accent, and sequestered himself in one of the mansions that collected along the coast. He told his neighbors that he lived off the income of his vineyards—a commoner made good—and no one cared to ask further. Marseille made a habit out of being discreet—most everyone here had something to hide—as long as everyone stayed out of trouble. Grey was counting heavily on that.

Demyan caught his eye from across the room. He was sitting in a pew with his legs propped up on another, his feet dangling in the air. A long cigar stuck out of his mouth like a tank turret. It was unlit; Grey wasn't sure if he was being reverent or simply hadn't gotten to it yet.

Grey crossed the room, composed and wary. He sat on the edge of a pew across the aisle from Demyan.

"The great Grey Stark," Demyan said, smiling with teeth too big and white to be real. "You cannot even imagine my surprise to hear from you."

"I need some information."

"And you think I might give it to you?" Demyan swung his feet to the ground, leaning forward. His clothes might speak of manual labor, but his beach-ball stomach and flaccid arms argued that he hadn't lifted anything heavier than a forkful of steak or a glass of wine for at least a decade. His eyes were sprinkled with cinnamon and, even though it was early, his breath was bitter with alcohol. This is what happens, Grey thought, when men like us retire. We have nothing left to do but kill ourselves.

"I'll pay for it," Grey said.

"I'd like to see you pay. Tell me, is it true the Americans are building an oil pipeline from the Caspian Sea to the Gulf of Aden? And that they're going to overthrow every country in between?"

Grey took out a stack of money, everything from his wallet; if Demyan told him what he wanted, he could go home tonight. "You heard about the bomb in Paris?" he asked.

"You can put your money away," Demyan sneered, "it won't buy you anything here."

Grey set the money on his knee, hoping it was a temptation. The Russian wouldn't need it, but he might enjoy taking it from Grey. That he had agreed to meet Grey at all meant that he expected to get something out of it.

"I hear you have the plans for some new type of nuke," Demyan said. "Any truth to that?"

"None at all."

"Oh." Demyan regarded him with disappointment. "You're as talkative as usual."

Grey shrugged.

"Let me fill in the blanks," Demyan continued. "Your government thinks the North Koreans built this nuclear bomb and the Iranians planted it in France. You're not buying it personally, but you'll need proof if you're going to stop the war. Right so far?"

Grey didn't answer and Demyan didn't care: "So Vladimir points you to the Major—the sniveling hyena actually called up to tell me. Didn't want me claiming his reward money. You came down here to see Jacques and arrange a meeting with the Major, but figured as long as you're in town, you might as well ask me first. Especially since you figure that, unlike the Major, I wouldn't risk my comfortable retirement for a chance to feel your warm blood trickling through my fingers."

Demyan smiled at Grey, folding his hands on his lap. Grey felt long-forgotten hate for this man rise inside of him. He replied as tonelessly as possible: "I need to know if the Russians ever got the plans for the Deadfall Project. I know you were administering your trade in Berlin at the time. You must have heard something."

Demyan filled the empty cathedral with laughter. He went on for a long time, rolling with the easy gait of ripples on a pond. The old woman at the altar cut short her prayers and made a quick escape. They were alone when the laughter tapered off.

Demyan's face was red from the effort. He patted his brow with a delicate silk handkerchief that cost three times his pauper's outfit. After a couple of sedated wheezes, he folded the handkerchief into a careful triangle and stowed it in his jacket pocket.

"You're wrong about one thing," he said. "The Major's not the only one you should be afraid of."

He moved so casually, Grey almost missed the knife. It came out of the handkerchief pocket, flashing in the dim light as it shot towards his neck, Demyan's whole body in tow. The neck was a tough target, even with the element of surprise, but Demyan was good.

Grey kicked the floor, throwing himself backwards and sliding off the pew. The knife pierced the skin of his neck and drove up against his jugular, but Grey's retreating body made Demyan's thrust fall short. The knife got no more than a spoonful of blood as Grey crashed between two pews.

Grey's arms were constricted and his good knife out of reach in his boot. Demyan drove his blade toward Grey's crotch, the only fatal target in range. Grey cocked his leg up, ramming his heel into Demyan's chin. The knife went high, slicing across Grey's thigh.

Grey flipped up to his knees, pulling a flat blade from his belt buckle. It was only two inches long, wide and flat like a tree leaf. The stem passed through his fingers to a cross-bar handle. It was the worst weapon he had on him, incapable of anything but short thrusts, but it was the only thing he could reach.

Demyan saw the knife and pulled back into a crouch, his own knife extended defensively. Grey rose slowly, using a pew for support. His leg stung and he felt warm blood running down his neck.

"Really, Demyan, in a church," Grey said, walking cautiously into the aisle. He felt ridiculous wielding the small blade, but the cut on his leg would hinder him if he reached for the one in his boot; Demyan wouldn't miss the opportunity.

"You know that real Russians are atheists," Demyan replied. He smiled, but fear quivered his voice. He began a slow retreat.

"You could still tell me what I want to know and walk out of here."

"You think I am a heartless man, but a lot of my comrades died on your great eastern pilgrimage."

"Someone will tell me—why not you?"

The Russian spat out a laugh, the kind a trapped rat might. "No one will tell you. The Major has ordered you to be delivered to him."

"The Major doesn't give the orders anymore."

"Who are you kidding?" The wall came up behind Demyan and he flinched as it touched his back. Grey stepped in tight, keeping his opponent off balance. Demyan was out of shape, but he had the better weapon—Grey didn't have much of an advantage, so he didn't press his luck.

Demyan lowered his knife like he was giving up, but then rolled it in his fingers—pointing the blade downward—and swung his arm roundhouse at Grey's ribs.

Grey's free hand caught Demyan's wrist, stopping the knife as it cut through the fabric of his jacket. His other hand snaked low, coming up under the Russian's arm and into his exposed armpit. The blade sank to his fist. He jerked it out and blood spurted from the severed artery.

Demyan brought his free hand up to stop the bleeding, but Grey dropped his knife and pulled the Russian's hand into the air. Demyan tried to twist free, but the effort only sped his decline. Grey held both wrists firmly until the strength left them. When he let go, Demyan's legs buckled and he dropped to his knees. Gritting his teeth stoically, the Russian struggled to his feet and raised his knife. But he couldn't hold himself up: he fell back to his knees, splashing in a pool of his own blood. He smiled, trying to cover his pain, but he might as well have painted a flower on a gravestone.

Demyan died slowly, his body convulsing, his throat gurgling. He kept the smile on his face as he flopped against the wall and slid down to the floor, leaving a red streak across several paintings.

Grey didn't want to watch him die, so he looked at a painting instead. It was an oil-on-canvas, circa the Second World War, of a plane crumpled on the ground. Its squadron continued toward the setting sun, an obvious gap left by the downed plane. In the upper corner, an angel looked down at the crash with the knowing sadness of a mother fated to watch so many of her children die at each other's hand. This was a painting that belonged in a church, playing on a man's feelings of mortality by reminding him of the dead.

Finally, Demyan's body ceased even reflexive spasms. Grey picked up his knife and wiped it on Demyan's cotton shirt. He thought about closing Demyan's eyes, but, even in death, found the man too repulsive to touch.

Grey found his money scattered under a pew. He dropped a hundred Euro bill in the donations box and left. The money was merely a courtesy for the mess he left behind; Grey hated churches.

Jerard watched Grey leave the church. The CIA man looked calm, but walked much faster than when he had entered. Something in there had set him off, but Jerard didn't know what.

So far, he had been unimpressed with the American's acumen. Grey must have known that practically every security camera in France was networked, and that the DST had direct access to all of them. Grey's attempt to ditch him was ridiculous, as he merely punched up the building's address and watched him right through the screen of his phone. And when Grey slipped out the back, used his phone's electronic map to locate the mouth of the alley, and waited there to pick up the tail.

Unfortunately, Jerard had no idea what had transpired inside the church. The stone hallway at the entrance had carried his footsteps, so he was unable to sneak in. He tried his parabolic microphone, but couldn't find a good angle. He heard two men talking, but he couldn't understand what was said.

He went back outside and, pulling up a satellite photo of the church, made a quick survey of the property. He figured that, unless Grey planned to jump down a fifteen foot wall, the American would leave the way he had come in. So Jerard positioned himself on the second story balcony and waited.

Now, as he watched Stark head down the hill, he decided not to follow. He was more interested in who Stark had met with. But, after ten minutes, no one else emerged from the church. So he went down to the entrance and, deciding it would look ridiculous to do otherwise, strode in like a tourist.

In the sanctuary, Jerard found a man lying on his back. As he approached, he saw the wide pool of blood and felt the dead eyes stare at him. His stomach turned and bile rose inside his throat. He just managed to turn away as his breakfast surged to the floor. He dropped to his hands and heaved, his stomach empty long before it grew still.

Jerard looked back to the body, finding that it no longer upset him. In fact, he was elated: he had finally discovered something worth reporting.

Wiping his hands on his socks, he got to his feet and snapped a couple pictures with his phone's camera. He flipped out the little keyboard and thumbed up a status report, attaching the photos.

He considered sending the report directly to Denis, but thought better of it. He loved Denis dearly, but as his boss, Denis made too much of a fuss over him. As a result, Jerard lost—rather than gained—respect for his accomplishments. Denis didn't understand that he needed this respect. He was a captain now, soon to be running his own operations. How could he do that if his own men didn't look up to him?

No, Jerard thought, I won't even copy Denis on this. Let him get the report through normal channels for once. Besides, Jerard looked forward to the scandal: Grey Stark had just murdered a man on French soil. The CIA wasn't allowed to do that, not without permission. He knew that Denis would cover for Grey, but he wanted to see what would happen if he didn't get the chance.

III

*T*he restaurant was supported by thick wood pilings that extended across the beach and out over the sea. They were south of Marseille and the land curled back around, affording Leigh and Grey a view of the city across the water. It was early evening—the sun was still in the sky—but a candle burned on their table. A bartender polished wine glasses. Other than him, they had the place to themselves.

Grey had brought Leigh all the way out here to convince her to return to Paris. But so far they had picked through a plate of fried calamari, a course of pasta, the local fish in butter sauce, and neither of them had said a word to each other. Even the slice of cheesecake they were sharing—a habit since their very first date—had been ordered without discussion. They ate it with coffee while the incoming tide gently rocked the floor below them.

Grey fingered his neck. A wad of toilet paper was taped just below his collar. He hadn't dared to go to a hospital—by the time they stitched him up, someone would have tied him to Demyan's death and brought the cops in. Dealing with the cops would have meant bringing in the DST, which—in the best case scenario—would clip his wings for the rest of the investigation. So instead, he had asked Leigh to stitch him up in the hotel's bathroom, using the complimentary sewing kit. She was a good sport and didn't ask any questions. All she did was kid him that he must not have liked the clothing she picked out for him, getting it all bloody and cut up. She apparently decided there was something to that, because after she fixed him up, she went out and bought him an outfit that was more his style. She had been nothing but supportive since he returned from the church, making it hard to broach the topic of sending her home.

Grey put his fork by the dessert plate, sliding the remaining inch of cake toward Leigh. He cleared his throat and Leigh looked up expectantly, but he didn't say anything. He didn't know how to start, and the truth was he didn't really want her to go. Not now, when they were getting along.

Leigh forked off half the remaining cheesecake and pushed the plate back to Grey. He smiled at her, took his fork and, edging it down the middle of what remained, leaving a thin sliver that quivered on the plate. He eased the plate back to Leigh slowly, so as not to topple it. Leigh grabbed her butter knife and, using her fork as a guide, halved what remained with surgical precision. She chewed a miniscule bite slowly, exaggerating her satisfaction. She rubbed her hands together, then slid the plate back in short stages, laying her hands flat on the table and pressing with her thumbs.

Grey inspected the impossibly slender tower. He pulled the long knife from his boot, catching the low sun on the blade as it snapped open. Leigh leaned forward, bright with anticipation. Grey lined the knife up and secured the plate with his free hand. The moment he touched the plate, the cake plopped to its side.

Leigh burst out laughing, covering her mouth to protect Grey from airborne cheesecake. Grey shook his head, chuckling. Leigh leaned over the table and inspected Grey's face, suddenly concerned.

"What?" Grey asked.

"I didn't know you laughed anymore." She was teasing, but it hit Grey like a snowball in the face. He let the knife clatter to the plate and looked out at the crashing waves, admiring their tenacity.

"Listen," Grey said, keeping his gaze on the horizon, "we can go to a notary in the morning and get the divorce paperwork signed."

"You want me to leave?"

"You need to," he said, facing her.

Now Leigh looked away. She watched a breaker crash and followed it up the beach, its strength undercut by the wave that came before it. After a minute, she turned back to him, "He's going to kill you, isn't he? This Major."

"Probably."

"I'd like to know something about it."

There was only one answer. Grey tried his best to sound apologetic: "It's classified—"

"Declassify it," Leigh said, glaring. Grey looked down, but Leigh bent low and looked up into his eyes. "I'd like to know something about it because I'd like to know who my husband is. Especially if he's going off to get himself killed tomorrow." Her voice broke under the weight of the words, her throat tightened.

Jaw clenched, Grey shied away further. Leigh moved with him, keeping his eyes trapped in hers. Behind them, wine glasses squeaked under the polishing cloth. The bartender shined several glasses before Leigh gave up.

"Okay," she said. "I'll leave in the morning."

"I tried to kill him once," Grey said, his voice trembling from the effort.

Leigh looked up, surprised.

Grey pulled the story into his head. He had told it many times, and it came to him as if from a history book:

"If there was a hall of fame for double agents, Major Nicolae Dragos would top the list. Back at the height of the cold war, he was the KGB's top field operative. The man was smart and ruthless, climbing his way to the top on a pile of dead bodies. And he was 'hands on,' which means he liked to do his own dirty work."

"Dirty work?"

"Yeah," Grey said, reviewing events in his mind but sparing her the details. "Killing people, framing them, extortion, blackmail, harassment. That was the job, both his and mine. But I like to think I didn't relish it the way he did."

"I'm sure you…," Leigh started, but realized that she wasn't sure of anything.

"Berlin was the center of all intelligence activity," Grey continued. "The world's two largest powers, separated by a distance you could chuck a stone across. It was the ideal place to pass information through the Iron Curtain—both ways. When you couldn't sneak it across, you could usually just make a run for it.

"The wall went up overnight, cutting a lot of people off from their family and friends. Combine that with the decades of oppression the East Germans had suffered since the war, and most of them would trade anything they could to get over to the West. Better still, there were some who would stay and offer their help, no matter what the risk.

"Because of these people, we had been winning the war in Berlin for years. Until the Major showed up. Rumor was he volunteered, saw it as an opportunity."

"So you worked in Berlin?"

Grey stopped. Everything that mattered in his life had happened in Berlin, and yet he'd never so much as admitted to his own wife that he was stationed there. He could see the empty canyon that divided them, and that he had put it there.

"Yes, I worked in Berlin," he said. "For twelve years. I was the Head of Operations. I pretty much ran the place."

"Oh," Leigh replied. His admission should have been a victory, but right now it didn't seem important. "That explains a lot," she added.

"Like what?" Grey asked, eager to be sidetracked.

"Finish your story."

"Yes. Berlin had a reputation for being dangerous, but, outside of a few notable operations, it was rare that anyone was actually killed. More often, we just conned and extorted information from their key officials, and they did the same to us. But the Major changed all that. He thrived on violence, taking risks no one else would. And he reported directly to Moscow, with little care for what the East Germans thought of him. As a result, he operated without constraint, moral or legal.

"We quickly figured out that he was a rough player, but were shocked by his audacity when he crossed to West Berlin and kidnapped the daughter of a visiting American senator. His operation was perfect, I'll give him that. He caught them en route to the embassy, coming back from dining at the mayor's mansion. There were fourteen policemen in escort, but the Major's men grabbed her without even one of them noticing a thing.

BRETT JAMES

"The Russians demanded a trade. They wanted one of their high-level colonels back, a man who had defected years previous—bringing with him a veritable encyclopedia on the Russian military. What we had promised him in return was immunity and a good life in the States.

"I really didn't think there was a chance in hell we'd give him up, but I was wrong. It turned out the Major had picked the right hostage. The Senator had the pull and a week later the poor colonel was shipped back to Russia, where he no doubt had a brief and painful life."

"I thought you didn't make deals with terrorists?"

"They're only terrorists if they don't work for super-powers," Grey replied. Leigh frowned, so he added: "Not my opinion, just how it works.

"As for the Major, he got himself a pat on the back and a promotion. In one fell swoop, he had brought a traitor to justice and destroyed the CIA's credibility with potential defectors. After all, would you trust us with your life if any of a hundred senators could send you back to the very people we asked you to betray?"

"Which senator was it?"

"It's not important. Only a few people even know it happened. What matters is that one of the Major's men got a little rough with his daughter. She was just coming of age."

"How rough?"

"Rough enough. After the Senator found out, he raised hell. He grandstanded on the Senate floor about how ineffective the CIA had become, and he called every general in the phone book and said the same. So a few months later, we got the order to take the Major and his team. Alive. Lord knows what they intended to do to them."

Grey traced the edge of the dessert plate with his fork, letting memories unimportant to the story play themselves out in his mind. Then he dropped the fork with a clink.

"I built a trap. One of our informers was an ambassador's assistant with family in West Berlin. He'd been giving us intel for years, and wanted to defect. I had promised to work something out. He was a good kid, sincere. I didn't want to burn him…"

"But you had orders."

"I made the choice—"

"You had orders," Leigh said firmly. Grey nodded, surprised. He hadn't expected her to understand. It wasn't the first time that he had underestimated her.

"We also knew the Soviets had a mole in our accounting department, so we submitted several false budget requests and the money shows up in the kid's bank account. It was the best kind of misinformation: hinting but not telling, getting the Russians so excited that, when they put the pieces together, they didn't stop to think that it might be a trap. Some traps are so well set that you're an idiot if you *don't* fall for them. The Major wasn't."

"So I gather."

"We'd never tried anything on this scale. I don't know that anyone had, and for good reason. It's complicated enough baiting a single agent, but the Major had nineteen operatives on his team and we were to capture all of them. That is, capture as many as we could. I wasn't going to risk the lives of my men just to placate some senator's ego. I ordered them to shoot at the first sign of trouble.

"I wasn't allowed to participate myself. I had just been promoted to GS-16 and my new rank made me officially too valuable for fieldwork. So while my men laid the trap in an old airplane factory, I was stuck in a safe house ten miles away, babysitting the brass that had flown in to 'observe the operation.' It was a goddamn party; they had cocktail waitresses.

"It was just past three in the morning when word came in: the factory had exploded. By sun-up, the West Berlin fire department had pulled thirty-five corpses from the rubble— my entire team, and not one of the Major's."

Grey was silent for a long time. The waves grew louder as the tide came in and the evening chill blew inland. Leigh slid her hand over Grey's. He came back to life and said:

"Not one man had died in the explosion. Every single one had been shot beforehand. Many had been tortured…"

Leigh squeezed his hand supportively. Grey pulled it away—he wasn't ready for pity; there was more to tell.

"I knew there would be a huge inquiry. And I knew that while it happened, I would be suspended. They would ship me back to Langley to cool my heels. No retaliation would take place, ever. There would be no vengeance for my men. They didn't rank up there with a senator's daughter.

"I had lived and worked in Berlin for twelve years. Every friend I had died that night. I drove straight from the smoking rubble of the factory to headquarters, where I took our files on the Major and his men. All of them."

Grey looked at Leigh. She seemed braced for what was coming, but she couldn't know how bad it was going to be.

"What I mean is, I stole the files. I slipped into East Germany that night and began tracking them down. I found the first three in a brothel outside Potsdam, celebrating. I killed everyone in the building and burned it to the ground. The next one was in bed with his girlfriend. He tried to shield her with his body. I even killed her dog.

"By the end of the week, I had worked my way through the list. I had saved the Major for last because I wanted him to be scared. I wanted him to see his men die one by one and know that I was coming for him." Grey's fists were tight, his face red, as if it were all happening right now.

"But you didn't kill him?" Leigh leaned back, folding her arms. The sympathy was gone from her voice.

"I knew getting to the Major would be difficult. I needed help, so I called in a favor. A man I thought I could trust. But I was wrong: he turned me in, told the CIA where to find me.

"I blamed him at the time. I even wanted to kill him. I lost my head; I had gone too far."

Grey gazed out at the ocean.

"They say I killed seventy-two people. It's probably true. By all rights, they should have executed me. Or at least handed me to the Russians as a peace offering. But no one wanted to give the Soviets access to what I knew. And I guess I still had some friends left upstairs; they spared my life. But they didn't want a mad dog like me running around America, so they stuck me where they could keep an eye on me. Here," Grey drove a finger into the table, "France. And then they pretended the whole thing never happened. Soon after, the Berlin wall came down and all the action moved to China and the Middle East. I was sidelined completely."

"Sidelined to Paris," Leigh said. "Is that so terrible? It's where you met me." She was surprised to find herself relieved by Grey's story. His dark past had cast a shadow over their entire relationship; it would have hurt more to learn that it wasn't so dark after all.

"The thing is, I never regretted killing—"

"Stop," Leigh commanded. "I don't need to hear your psychosomatic regrets or your private theories about why this fucks you up. I can figure that part out by myself."

Grey drank the last splash of stale wine from his glass, wishing he had something harder. "I must seem like a completely different person to you now."

"What I can't figure out is how you killed so many people when you can't shoot the broad side of a barn."

Grey laughed nervously, "Yeah, guns aren't my thing."

Leigh smiled. She shouldn't smile after such a story, but it had all happened such a long time ago. She had never met that man. The one she knew was ready to die to save the world.

"Don't go," she said.

"If the plans for the Deadfall Project are out there, I need to find them. And fast."

"Leave it to someone else."

"There is no one else."

"Then just leave it," Leigh said, choking up.

"Do you know what we're dealing with? It's a nuclear bomb that can be carried in a briefcase. The materials aren't radioactive, so they can't be detected, and all you need to explode it is some household chemicals and an electrical outlet. Any man with one becomes a superpower. Car bombers could blow up entire cities. If my government wants to use the bomb as an excuse to invade Iran, fine, but I still have to contain the plans before something really terrible happens. This isn't about who built the last bomb, it's about who is going to build the next one."

"And the Major can tell you this?"

"If anyone can. I have to ask."

"In exchange for your life," Leigh said. It wasn't a question. From what Grey had told her, there was no question about it.

"There is no other way."

Leigh opened her mouth to respond, but a car horn from the street cut her off. Other horns joined in and soon they echoed all along the cape. A distant roar came over from Marseille, as if from a soccer match. A man from the kitchen rushed to the bartender and whispered excitedly.

The bartender let out an elated howl. Leigh and Grey looked over and he bowed apologetically. "Pardon my outburst," he said, his voice fluttering with excitement, "but France has joined forces with the Americans. We will go to war!"

Grey paid the bill at the front, not wanting to wait for the check. He held Leigh's rawhide overcoat for her and she hooked her arm into his. He watched her as they walked down the sidewalk. She would be leaving in the morning. It was right for her to go, but it made him sad. He had been working alone for so long that he had forgotten how nice it was to have someone along.

He steered her down to the beach; she didn't object. Side-by-side, they plodded along the waterline. They found a lonely bench on a small grassy hill and sat leaning against each other, watching the twilight fade. They were far from the city lights and, as he gazed upwards, Grey felt like he was falling into a sparkling black pool.

They sat quietly until it was late, then shared a cab back to the hotel and slept in their separate rooms.

IV

The dark-windowed Mercedes sedan bounced over the curb and into the dirt parking lot of the Buoux train station. Buoux was a resort town in southern France, small enough that there would be few people around, but not so small that the arrival of a stranger would be an event.

Richard steered the car into a parking space and cut the engine, leaving the key turned so the radio would play. He had grown fond of western music, listening to it whenever he got the chance. The dash clock read 6:45 in the morning. He had fifteen minutes to wait.

He looked around the car, inspecting the dark tinted windows. He had tinted them himself, cutting the sticky plastic sheets from a roll and pressing them on with a squeegee. The tint was limousine dark—illegal for regular cars—and no glass shop would have even done the windows, much less the windshield. It had been a lot of work, and he hoped his brother took better care of this car than he had the last.

Four songs later, the train from Marseille rumbled in and squealed to a halt, overshadowing the small shack of a station. The first person off was an old woman, who called the conductor for help unloading a breadbox-sized suitcase. After her came Amin, dressed in a dark blue businessman's suit. It looked better on him than Richard would have expected, but he walked as if it were made of fiberglass.

Richard switched off the radio, leaned over and swung the passenger door open. Amin got in, closing the door behind him. Richard inspected him for any sign of injury, but only saw that his brother was deeply tired.

"How did it go?" Richard asked.

"It was simple," Amin replied, but his voice said otherwise.

"No witnesses?"

"None but Allah himself," Amin said, trying to put strength in the words. They came out hollow.

"Good," Richard announced, and then, because it didn't feel that way, he added another: "Good." He opened the center console, retrieved Amin's revolver and handed it to him. His brother looked relieved just to hold it.

Amin flipped open his jacket, removing the small automatic that peeked from his large shoulder holster, and handed it to Richard. It was a Beretta Tomcat. Richard sniffed the barrel.

"How many shots?"

"Just one."

"You're really very good."

Amin ignored the flattery. The train pulled away from the station, shaking the car as it picked up speed. Amin watched it pass as if death were brushing by. Richard stashed the Beretta.

"And the box?" Richard asked.

Still watching the train, Amin passed over a device the size of a thick pen. Richard pressed a button on the end and a small LED screen displayed three sets of numbers: global co-ordinates, down to the centimeter. He nodded gleefully and slid the device into his jacket pocket. As he reached toward the key, Amin said quietly:

"He begged me for his life."

Richard flushed. "The coward! I hope you made him beg. When I think of the women and children murdered by their bombs—"

"It isn't that," Amin cut in. "I just… Just explain to me again why it had to be done."

Richard hesitated; no answer came to mind. "There is no time to explain what I know, and I don't know half of it. The orders came from Il Siyâh. They are sending a new bomb."

"Yes," Amin said flatly. "You said."

Richard twisted around, grabbing a paper bag from the back seat and dropping it on his brother's lap. "Here. You will feel better when you eat. We have much to do today."

Amin inspected the bag's contents. The warm smell of lamb filled his nose. He was hungry and the hunger drove all other thoughts from his mind. He opened a Styrofoam container and greedily mixed the heavily sauced meat with the yellow saffron rice.

Richard backed the car out and started down the road, pleased with himself. The halal food had done the trick; he had guessed correctly that his brother would be too wound up to feed himself. He watched Amin slurp down the food. He would feel better when he was full, and feeling better, he would forget all his concerns, especially those about Richard. It was for this reason, Richard thought, executioners were always generous with a prisoner's last meal.

He had thought it unlucky when Amin survived his first encounter with the American agent, but his brother had since proved to be very useful. But now that usefulness had passed and it was time for his final task. It was Amin's deepest desire to die a holy warrior, performing the will of Allah. As far as he would know, that's exactly what was going to happen.

"I have good news," Richard said. Despite Amin's hunger, he lowered his fork. "We have new orders. We're going after the saboteur."

Amin brightened. "When?"

"Today. This afternoon. Get the map from the glove box."

Amin tossed his half-eaten food into the bag and reached for the map.

V

"**I**dentification."

The black-skinned clerk didn't look up from his computer as he held out his pink-white palm. There was a large blue sign above his head titled, "Prison Visitation Policy." It listed useful information like visiting hours and time restrictions, but also spelled out rules like: "Do *not* spit on prisoners" and "Do *not* give weapons to prisoners."

Grey was here to see Jacques because Vladimir told him that Jacques set up meetings with the Major. He remembered that Vladimir was amused by this arrangement, but Grey couldn't see the humor; meeting Jacques to see the Major was like having to defeat Cerberus to pass into the gates of hell.

Grey pulled out his Parisian Police ID. He had a half-dozen choices of how to identify himself, but only a few of them would get him into here, and all of those would raise a red flag back at the DST. The police badge was the most innocuous, and it might speed up this interminable check-in process. The waiting was doing nothing for his nerves.

Grey handed the ID to the clerk, leaning across the two-foot wide expanse of red-taped floor that separated him from the desk. The clerk wasn't impressed. He set it by his keyboard and pecked at the keys like a bird searching for worms.

The only other person in the room was a pasty guard who stood at lazy attention by a metal door labeled, "No entry without authorization." The guard's body drooped into a bulging lumpy stomach, like he was hiding a sack of potatoes. His stomach was so large that only the very tips of his shirt-flaps could be tucked under his belt. He eyed Grey with mild animosity; he probably had a chair stashed away that he was being kept from.

The paperwork finally sorted, the clerk handed Grey back his ID. The guard and his stomach led Grey through the door and into a two-gate lockdown. It was tight quarters for the three of them. Next came a long hallway that led to more gates, beyond which was a riveted steel door—Grey's private meeting room.

Jacques was a former button man for the KGB, neither a shooter nor a slicer, but a monster of a man who killed with his bare hands. He was famous for his temper, which was plenty short even when he wasn't hitting the bottle. And he rarely wasn't.

BRETT JAMES

Despite the staggering number of murders he had performed—KGB ordered and otherwise—what finally put Jacques in jail was killing his ex-wife.

Jacques had retired from the Major's team just before the trouble started, returning to his childhood home of Nice and marrying a former trapeze artist named Rosanna. She had a wide muscular body—nearly as strong as his own—that was generous in all the right places. Her skin glistened in permanent tan, her hair was full and dark, and her face brutally scarred.

They beat each other up for kicks, both in public and privately. But when the pain lost its novelty, Rosanna sued for divorce. Neither of them could afford a new place, so they plastered new walls down the center of their house, dividing it in half.

As terrible as they had been together, they were worse apart. Jacques continued to beat Rosanna, though no longer with her permission. And she found new tortures for him.

She set her bed against the wall of Jacques's bedroom, the bed they had once shared. She went down to the docks and picked up sailors, sometimes two or three a night. Men off the sea were too anxious to smell the danger in a woman. She brought them back to that bed and gave them a hell of a workout, moaning wildly while the brass headboard pounded against the wall. Then she would beg for more.

And Jacques, the man the Major called on when he needed a particularly brutal murder, sat quietly on the other side of the house night after night, just drinking and listening.

Rosanna gave those sailors something they would never forget, particularly the last one. The story says it was some kid in from Corsica who probably hadn't seen much of the world except the village he was born in, and the sea between there and here. He was the only one surprised when Jacques kicked in the door and ripped his ex-wife apart, piece by piece. For the rest of the world, the only surprise was that he had held out for six months.

The steel door creaked ominously as the guard pulled it open. Inside was a dim metal room divided by a cage of pencil-thin steel bars. The guard motioned Grey in, clanging the door shut and turning the lock. He was alone except for a few dozen flies buzzing around the cage.

The room was dark, the only light from a small high window with thick bars, offering little hope of escape. Grey fingered the cage, not daring to test the strength of the thin metal—he'd rather not know. It was barely ten in the morning, but he needed a drink.

A loud buzz sounded, followed by the thump of a dead bolt. The far door opened and a small guard led Jacques into the cage, his hulking body filling the large doorway. His face was flat like the back of a shovel and his eyes hid below a single thick eyebrow.

The two had never before met, but Grey knew of his exploits from reading his file. Jacques would have read Grey's as well. Or had it read to him.

The guard left. Jacques remained standing, studying Grey as if to figure out which parts came off the easiest. Grey waited for Jacques to speak, feeling the sweat in his armpits.

A fly took interest in Jacques, circling his head. He barely glanced at it, flicking it away with his finger. He struck it in mid-air and it sailed across the room, cracking into the far wall. Grey heard himself gulp. Jacques spoke:

"Geneva. Day after tomorrow. You know the walkway that leads out by the water jet?" His voice was soft and rich, which threw Grey more than anything.

"I can find it."

"Ten A.M. sharp."

Without waiting for a reply, Jacques turned and banged on the door behind him, telling the guard he was done.

VI

*F*aison bent over his desk, flipping intently through a stack of six hundred printed pages. Each page was divided into two columns of fourteen-digit alphanumeric codes that looked like well-ordered gibberish. The first column was a list of transmitter codes for location bugs, the GPS trackers that operatives placed on suspects or their cars. The trackers dialed into the cellular network, reporting their exact location every ten minutes. The list in front of Faison did not tell him which trackers were assigned to which operative—that was far too classified to ever put down on paper. What he had was a list of what trackers had been used in which of the Directorate's past operations, the code for which was shown in the second column.

Faison had memorized the codes for every operation Jerard had ever worked, and when he found a match, he made a note of it. He was trying to determine, by inference, which trackers Jerard was carrying right now. And when he found them, he could use their codes to discover the location of Agent Stark.

This was not the usual process to get this information. Normally, Faison would simply call Control, but they claimed their computer was down for maintenance for the rest of the week. A thin lie, he thought, and there was no doubt that Denis was behind it. Surely Denis hoped to discourage him, but the effect was quite the opposite: Denis's attempt at subterfuge had piqued his interest. After all, why would Denis bother to hide what wasn't important? And he was hiding something.

Jerard could monitor his own bugs from his personal tracker, but he was also required to report any that he was using, and what he was using them for. They would then appear on the big map, along with his name. Since there weren't any up there, one would believe that he wasn't using any. But Faison himself had told Jerard about Grey's car, and even Jerard wasn't foolish enough to tail him without setting a tracker. No, Denis was keeping the transmitter codes a secret. As Peerson had said, Denis trusted Stark to a fault. That would be his undoing.

Even without the transmitter codes, Faison had a pretty good idea of where Grey was and what he was doing. When he learned that Grey was heading south, Faison took the precaution of calling every local law enforcement agency down there, asking them to report anything unusual. It was these details that no operative ever bothered with, and it was the sort of initiative that got ignored when promotions were handed out. But this morning it had paid off.

Faison received a call from the Grasse Maximum Security Prison, just outside of Marseille. Apparently, a Paris Policeman by the name of Grey Stark had visited an inmate named Jacques Moreau. Faison knew who Jacques was—it was a rare year that his name didn't come across telex, usually for murdering one of his fellow inmates. And Faison knew there was only one reason why Stark would have gone to see him.

Faison closed his eyes and cleared his head. Poring through this much data would take any other ten people the longest week of their lives, but he had a mind for numbers. He could order concurrent codes in his head, and easily locate the duplicates. There were around forty thousand codes listed on the pages in front of him; he figured it would take him the better part of the afternoon to sort them out.

There was a knock, and the door opened before Faison could even look up. Peerson shoved into the room, supporting his girth with an orthopedic cane of dull aluminum.

"Hello, old boy," he said, as if feeling the need to remind everyone he was English. He crossed the room by a cumbersome process, planting the cane and rotating his body around it. It took six repetitions before he plopped into the chair opposite Faison, wheezing like Atlas at the end of his shift.

He raised the cane and said, "Slept on my leg wrong last night. Happens to me a lot, I'm afraid. The thin mattresses in these damn hotels."

Faison used Peerson's long walk to pile the transmitter codes up and slip them into his desk. He was irritated by the interruption—it would take time to get back into the rhythm of his work—but he didn't want Peerson to think it was anything important, so he acted like it was a bit of tedium that he was happy to set aside.

"I was wondering if Jerard has moved?" Peerson asked.

"Not that I've heard," Faison replied, folding his arms on his desk.

"I'm starting to think that our young operative has lost his quarry and is just too embarrassed to tell us."

"You must not talk to Denis much. Jerard's the best we have."

"I can understand why you would be jealous."

"Jerard and I are in different fields," Faison said without conviction. "There's no competition between us."

"Except that his field is prone to advancement, apparently. And that he himself seems especially prone."

Peerson was fishing, but Faison couldn't tell for what. He wondered about it for a fruitless moment, then said, "You have his personal transmitter code, you could have checked Jerard's position with Control."

"Yes. I could have. But I was also wondering: wouldn't Jerard have planted a transmitter on Agent Stark or his car?"

"It's possible," Faison said, suddenly leery. It made sense that both of them would be asking the same questions, but it still felt like Peerson was reading his mind. "But he would have reported it to Control."

"What if he didn't get a chance to?"

"Why wouldn't he?" Faison asked, his voice on edge.

"Plenty of reasons, certainly. I'm only speaking hypothetically."

Faison nodded, pretending to consider the subject. "We could check all of the transmitters assigned to him."

"I tried that, but they can't give me that information. Some computer problem." Peerson waited, but the only response he got was a thoughtful nod. "That doesn't strike you as suspicious?" he pressed.

Faison tried to laugh, but he wasn't very good at it. It came out as a gargling sound. "Why would that be suspicious?"

"Do you think Denis might be keeping information from us?"

The conspiring 'us' in Peerson's question irked Faison. He looked at the man's cane, wondering what sound it would make if it was cracked over his head. But he let it pass. This conversation was nothing but a waste of his time—the shorter, the better. "It's unlikely," he said, "but you'd do better asking Denis than me."

"I might just do that," Peerson said, lofting himself up like a hot air balloon. He teetered precariously before finding his balance, then hobbled out. Faison waited patiently for him to leave, but when he got to the door, he turned back, donning an embarrassed smile.

"One other thing," he said. "Why do you think Stark might be spending so much time in Marseille? Assuming he is indeed still there."

Faison splayed his hands out. "If I remember correctly, Marseille is where you allegedly followed an Iranian terrorist into France just last week."

"Yes. You do remember correctly." Peerson considered Faison for a minute, wondering if he had underestimated him. "Just thought I'd ask," he said, rotating out the door and shutting it behind him.

"Yes," Faison said to himself, "I'm certain you did, *gros lard*."

Peerson's suspicions confirmed his own, Faison thought: while he knew Jerard was still in Marseille, it was obvious that Stark was long gone. He would be en route to Switzerland by now, and Faison might be the only person in the building who knew that. Even without the tracking code to Stark's car, he could still arrange for him to be captured. But if he could get the code by this evening, there was no limit to how far he could exploit the information.

He pulled the transmitter codes back out.

VII

The sun rose on noon as Grey left the prison, the hot air drying his lungs. He was anxious to put Marseille in his rear-view mirror, but—and maybe he was just being paranoid—it seemed that there was one more person to deal with before he could. So instead of heading back to the hotel, Grey parked by the harbor and set out on foot. After a couple blocks, he found the courtyard of a small chapel. It would do.

Two grandmotherly nuns manned a small shed, the 'donations' bucket set on a chair beside them. Grey dropped a one-Euro coin in as he passed. The courtyard was filled with benches, all of them directed at an alcove near the roof of the chapel, where a statue of the Virgin looked down with holy bliss. The statue's religious significance escaped him, but apparently she could draw quite a crowd. Fortunately, in the heat of the October afternoon, the courtyard was abandoned. Grey walked alongside the high stone wall that separated the grounds from the street and leaned into the corner—not hiding, but making himself harder to spot.

The better part of a minute passed before a thin Asian man walked through the gate. He had been tailing Grey since the prison, hanging back so as not to be noticed, but his outfit—a purple suit with bright yellow pinstripes—was so loud that he might as well have worn a siren.

Grey figured either he wanted to be noticed or was insultingly incompetent. The shocked look on the man's face when he noticed Grey staring right at him suggested the latter.

The man's hand went into his jacket, to a gun holster. Grey leaned casually against the wall, crossing his arms unthreateningly. The man was confused at first, then nodded his head curtly—as if Grey had passed him some signal—and let his hand drop back to his side.

The nuns eyed the newcomer suspiciously, but he didn't seem to notice them or their bucket. He strode over to Grey, a bitter face like he was chewing aspirin. He came up to Grey until his forehead was within an inch of Grey's chin—he was tall for an Asian, but that meant little in the West. He was trying to be intimidating; Grey had to choke back a laugh.

"You have something we want," was his opening line, abrupt even in this business. Grey sized the man up. His tight-pointed eyes hinted at Korean blood, and, since the American government was about to declare war on North Korea, Grey figured it was more than just an educated guess.

"I have something that everyone wants," Grey replied.

His answer irked the Korean: "Is there going to be an auction?"

"I can't say for sure, what am I selling?"

The Korean's face turned red. "Do not make light of us, Mister Stark. You would soon regret it."

"I already do."

The man's hand went back into his coat. This time it came out with a gun, a small nine-millimeter of a make Grey didn't recognize. He held it close to his stomach, hiding it from anyone in the courtyard. There wasn't anyone in the courtyard. Definitely a North Korean agent, Grey decided, and not a very good one.

The Korean was left handed, so Grey stepped to his right, pushing the gun outward. If he had wanted to kill Grey, his shot would have gone wide. But the man didn't fire, which Grey took as a good sign.

Grey whipped out his Berretta and drove the butt into the man's fingers, smashing them against the grip of his own gun. The Korean yelped as Grey yanked the gun from his hand.

Grey pocketed both weapons and smiled at the nun who peered out of the shed to see what the fuss was. He pointed the Beretta inside his pocket at the man, who was sucking his fingers.

"What am I selling?" Grey asked.

"The plans."

"Which plans?"

"We are talking of the plans for the bomb that you built in Paris. My government is interested in purchasing them, but we want an exclusive—"

"Hang on," Grey interrupted. "How did you find out I had the plans?"

The man hesitated. "Sources."

"Which sources?"

The man didn't respond, so Grey grabbed one of his broken fingers and squeezed. It was a dirty trick, but he didn't have a lot of time. It must have hurt, but the man took it longer than Grey would have expected.

"We got a call this afternoon, from a reliable source, an ally," he said, his voice wavering. "They told us you were selling the plans and that you would be at the prison this morning."

There was a lack of detail to the story that Grey didn't like, but chances were the Korean was telling him all he knew. "So you're just the local boy?"

"I work at the embassy in Madrid. I'm a clerk. I was just close by."

"Oh." Grey felt suddenly guilty for strong-arming him. He released the man's hand and let go of his gun. He spoke in a soft firm voice: "Listen carefully: this is all a mistake. I don't have the plans. I don't even think they're in France. If I seem blunt, it's because I've got enough trouble without having you people around."

"I see," the man said, though he was obviously unsure. Then he remembered why he was here. He composed himself and—forced by his injury to use the wrong hand—reached awkwardly into his breast pocket and produced a business card. "If you change your mind, we will be the highest offer. Since you're being blunt, I'll do the same. I am to threaten you, to say you must respond in the next twenty-four hours. I believe the threat is to be realized by someone more capable than myself. Have a good day, sir."

Without waiting for a reply, the Korean turned on his heel and walked out of the churchyard. He moved quickly, either shaken by the encounter or anxious to get his hand fixed.

Grey rubbed his lip, wondering who had told the man that he had the bomb's plans. It didn't seem likely that Vladimir would spread such a rumor; he would love to cause Grey trouble, but not at the expense of his own reputation. Demyan certainly didn't tell anyone—in fact, he had heard the same rumor.

It was always possible that the Koreans were trying a double-bluff, pretending they wanted to buy the plans to throw off suspicion that they already had them. But they knew he would be at the prison this morning; that information had to come from somewhere.

Grey stuffed the business card into his pocket and walked out of the courtyard. Outside the gate, a man with shockingly blond hair struggled to balance a camera on tripod—it had a megaphone-sized lens, the sort used at sporting events.

"Pardon," the man said, and Grey realized he had stopped right in the man's way.

Grey excused himself and walked halfway down the block, stopping to scrape something off his shoe. The photographer energetically snapped photos of the churchyard, occasionally consulting with a light meter. Grey shook his head; now he was being paranoid.

He started back to his car. He had two days for a drive he could do by nightfall, but he also had to drop Leigh off, preferably somewhere that didn't give away that he was heading to Geneva. It was too dangerous for her to return to Paris; he had no doubt that Jerard would have reported that the two of them were together. And the man who had attacked him outside of DST headquarters had also gotten a pretty good look at her.

He dumped the Korean's gun in a trashcan and walked all the way around the harbor, just to be sure no one else was following him. Considering how his luck was running, he was surprised to find that no one was.

VIII

*L*eigh's hair flowed in the wind. Her red streaks blended with her black hair until they were the color of the fall leaves, like those ruffling on the trees as the MG blew past. The crisp air held the first inklings of winter, but the sun was warm on her skin. Leigh leaned back in the passenger seat, her eyes closed. A distant smile hung on her lips, as if this was nothing but a drive in the country.

The highway twisted along a thousand-year-old trade route, passing through the rolling hills of the Lot region. The road was level, cutting through ancient hand-dug tunnels and over modern bridges that spanned precipitous gorges. As they crossed such a bridge, Grey risked vertigo to peer down at the distant stream. The scenery looked like it had been copied from a painting.

This area was popular in the summer, offering endless hiking and fishing, but it was fall now and Grey had the road to himself. It felt good to be driving, to be out of the stink of

Marseille and to feel like he had somewhere to go. Even if that somewhere was grim.

Grey had been varying his speed, checking if he could catch sight of their tail. But Jerard had apparently wised up—with a GPS tracker, there was no reason for visual contact—but Grey needed to be sure he knew that. Grey's plan was to drop Leigh, drive for another hour or so, and then dump the tracker on some other car before turning toward Geneva. For Leigh to get away safely, it was critical that he wasn't seen driving alone.

Grey felt a pang of guilt. He liked Jerard and knew how it felt to be duped. He considered taping an apology to the tracker, but knew it would feel like a jeer. It was odd that, playing for such high stakes, he would worry over such a little thing. But Jerard had that effect on people. He was the bright-eyed kid that no one wanted to disappoint. Grey shook it off. The lesson would do him good.

He pressed down on the gas pedal, drunk from the warm sun. The MG's engine deepened from baritone to bass and the seat pushed against his back. The wind roared, but Grey thought he heard Leigh giggle. He glanced over: she certainly wasn't frowning. She arched her back lazily, pressing her chest to the sun.

Grey stared too long and nearly drove off the road.

Seventy-two hours ago he was ready to forget this woman; now he searched every smile and glance for a glimmer of hope. This moment felt so perfect that he forgot the years of bickering, and all the battles between them. While he knew he shouldn't trust his feelings, right now all he wanted was her.

Grey pushed hard into the next curve, the seatbelt digging into his side and the wheels chirping against the road. Now both of them were smiling.

The land flattened as they entered a valley. Grey slowed, turning across a short stone bridge and crossing over a gentle stream. They drove into the town of Figeac.

The first thing he saw was a modern hospital, eight stories tall and just as broad. It was out of place in these country hills, as if the builders, intent on Lyon, had gotten lost along the way.

A few blocks later, the asphalt turned to cobblestone and the buildings grew older by centuries. Grey navigated through curvy, narrow roads and arrived at a circular courtyard. He parked in front of a stone-cut church. Gargoyles looked down at him from the roof, seven hundred years of disdain on their faces. They were no more inviting today than they had been for the armies of Edward the Third.

Leigh stretched, turning to Grey without opening her eyes. "Is this where I get out?" she asked, a touch of disappointment in her voice.

"We'll go one more town, just to be safe," Grey said, dropping the car back into gear. Moments later, they were speeding down the highway. There was no rush to drop her off, he decided. Who knew when he would see her again. If ever.

"Just one more town," Leigh said, casually resting her hand on Grey's leg. It was warm through his slacks. Grey brought his hand down toward hers, but the car jolted forward with tremendous force.

Leigh wasn't wearing a seatbelt. Her seat pressed forward, then flung her at the windshield, which shattered against her head. She flopped back, unconscious, red dampening her hair. Grey reached for her, but the car jolted again.

He jammed the gas pedal down with all his strength. The rear view mirror was crooked. He adjusted it, confirming his fear: a black sedan with tinted windows was chasing up behind them.

Grey downshifted and the engine growled. They were already going eighty, but the tires still left a black footprint on the pavement as the car shot down the road.

The Mercedes faded, unprepared for the sudden acceleration. The MG's tachometer flew past the red line and the needle pegged at the top of the gauge. Grey kept his foot on the gas. They would be across the valley soon, and the curves ahead would give him the edge he needed. He resisted the urge to glance over at Leigh. He shifted up two gears, giving the engine a rest.

Hills rose on either side of the road and the Mercedes disappeared as Grey hit the first curve. He hoped for a fork or a turn off—somewhere to slip off the road while he was out of sight—but nothing appeared. At the end of the curve, a rock cliff cut across the road, a two-lane hole hewn into its face. The MG plunged in.

The tunnel was cold and damp. The MG's engine thundered, echoing until it was as loud as warfare. Grey left his headlights off, watching the rearview mirror. He saw nothing but the retreating entrance, a dot of light floating in the dark.

The road was straight, so he risked a glance at Leigh. In the dark, he couldn't tell if she was moving or just being shaken by the car. He pressed his hand against her chest and felt her draw a slow, small breath. He looked at her unfastened seatbelt. At this speed, he couldn't risk leaning over.

Grey put his hand back on the wheel and checked the rear-view mirror. The Mercedes appeared at the tunnel's entrance, a black shadow. Grey's speedometer said he was going a hundred and forty miles an hour. This car wouldn't go any faster, the Mercedes could. He had the advantage on the curves, but the hills didn't go on forever.

The engine seemed to cut off as he shot out of the tunnel and into the blinding sunlight. The road ahead was a wide 'S', banking first to the right, running parallel to a deep gorge, then to the left, crossing a narrow stone bridge. Grey looked at Leigh. Blood pooled up in her collar and poured down her body like a crimson fountain. She wasn't going to last long.

He took the first turn as fast as he could, his forearms straining against the steering wheel. Leigh flopped onto him, blood spraying on his shirt. He slid his arm down the back of her blouse and grabbed her leather belt. The stone bridge raced toward them, barely one lane wide.

The Mercedes emerged from the tunnel, slowing as it came into the first curve. Grey let off the gas; he wanted it closer.

He rotated Leigh's body, laying her across the center console. She moaned as the gearshift dug into her ribs, a reassuring sign of life. He unclipped his seatbelt—holding the wheel with his knee—and reached for Leigh's rawhide coat down on the floorboards. It was thick leather; he hoped it was thick enough. He draped it over her.

They were a few seconds from the bridge—just enough time for him to decide his plan wasn't going to work. But the Mercedes was on top of them and it was too late to change his mind. He punched the gas again. This time the Mercedes was ready, staying tight on his bumper. They were going an even hundred when they reached the bridge. Grey whipped the wheel to the left and the MG spun sideways, the driver-side tilting up off the ground.

The car was longer than the bridge was wide, and it caught the low stone railings on both sides, flipping onto its side and flinging Grey and Leigh into the air. The Mercedes, not ten feet behind, struck the underside of the MG like thunder clap. The MG folded around the Mercedes. The combined mass of metal ripped across the bridge, pulverizing the stonework, which plunged down the gorge to the stream far below.

Grey somehow got the leather jacket around them. They hit the ground halfway down the bridge, his ribs cracking under Leigh's weight. His bare forearm ripped along the pavement, and pain seared through his body. He yanked the arm into a rawhide cocoon, and they slid down the road. The giant metal cannonball bore down on them, plowing apart the bridge and shredding it to rubble.

The pavement chewed at the jacket; it burned against his skin. Grey felt the MG slap against his foot, but then the car caught on the wall—stopping instantly. They slid away.

The MG swelled, stretching momentarily, and then pulverized. The rear end of the Mercedes rose up behind it, disintegrating to scrap. Jagged chunks of metal shot down the road.

Grey rolled on top of Leigh, covering her body with his. Something pierced his leg and it went numb. The thick smell of gas filled his nose, followed by that of fire. The leather jacket ground to a halt. Grey rolled off Leigh, his arms flopping out. The world faded away.

— — —

When the world came back, the sky was black with smoke. A car grill lay over Grey's face, but he couldn't tell from which car. He pulled his head up and saw a bonfire roiling with frantic energy. Nothing moved inside it. Nothing could be alive in there.

One hand was still on Leigh's belt. With the other, he clawed at the road, trying to pull them to safety. But the road was covered with blood or oil or both; his hand slipped across the surface. He reached for the trees in the forest, but they must have been further away than they looked, and besides he couldn't stay awake any longer.

Darkness tightened around him.

BOOK
FOUR

1

*D*eniss's hollow gaze was fixed on a map of downtown Marseille, so large it draped down the sides of his desk and offered details down to the individual building. Large X's and arrows had been scrawled over it in red pen—he had used Jerard's GPS log to re-trace the young captain's steps over the last three days. The X's marked any place where he had stopped for at least an hour. One particular X had been run over so many times that the pen had dug through the paper. This was Jerard's last known location, as of twenty hours. According to his GPS tracker, it was also his current location.

It was a hotel, presumably the one Jerard was checked into, since he had stayed there every night since his arrival. It was the curse of technology that Denis had to make that assumption. Ten years ago, agents called in to regularly update their status. But now, knowing their every movement was tracked, most of them had grown slack. And the younger agents, like Jerard, rarely bothered to check in at all.

Denis had been sequestered in his office all evening, scribbling madly on the map and trying to divine an answer from it. The question on his mind was if he should send someone to check up on Jerard. To do so would be to risk interrupting a delicate operation. Or, worse still, draw Jerard's ire for mothering him. He'd been accused of that in the past.

Jerard was sensitive about what the other agents thought of him, and of his rapid promotion. He had earned it, certainly, but there were those who said otherwise. And jealousy often took a petty form, especially from the older agents—those who felt seniority was more important than talent. Denis had been quite young himself when he took over the Directorate, and so knew first-hand what Jerard was up against.

He turned back to the map. It was unlikely that Jerard was in any danger; his GPS tracking system had a built-in alarm with a dozen ways to trigger it. It even monitored his vital signs, and would alert the Directorate's control room if his pulse so much as slowed. Bypassing the alarm would not only require amazing timing, but an intricate knowledge of the system that few people had. All this was very re-assuring, but not as much as just hearing the sound of Jerard's voice.

He was tempted have Control track down the bugs that Jerard was carrying, but to do so would probably give up Grey's position as well. He had suppressed those codes to protect the American's movements, and if he asked for them now, protocol would require that Control put them up on the big board. That was a regulation even Denis couldn't bypass. So it had come down to Grey or Jerard. The choice was obvious.

Denis was punching Control's number into his phone when there was a knock on his door. Normally, Denis would have made them wait, but there was something authoritative in the knock—it was loud and firm, which didn't sound like any of his employees. He set the phone down and buzzed the door open.

The hand that opened it was well-manicured, with thick hairs like silver wire. The hand extended out from a dark blue suit that cost more than most cars. Inside the suit was the Minister of Defense, Denis's boss.

Denis was immediately on his feet. "Sir," he said, running his hands down his jacket in the hope of making himself presentable.

The Minister had a stern face, a beaked nose, and waves of pewter hair flowing back from his forehead in perfect uniformity. He looked such the model of leadership that he might have been a caricature. He smiled, but it wasn't warm.

"Sorry to interrupt your work, Denis," he said in a quiet, forceful voice—one accustomed to the attention given to a symphony orchestra.

"Not at all, sir."

Two uniformed officers followed the Minister into the room. Something terrible was happening. Denis felt his legs waver and dropped into his seat before he lost his balance.

The guards stepped to either side of the door. Peerson hobbled between them on a cane. Faison skulked in last, closing the door with the care of a locksmith.

"What is all this?" the Minister asked, gesturing at the map-covered desk. It was typical of him to start with small-talk, no matter the occasion. "Do we have an important new lead?"

"No, sir." Denis tried to fold the map, but it was too big and crumpled in his shaking hands. "Just an agent we're trying to locate."

The Minister frowned. "I should think the head of France's internal intelligence would have more important things to focus on during this time of crisis."

"Yes, sir," Denis said, unable to think of anything better.

"Enough of that. The reason I'm here is that Doctor Peerson has leveled some serious accusations against you and we're going to have to straighten this all out."

Denis nodded. The Minister looked to Peerson, who cleared his throat as if to read a well-practiced speech. It probably was.

"This morning," Peerson said with trembling anger, "I received this on my desk." He slapped a photo on the desk. It was a black and white of a man lying in a pool of blood. It was no one Denis recognized.

"His name is Demyan Ermolov. He is a former KGB agent, murdered in a church in Marseille yesterday by a man who matches the description of Grey Stark. The photo and the information came to me from NSC headquarters. No one around here seems to be giving me any information at all." Peerson delivered the last line directly to the Minister.

It was a good performance, Denis thought. Peerson was keeping the edge in his voice but not losing his temper. But it was still just an act, put on for the benefit of the Minister. The NATO Security Council, it seemed, was making its move.

"So I started to ask myself," Peerson continued, "why would one of our own agents, supposedly investigating a bomb in Paris, be meeting with a retired Soviet agent in Marseille? Again I had to go to my own people for the answer. They sent me this." Peerson put a manila folder on the desk, laying his evidence out like a trial lawyer. "It turns out that the plans for the bomb passed through Berlin while Grey Stark was Head of Operations.

"I was upset at my own people, chastising them for not providing me with this critical information, but apparently they had already given it to me. They had included this in my initial briefing material, though I never saw it. And it seems that, shortly after I shared my files with the DST, Denis himself put in a phone call to the CIA, during which this very information was discussed. I have the transcript right here—"

"There's no need for dramatics," Denis interrupted. He could see where Peerson was heading and needed to derail him before he got there. It wasn't so much the facts, but how they were presented, that would sway the Minister's judgment.

"I knew that the plans had passed through Berlin," Denis said offhandedly, as if it were a mere detail. "I contacted Tom McGareth about it and I imagine he discussed the matter with Grey. I never heard back on it, so I assumed nothing came of it."

"You did all this without telling me."

"Grey is not one of my agents, I have no authority to release his personal information. Not even to other French agencies."

"It's not personal if it's relevant to the investigation, is it?"

Denis didn't like the triumphant smile on Peerson's face, but there was only one answer he could give: "Of course not."

"And was it relevant when I asked you why Grey was cavorting with Russian agents right here in Paris?"

Denis shrugged. "There's no reason to suspect Russian involvement. According to the report, they never got ahold of the plans."

"But Grey Stark did."

"And he saw they were destroyed."

"According only to Stark himself. There were no witnesses in no-man's land. He could have easily hidden it on the body of the Russian agent, later to be retrieved by one of his Soviet colleagues."

"You can't seriously think Grey provided the bomb's plans to the Iranians."

"I can and I do. He could have arranged for the bomb to be planted in Paris, to ensure his own involvement in the investigation."

"The bomb was a dud."

"A carefully engineered dud. If it had blown up, what use is it to him? But an unexploded bomb, its authenticity confirmed by no one less than the President of the United States... Now that's a good way to advertise that you've got a new product to sell. In fact, we have reports that a bidding war is already in progress."

"But that's inconceivable. Why would he do something like that?"

"I can think of a hundred reasons starting and ending with money. Did you know that Grey Stark has a private Swiss bank account he keeps under an alias? There's quite a bit of money in it."

Peerson was tying his story together with innuendo. That Denis could handle: "I've been running the DST four times longer than your organization has even existed. I oversee a thousand operations a year. I've seen double agents, I know them a mile away."

"You're such a good judge of men, are you?" Peerson sneered.

"Call it what you will."

"And using that good judgment, you gave us a top-notch operative. Your very best, if I remember your words correctly."

"You do," Denis snorted. "And I stand behind them."

"And this highly-decorated operative, so frequently promoted in your own department, how did he perform? It seems that your inflated judgment of his abilities got him in over his head. It got him killed."

"What are you talking about?" Denis asked. Peerson's words echoed in his head. His stomach sank.

"Killed," Peerson continued, "by a thirty-two caliber bullet bearing the rifling marks of a Beretta Tomcat, the very gun carried by Grey Stark. The agent's personal GPS transmitter had been rewired, bypassing its medical emergency alarm. Grey Stark is one of the few people with the knowledge to do that, and very likely the only one in the city of Marseille."

"Who was killed?" Denis shouted, his mind already rejecting the answer. The Minister raised his hand to Peerson, who begrudgingly held his tongue. He stepped close to Denis, speaking in a soft warm voice: "This is not how I would have chosen to tell you. Jerard's body was found this afternoon in a hotel room. I only just found out myself. He was due to check out and didn't answer the door."

Denis felt the blood drain from his face.

"But that's not really the point," the Minister said, his voice growing hard again. "The issue here is that you had strict orders to co-operate with the NSC, and by all indications, you withheld key information from them on several occasions."

The Minister waited for a response that didn't come. Denis might as well have been in another room, or another building, or on another planet.

"There's nothing I can do about it," the Minister sighed. "I'm temporarily suspending you. We need to sort this mess out, but this obviously isn't the time." He motioned to the guards and they eagerly charged forward.

"Gently, men," the Minister cautioned. "We're not hauling in a criminal, we're escorting an important man."

The guards stopped, perplexed. One of them got it: he extended his hand. Denis took it and the guard helped him up from his chair, leading Denis limping from the room. The Minister held the door, regret on his face. But when the door closed, his expression switched with the draw of a breath.

"Doctor Peerson, I am very sorry for this. Denis is a good man, with years of faithful service. It's a shame you two couldn't get along. I think sometimes it's just hard for different teams to work together, even when they have the same goals."

Peerson managed an equally equitable look, one of sadness and appreciation, and said: "It's water under the bridge, sir. My biggest concern is how to move forward."

"Yes," the Minister nodded. "I shall officially assume Denis's duties until we can get someone interim. I'll see that you get whatever you need. I won't have much time to attend to you personally, I'm afraid. Did you have a preference of who your contact is?"

Peerson nodded at Faison. The Minister turned, having forgotten there was anyone else in the room. "Lieutenant…?" he said, as if his name were on the tip of his tongue. In truth, he had ignored the man when they were introduced.

"Faison, sir," Faison said, straightening to his full height.

"Lieutenant Faison, you are now the senior officer on the case, regardless of rank. I hereby make you interim Director of Operations. Give Doctor Peerson everything he wants." He turned to Peerson. "Let me know immediately if you're not getting everything that you need."

Peerson nodded, barely masking his look of triumph. The Minister strode out of the room and, for a moment, everything was still. Peerson turned to Faison, who was grinning euphorically.

"We're going to need more operatives," Peerson said, "at least ten. Let's get them looking for Agent Stark immediately."

"That won't be necessary," Faison replied. "I already know where he is."

Peerson tried to cover his surprise. "Then send a team to go pick him up. And make sure they get the plans. I don't care how they do it." He started toward the door, glancing at his watch. "I'll be back early tomorrow morning. It'd be a nice surprise if you had him waiting for me."

"Where are you going?"

"Stark is the CIA's man, so he's the CIA's mess. It's about time they came and cleaned it up." Peerson stopped at the door, fondling the lapel of his jacket. "And one other thing: have a proper badge waiting for me when I get back."

II

The first thing Grey noticed was someone turning on a light. Or maybe they drew a curtain. He couldn't really see the light so much as he was just aware of it. Soft footsteps circled him and then the light went away. Grey felt tense, but he had no idea why. He just knew that something was wrong—desperately wrong—and that he had to do something about it.

His eyes were open. He could feel them blink, but whatever they saw, they weren't sharing it with the rest of him. His mouth was packed with tasteless sand. His ears pulsed like his heart had been knocked up into his head.

The visual isolation went on for years. All he could do was lie in the dark and think, but he had nothing to think about. His mind was blank. He didn't know where he was, and he couldn't say how he got here. He wasn't even all that sure who he was. Memories flashed through his mind, images with no context. The more he grabbed at them, the faster they slipped away.

The room brightened like the slow coming of dawn—first to white, then with blurred splatters of color. Footsteps approached. Someone, or something, bent over him and stabbed something between his dry lips. He smelled perfume and thought of Leigh. He felt pressure on his wrist and the pounding in his ears grew heavy. And then everything came into focus.

He was in the hospital and a plump, middle-aged nurse was taking his pulse. Her hair had too much henna in it, making it the color of dried cedar. Her sloped nose was too small for her face, and her teeth were placed randomly about her mouth. Her uniform was fifteen pounds overdue for replacement. She frowned at his wrist, letting it drop back to the bed.

Grey suddenly remembered that he had been in a car accident, and that memory formed the keystone that his other memories built on. Half a minute later, the nurse plucked the thermometer from his mouth and Grey had reconstructed everything that had happened to him over the last week.

He asked about Leigh, but his mouth didn't open. The nurse scribbled on a clipboard and hung it at the end of his bed. She left him alone with the soft beeping of electronics.

He waited for a month or so for her to come back, but then let his eyes close, because they very much wanted to.

— — —

The next time Grey woke, it was to the smell of warm cheese. He opened his eyes and saw a small wheel of brie hovering over his lap. It was on a yellow plastic tray, which in turn was on an adjustable table. Keeping the cheese company was a fried egg, a pastry, and a small loaf of steaming-fresh bread.

Grey could not remember being this hungry. He leaned forward and pain rippled through his back. He started to fall, but a pillow appeared behind him, set there by the henna-haired nurse. He hadn't noticed her there. She wasn't the only one he hadn't noticed.

"It isn't broken."

Grey turned as fast he could—which wasn't very—and saw a doctor standing in the doorway. He had wisps of silver hair at the base of his skull and wrinkled, muddy-tan skin. Grey put him at seventy. The doctor inspected him with deep concern. Or perhaps disdain.

"Your back," he explained. "It isn't broken, it's just been badly compressed." He knows about me, Grey thought, enough to speak English. He asked about Leigh, making an unintelligible sound like he had a frog hidden under his mattress.

The doctor raised his hand. "We will talk later. Eat now, to recover your strength." As he left, Grey saw something shiny in his hand, like a knife or a scalpel.

The warm brie called for his attention. He reached for his fork and knife, and discovered that his left arm was cocooned inside a tube of plaster. He took the knife and tried to slice the brie, but his hand was too weak to puncture it. He grabbed the cheese in his hand and bit off a big chunk. It was as rich as melted butter.

"You don't support the war, do you, Tom?"

The dark small room felt exactly like what it was: a place where secrets were discussed. Four men sat in ornate Victorian chairs around a square marble table. Expensive china was laid out for coffee service.

The man speaking was Senator Terry Johnson, the senior Republican from Missouri. He was tall and thin, with a slight hunch to his wide shoulders. He had hit his sixties with an easy stride, his red hair not so much turning white as fading to clear. His suit was cut plainly, as if from a Sears catalog, but it was hand-tailored from expensive wool. Though he had lived in Washington for three and a half terms—twenty-one years in all—he made a point to keep his lispy Missouri accent. If he ever lost it, the people of his native state wouldn't see him as one of their own. But the truth is, he wasn't.

As the Senate Majority leader, Terry was the most powerful man in Washington, barring the President himself.

When he personally called Tom and asked to see him, there was no way to refuse.

"It's okay that you don't," the Senator continued. "Most of you CIA guys don't."

"The CIA doesn't have access to the conclusive information that the NSC apparently does," Tom said. "And we all know how well that information has served them in the past. Speaking of which, how is the search going for Iraq's nuclear arsenal?"

"No reason to be prickly, Tom. No one said the NSC hasn't made mistakes in the past. They were just a fledgling organization back then, and perhaps a bit overzealous. And that was years ago. We don't waste our time digging through the CIA's past mistakes, now do we?

Tom was about to retort when the Senator cleared his throat. "But that's not what we're here to talk about," he said, then waited with some satisfaction while Tom swallowed his words. "The President asked us to speak with you. Well, he asked me and I asked Jim here because I know he's an old friend of yours."

Jim, in this case, was Senator Jim Thomas. He was tall, thin, and strong the way bamboo is. He wore the same flattop as Tom, but his hair was powder white. His neck bent at his prominent Adam's apple, earning him the nickname 'Pelican' back when he was a marine. Tom had first met Jim in the Corps. They had seen action together and, ever since, Jim had championed Tom's career. Jim was a Democrat from New Hampshire and the Chair of the Senate Intelligence Committee. Tom wouldn't be sitting in this room if Jim hadn't pulled him up the ladder.

The last person in the room sat back from the table, as if a mere observer. His name was Doctor Peerson, and he filled his chair like a sack of milk. Tom had been hearing a lot about this man recently. The last he had heard, Peerson was in France. Tom hoped that he hadn't come back just for this meeting.

Tom looked through the photos that were laid out on the table. One was of Grey and his wife leaving a Russian-owned bar, another showed a French agent shot through the forehead. After that was an ex-KGB agent lying in a pool of blood. The last, and most worrisome, was Grey having an apparently friendly conversation with a garish Korean agent. All of the photos were stamped with the gold DST logo in the bottom corner. It seemed that Denis had betrayed him by having Grey tailed—but not nearly as much as Denis had betrayed Grey.

"The operating theory," the Missouri senator continued, "is that our man over there has been selling the plans for the nuclear device that, but for an act of God, would have murdered millions of people. He's been on the move ever since we uncovered the bomb, and spending a lot of time with his old KGB rivals. We don't know why. They might be holding the plans for him, or they might be brokering his private auction. An auction, I am assured, to our most outspoken enemies." The Senator looked to Peerson for confirmation, letting on who had done the assuring.

Tom looked over at Jim; he gave Tom a nod, letting him know that he was still on his side. "I ordered Grey to investigate the link between the plans and Russia," Tom said. He had expected this to come as a revelation, but no one in the room looked surprised.

"Believe me," Senator Johnson said, "I appreciate the irony of the situation. You made a… a curious choice, but not necessarily a bad one. You couldn't have known at the time that Agent Stark already had the plans."

"And we know that now?"

"The evidence is conclusive enough for me," the Senator said.

"Why would he do that? How could he do that?"

"I don't know," the Senator said impatiently. "Hell, I don't care. Right now we need concern ourselves with containing the damage."

"Even if Grey has proof that Iran isn't connected to the bomb?"

"Proof?" the Senator spat the word back at him. "We've had proof of the opposite for days now! And it's moved way beyond that. I can tell you, confidentially, this will be a shooting war by week's end. That should help you appreciate our position. As well as your own."

Tom nodded and kept his thoughts to himself. Politicians had their own truths. "What do you need from me?" he asked.

Johnson glanced at Peerson and the heavy man leaned in, speaking for the first time. Tom had cast him as an Iago, sowing the seeds of spite with a hissing whisper to the ear, but his voice was rich and commanding.

"I need you to come to France and help me find Agent Stark. You know him better than anyone. You've been his boss for years, and before that you worked alongside him in Berlin. I understand that you consider him a friend."

The insinuation was clear: prove your innocence by delivering Grey. It was the kind of deal Judas would hang himself over.

"And when we find him?" Tom asked.

"We bring him back," Peerson said, as if it were the most obvious thing in the world.

Tom wasn't buying: "Alive?"

"Only your knowledge could make that possible."

"Our principal concern," Senator Johnson added, "is to get him off the streets. After that, well, this is America. He'll get a fair trial."

Tom wasn't much for speeches, so he didn't make one. "I'll help you find him, but that doesn't mean I suspect him. It only means I know how to do what I'm told."

Peerson smiled. "Good," he said. "Your skepticism will help us reach him. I assure you that we're not out for his blood.

Quite the opposite, we want to know how all of this happened. And, if he is innocent, we will owe him an apology." Peerson pushed to his feet. "If you'll excuse me, I must be getting back to Paris. I trust you can arrange your own transport?"

Tom said he could and the meeting broke. Senator Johnson left with Peerson. Jim waited behind; he had more to say.

In the hall outside, Peerson shook Senator Johnson's hand and received praise for his work. A long black car waited for the NATO man outside. It whisked him down Pennsylvania Avenue to Bolling Air Force Base, where a supersonic jet was warmed up and on the runway. He would be back in France in less than three hours.

IV

*G*rey sat in bed reading the morning's newspaper, relieved to learn that not even a full day had passed during his endless stupor. His meeting with the Major wasn't until tomorrow. He still had time to make it.

The date was the only good news that paper brought. Every story was focused on the upcoming war. The front page had a photo of a French helicopter pilot waving as he climbed the gangway to the Jeanne d'Arc. The cruiser was to sail for the Persian Gulf this afternoon. The pilot smiled like an athlete heading to the game.

Grey's health had improved, which meant that his numb disorientation had been replaced with acute pain. His forearm, hidden inside thick plaster, felt like it had been run through with needles. His leg only hurt when they changed the bandage, but the way it hurt then more than made up for the rest of the time. His back was better: sore, but he could sit up on his own. He still wasn't hearing any answers to his questions, but he doubted there was anything wrong with his ears.

Grey folded up the paper as the doctor appeared at the doorway. He had been wrong before: the doctor wasn't holding a knife. His hand was a metal hook, sticking out from a plaster wrist.

"Bonjour," he said. "You can walk?"

Grey nodded.

"Then come now." The doctor offered no help as Grey struggled to his feet. He led him down the bustling hallway to an elevator. The hospital was eight stories tall; Grey was on the third. The elevator raised them up to the fifth and opened on a hallway as quiet as a morgue. The doctor went silently to the double-doors at the end. They were labeled, "U.S.I." Behind them was a room with three large windows, each offering the view of a bed that was surrounded with massive stacks of medical machinery. Only two of the beds were occupied. Only one of those interested Grey.

Leigh lay in a hospital gown, motionless. Grey's heart jumped when he saw a scar running down the center of her face, but at second glance, realized it was only an oxygen tube. Wires and tubes formed a spider's web across her body, feeding into the surrounding machines and making them flash and twinkle. A plastic brace locked her right leg straight.

The doctor closed the door behind them. "She lost much blood," he said. "She has a powerful compact, and has turned her ankle. She'll recuperate."

"A compact?"

"A compact to the head." The doctor searched for the word: "A concussion."

Grey wanted to go in and see her, but wasn't sure how to ask.

"You know her?" the doctor asked.

"She's my wife."

"Oh." The doctor looked surprised. "That is an unfortunate chance. You are not German, and you are not French."

"American," Grey said. "I've lived in Paris a long time."

The doctor frowned. He leaned toward Grey and whispered confidentially: "I do not mean to press, but there is a thing we must immediately discuss.

"I admitted you myself. You were brought in directly, not by the police. You had a number of passports." Grey's face flushed and the doctor quickly added, "Only I know of this.

"You had police credentials as well. I was in the military. I lost this," the Doctor held up the steel hook, "at Algiers. So I know of undercover agents. I chose to conceal your many identities until I better understood your position."

Grey experienced the strange sensation of being both alarmed that his cover was blown and thankful that the doctor had kept his secret. The important thing, he decided, was that they were safe. "Who am I registered as?" he asked.

"Jeffrey LeRoit. It was the least stamped passport. I took further precaution by misspelling the name. The woman had no ID. Perhaps she had a purse? The only thing on her was an impressive handgun. Your cars were both incinerated. Even the license plates were destroyed. I feel no one knows that you are here."

"And the other driver?"

The doctor's face was blank. "Which other driver?"

"The one from the other car. The Mercedes."

It took a moment for the doctor to figure it out: "I see. I have talked with the police. They felt you were each driving a car. You were in the same?" Grey nodded. "The police are anxious to speak with you," the doctor added.

"That can't happen. We have to get out of here immediately."

"The woman can not go."

"Why not?"

"She is stable, but in no condition to travel. She needs the machines. They are keeping her alive."

"How long?"

"Another day in there," the doctor said, pointing at the intensive care room. "A week before she can leave. But even then she must rest. And the police will not wait so long. I should not even make them wait now."

The message was clear: the doctor had covered for them so far, but Grey had to convince him, right now, to keep what he knew a secret.

Grey went with the truth; he was too disoriented to make anything else work. "I'm a CIA agent and my wife is a retired police officer. We're investigating the bomb in Paris. I have good reason to believe that, contrary to public opinion, it has nothing to do with the Iranians.

"The thing is, I've over-extended my authority. If the police find me, they will haul me back to Paris and throw me in jail."

The doctor chewed Grey's words. "Your ideas are... assured?" he asked. Grey nodded and the doctor mulled it further. "Ah, bon," he said. "I must phone the police, to tell them you are well enough to speak. But I will wait, so that you may escape."

"You'd do that?"

"If you are telling the truth, you might stop the war and save many lives. If you lie, the police will get you soon enough. With what is at stake, mon Dieu. It is easy to think in which direction I prefer to be wrong."

"You're taking a hell of a risk."

"The risk is yours. Entirely so, if you don't say that we talked. As for me, this region is for the old; my time is spent issuing laxatives and death certificates. I am happy for the adventure."

"You'll get that."

"Now I suppose you will want to go in?" The doctor pointed to Leigh.

"Can I?" Grey brightened.

"Yes, but… do not get her excited." He smiled. "She is not well."

Grey entered the room quietly and kneeled down beside Leigh. She didn't move, didn't appear to notice he was there. The only light was from the interior window, and that wasn't much. The bed was surrounded by a small fortune in equipment, but the only sound was the whirring of a small fan in one of the machines. Even her heart monitor pulsed in slow silence.

She didn't look as bad as he had feared. Her skin was pale and her lips bloodless. Stitches ran along her hairline and a dark bruise covered half her neck. Other than that, she might be sleeping off a hangover.

Grey took her hand; it seemed the right thing to do. Her lips drew up into a smile.

"Hello, honey," she said, her voice barely a breath. He ran a finger down her cheek. She raised her arm—the one that wasn't riddled with tubes—and laid her hand on his. Her fingers squeezed with the strength of a ghost. Her eyes opened and found his.

Grey wanted to kiss her and she wanted to be kissed, but he hesitated and the moment was lost. So they just sat there, eye to eye, her hand over his.

Time passed and Grey knew he had to go. His whisper bellowed in the silence: "I have to leave you in a bad situation."

Leigh nodded.

"I'll need two days, at the most. I'm going to head up to… to keep that appointment. The police don't know who you are, and they are going to be curious about me. It's best just to pretend you can't remember anything."

Grey tried to pull his hand away; Leigh held it with new strength.

"Don't," she managed.

He shook his head. "It's the only way."

She drew the back of his hand to her lips, pressed it there, and then let it go.

It took some effort for Grey to turn away. He pushed to his feet and walked out the door without looking back. Then he bent his mind to the task ahead.

V

*T*om didn't think that Jim Thomas had offered him a ride home just to save him the cab fare. The Senator had something on his mind, though so far he had only tossed out some tidbits regarding the statues they drove past. Jim was an expert in American history, better versed than most professors, but Tom wasn't up for a history lesson right now; he was anxious for Jim to get to the point. But it wasn't until the limo pulled in front of Tom's townhouse that the Senator did:

"Do you remember the Bay of Pigs, Tom?"

It struck Tom as an odd way to open a conversation. "I remember what I learned," he replied. "I was only ten when it happened."

"It was a very public failure, very bad for the CIA. They had to fire their two top men and scores of others. Good people, career intelligence folks with decades of experience. It only took a single botched operation to bring the Company crashing down.

"You see, the CIA works for the government and the government for the people. So when you guys screw up and the public demands action, we give it to them, whether it makes sense or not. We do it or we get replaced by those who will.

"This country believes what it reads in the paper, and the press decided that the Bay of Pigs was an asinine idea. Politicians like myself—even those who supported the operation—had to dig up scapegoats. It was our job to clean out the CIA and to assure America that everything was fixed.

"These were smart men and women, people who worked hard for their country, and who never needed our support more. Instead, they were dragged into the spotlight and persecuted."

The Senator poured water into a whiskey glass and took a pull like it was single malt. "But this 'fix' for the CIA was quite the opposite. A year and half later, we had the Cuban missile crisis. The country cheered Kennedy for his fearless response, but it never should have happened in the first place. We knew the Russians were planning it months in advance, plenty of time to stop it quietly. But the newly rebuilt CIA was inexperienced, cocky, and plagued by internal politics. They blew a thousand opportunities to ward the problem off and—despite overwhelming evidence—the missiles had been in Cuba for over a month before the President was even told about them."

The Senator saw the confusion in Tom's face. "My point is, while Grey Stark may not have done anything wrong, they have enough evidence to condemn him in the public forum. There will be a huge shakeup in the CIA, and maybe even its complete destruction.

"The war is coming, neither of us can stop that. The Republicans want it and they hold the House, the Senate, and the White House. Even the Judiciary swings to the right these days. This country is essentially a one-party system, and I'm in the wrong party. I've fought against the invasion of Iran at every turn, as I did with Iraq, and they are anxious to get rid of me."

The Senator studied his water glass.

"They're going to burn us, Tom," he whispered. "They're tying me to you and you to this Grey Stark thing. I know you don't play politics—I've always respected you for that—but the balance of power in this country has fallen too far to one side. It's not democracy, it's a dictatorship with an agreeable name."

"You're right," Tom barked, surprised at his own venom. "I don't play politics. I work for the CIA. We don't belong to either party, we serve the people and whoever the people choose to elect."

The Senator took a long draw of his water. Tom knew he was wound up, but this was all coming at him too quickly. Jim was his friend; he owed it to him to hear him out: "If I did agree with you, what would you have me do?"

"After they capture Grey Stark, the Senate will hold a hearing to shake down the CIA and destroy what remains of its credibility. They'll embarrass me, force me to resign my seat on the Intelligence Committee. Next, they'll replace your boss with a pawn and methodically transfer all of the CIA's power to the NATO Security Commission. After all, who wants an American intelligence agency when you control an international one—one that is far less accountable to public opinion?"

Tom had never heard Jim sound so paranoid. He laughed, his instinct telling him it was a joke. But Jim didn't laugh back.

"Grey Stark's trial will make headlines for months," the Senator said. "He'll be pegged as a national traitor. Hell, I've already seen their press release. The longer the trial, the greater the damage."

"And?" Tom asked, his voice unsteady.

"It would be far better if there were no trial at all."

"You want me to kill him," Tom blurted.

The Senator retreated. His face froze over and the friend became the politician: "Decisions like that are entirely yours. France is your baby, Stark is your man. I'm sure you'll do the right thing."

Prompted by some unseen signal, the chauffer opened the limousine's door. Outside, the sky was dark and overcast, and the air thick from a coming storm. Tom rose stiffly, as if he had been worked over by a couple of thugs. The Senator threw some parting courtesy at him, but Tom's mind was far away.

The limo pulled away, but Tom made no move for his house. He stood in the cold wind, staring at nothing, and asked himself if he could kill a friend.

_VI_

The hut Grey sat in was a marvel of medieval engineering, its pencil-sharp, stacked-slate roof still intact after a half-dozen centuries of disuse. It stood next to an abandoned field, along the farmland trail on which Grey had been walking.

The Lot region was crisscrossed with trails like these, old trade routes that ran from one village to the next, allowing the region to be toured entirely on foot. Grey had planned to walk one town over before he caught the train, to obscure Leigh's location by putting some distance between himself and the hospital. But he had underestimated the damage to his leg, which throbbed terribly, forcing him to spend more time resting than walking.

He'd been on the trail for six hours, optimistically shooting for the town of Capdenac by sunset. He had no idea how much farther it was, but the sun had dropped below the distant trees and the forest burned orange from its light. The only good news was that the moon was nearly full, so he'd be able to travel at night.

Grey was cleaning his gun on the hut's flat stone table while he rested his leg. He clamped the barrel to the table with the tubular cast and slid it back together. He tested its action, sliding the chamber back and forth, and then checked the sights against the blazing trees. Satisfied, he holstered it.

He eased to his feet, leaning on the table to keep the pressure off his leg. He was wearing red-checked pants and a canary-yellow shirt, purchased in Figeac with the idea they would get him noticed—it was a long walk if no one saw him. Looking at his bright outfit, he wondered if he hadn't been a little overzealous. He pulled on a muted brown overcoat, to guard against being spotted too soon, and slid a brown cap low on his brow. He stepped out into the chest-high grass.

The hut was up on a hill, and he could see a river running down along its base. There was a road alongside the water and Grey started toward it. The road would be easier to navigate in the moonlight. At the edge of the forest, a giant boulder peeked out of the ground, rough stairs cut directly into its face, worn by centuries of use. They led down into the dark canopy of trees.

Grey took one last look behind him. Miles back and hidden by several hills, Leigh lay in her hospital bed. He had a strong urge to return to her side, to lie down next to her and let the world take care of itself. He had felt this way all day, and the feeling grew stronger with each step.

As he stood and gathered the strength to press on, he watched a hawk soaring against the dim sky. It turned tight circles, doing its best to dodge the unwavering attacks of a small band of crows. A hawk, for all its majesty, is no match for the thuggish brutality of the crow.

Crows are better suited to the world that man has built. Refuse is a fair substitute for the carrion of their usual diet, and they are better fed by a dumpster than anything nature provides. As the human population has flourished, so has the crow. And like humans, they are very jealous of their property. So when a crow moves into a hawk's territory, there's always a showdown.

Hawks have small light bodies, effortlessly supported by their glorious wings. Crows are heavy, expending a great deal of energy on even the shortest of flights. But the crow's ungainly flapping allows for greater dexterity, and they can attack too quickly for a hawk to strike back. A single crow can harass a hawk and keep it from feeding. A pack of them can knock it out of the sky. When the crows come, a hawk must either run away or die; there are no other options. Grace and beauty are no match for brute force.

By twilight, Grey was walking alongside a two-lane road that skirted the river. He cradled his plastered arm to his chest and limped to keep the weight off his injured leg.

The road had been empty since he turned onto it, but a pair of headlights came around the bend, ripping toward him like an earth-bound rocket. He lowered his arm, pulled down his cap and walked casually, hoping not to draw attention. He felt exposed and wished there was something to duck behind. But it was too late; whoever was in the car would already have seen him.

The car was a white Aston-Martin, new enough to still have the cardboard plates from the dealer. It glinted like a knife in the dim moonlight, and kicked up pebbles as it passed, stinging Grey's legs. Then it slammed on the brakes, painting wide black streaks on the pavement. The car reversed quickly, coming alongside him. Grey slipped his hand into his jacket and found his gun. The only thing he saw in the car's window was his own reflection.

The window slid down with electric precision. A well-tanned, shock-blond man leaned out and gave him a friendly smile. He looked familiar to Grey; he had the polished look of a celebrity.

"Excuse me," he said with a light Australian accent. "Do you speak English?"

Grey nodded and, trying to sound French, said: "A little."

"Great," the man said, flashing monstrously perfect teeth. "I am hopelessly lost. You don't know the way to Toulouse, do you?"

"The road is correct," Grey said, stumbling over his English, "but you travel the wrong way."

"Crap." The man pulled a map off the passenger seat and inspected it, then balled it up and tossed it out the window. Deciding this wasn't enough, he leapt from his car, stomped it flat and kicked it into the stream. He watched with satisfaction as it floated away.

The man thanked Grey and jumped back into the car. The car shot down the road, cut a tight U-turn and whipped past him in the other direction. It was almost around the bend when it again chirped to a halt. As the car reversed toward him, Grey found himself smiling at this man's antics, and wondering what was next. The man popped his head out the driver's window, on the far side of the car.

"You don't need a ride, do you?"

It was an easy decision: Grey's leg hurt terribly and he wasn't sure he could make it to Capdenac in time, much less at all. And Toulouse was a better place for him to be seen boarding a train; it was a lot further from where Leigh was.

"Merci," Grey said.

The man dropped down into the car and pushed open the passenger door, leaning out. "Where are you heading?" he asked.

"I was to catch the train here, but if you are en route to Toulouse—"

"Of course. I'd love the company."

Grey barely got the door closed before he was tossed into his seat; the car accelerated away.

VII

*H*is name was Dick Fiddich, and he wasn't a celebrity after all, but he thanked Grey for the compliment. He called himself a philanthropist, a word that rich unemployable men called themselves to justify the oxygen they consumed—his joke, not Grey's. He was from New Zealand, but most people just lumped him in with the Australians. He was part Maori, the aboriginal population there, which accounted for his darker skin. The white settlers didn't slaughter the Maori, but they didn't coddle them either.

Dick was the illegitimate son of a wealthy playboy. When his father killed himself in a drunken accident, his grandparents tracked his mother down and claimed them as family. Some sort of atonement, Dick figured, but he was only three at the time.

He was here in France on a hunting trip, and had driven up to Lot to meet a friend, a woman, but she had stood him up. So now he was heading back to Toulouse. Dick spoke in a rapid clip—everything was a story and every story led to another. He talked a lot, but that meant Grey didn't have to.

Dick did ask Grey about the ring on his finger. He was curious about marriage because he was engaged. Had been for years, he said. Grey made his reply painfully slow, dragging it out by pretending to struggle with English. When he finally finished, Dick didn't make the mistake of asking any more questions.

He insisted, absolutely, that they stop for dinner. He would buy, of course. Grey agreed because it would have been difficult not to. They stopped at the only restaurant they found, halfway between Capdenac and Toulouse, and right in the middle of nowhere. It could have been a house but for the pink neon 'Les Poissons' glowing in the window.

The house was right on the river, leaning out on a pier the way a drunk leans on a friend. It was a wonder the whole thing hadn't tipped over and floated away. A chapped rowboat was tied out back and there was a gravel parking lot that could hold four cars. It was empty until the Aston-Martin pulled in.

The inside hadn't been renovated for maybe a half a century, and looked more worn from the years than the use. A matronly woman, her chest shaped into a funnel by a tight corset, seated them next to a smeared window that overlooked the river. The table was covered with a yellowed tablecloth of embroidered linen, set with chipped flatware and silver that was dulled from age. She dropped a screw-top gallon of wine on the table—wrapped in twine to decoratively hide the label—and said, "Compliments de la maison." Neither man touched it.

A man sat alone at a corner table, tending his jug of wine and making no pretense about food. He had dirty hair that was sun-bleached to mustard, and the skin on his neck looked like charred bacon. He acknowledged the new diners by turning his chair to keep his back toward them.

When Grey took off his overcoat, Dick was amused by the clothing underneath. He asked Grey to translate the menu and wasn't bothered by the inconsistencies between Grey's description and what actually arrived. The food was surprisingly good: vegetables freshly pulled from the ground and fish so tender they could have served it with a spoon. Southern France bordered on Italy, and shared the Italian knack for food.

Dick asked Grey about his cast, as if just noticing it. He was impressed by the size and asked where he got it done. A wise hunter, he said, always knows where the nearest hospital is. Grey didn't want to give away Leigh's location, not even to this man, but knew almost nothing of this area. He made up a town that didn't exist and did his best to distance it from Figeac, both in location and description. He even recommended a fictional steakhouse there. "Tell them André sent you," Grey told him, "and they'll take care of you." The Kiwi said that he would. Grey didn't care either way; by tomorrow morning, he'd have much bigger problems than misleading a tourist.

Grey pressed Dick about the time; he had a train to catch. Dick apologized, and demanded the check.

While they waited for it, Dick asked if he could sign Grey's cast. He said it was something they always did back in boarding school.

At the station, Dick insisted on waiting, to make sure Grey was able to catch his train. Grey went to the ticket counter and bought a first-class ticket to Paris with a credit card that he knew would sound an alarm back at DST headquarters. While the ticket was printing, he shed his coat and gave the clerk a memorable look at his tacky outfit. Thanks to Dick, he was seventy miles away from the hospital.

He waved his ticket at Dick and the Aston Martin raced away. Grey stepped onto the train to Paris and walked down the aisle, moving from car to car until he reached the end. Then he slipped on his hat and coat and stepped down to the platform. He sat down on a bench and waited for ten minutes, then walked to an automatic ticket machine and bought a second-class ticket to Geneva. He paid with cash.

His train was just arriving and he boarded immediately. He stuck his ticket in the overhead clip so the conductor wouldn't bother him, then tucked himself in a window seat, pulled his hat over his eyes and did his best to sleep. His best wasn't very good: he only managed to doze for thirty minutes. He changed trains in Lyon and the second leg took two hours. Grey spent it staring at the dark window.

It was near midnight when he arrived in Geneva and the fluorescent lights in customs brought dull pain to his tired eyes. He flashed a Swiss passport and the agent didn't bother to write down his name.

VIII

*G*rey emerged from the train station into the night. The streets had a gentle glow, the way all cities do, but were nearly abandoned. He had never been to Geneva before—nothing of intrigue ever happened here—but even at first glance, he could see that this place was the complete opposite of Marseille.

Buildings were short and unassuming, and appeared to be scrubbed nightly by gnomes. The cars on the street were the finest examples of German and Japanese engineering, luxurious but practical, and every one of them looked like they had been bought this morning.

There was no such thing as a Swiss car—they didn't make them. The Swiss only made what they felt like making, which was mostly watches, knives, and chocolate. Unlike the rest of the world, they had no economic incentive to manufacture; they had been bankers as far back as any history book could remember, a living testament to the old line about getting rich by simply going back in time a thousand years and putting a dollar in the bank. Switzerland was a whole country of trust-fund babies and, Geneva, no more than a postage-stamp on the continent of Europe, had more money than Tokyo.

A baggage attendant in a sharp uniform was re-organizing the luggage from the train into alphabetical order. Grey asked him for directions to the lake. The attendant warned him it was halfway across the city and that he should take a cab. When Grey persisted, he looked down his nose and waved an arm down the street. It took no longer than ten minutes to walk there. Along the way, Grey caught glimpses of the famous water jet; nothing had prepared him for how impressive it was.

A lakeside plaque declared that twin pumps rammed five hundred liters of water per second to a height of one hundred and forty-six meters in the air. It went on to describe the amperage of the pumps and the candle-watt of the lights that lit it up. This array of facts held no more meaning for Grey than would an index of the colors used in the Mona Lisa. It would seem that, in the Swiss mind, the water jet's beauty was incidental to its technical accomplishment. But Grey didn't need to know the pump's rotor speed to be impressed by what he saw.

The jet was a towering, hypnotizing shaft of water that punctured an otherwise glass-calm lake and rose higher than the Great Pyramid of Giza. Mist trailed off the white column, fading from silken threads to ghostly shadows. At the very top, clumps of water lobbed for the heavens. They shattered against an invisible roof, raining down into the fog that swirled at the fountain's base like the set of a horror movie.

A thin walkway led out to the jet, passed near it and hooked off to the bantam lighthouse that was meant to ward ships away from the man-made hazard. Grey strolled down it, stepping cautiously on the smooth flagstones. There were no handrails, just a flat stone bar rising a foot above the water line. Right at the jet, he saw something in the water by his feet. He squinted to get a better look, raising his hand to the blazing spotlights.

It was a rabbit, pinned against the wall by the current coming off the fountain, its lifeless body rolling in the gentle waves. It wasn't a wild rabbit, but a big fluffy one that might have been a child's pet. Grey felt a chill: he would be standing in this exact spot tomorrow morning.

There was an audible click and the lights went out. Grey jumped back so fast he almost fell into the water. He found his balance and steadied his pulse, surprised at his own skittishness.

The jet shrank down and disappeared into its own foam. Grey looked at his watch: it was one A.M. on the dot. An automatic switch had shut everything off with Swiss precision. He looked for the rabbit, but it was too dark. He wasn't bothered by it anymore. It wasn't ill portent from the Fates, it was just a dead rabbit.

A light rain rolled across the lake, overtaking Grey as he made his way back to the shore. He pulled his collar up and walked to the nearest hotel, decorated only by a painted brass plaque at the front door. The night clerk stood behind a thick walnut counter, disapproving of the hour and of Grey's cash, but he took the money and gave him a key in return.

Grey asked for a wakeup call at eight, but was up by six. He didn't bother to check out.

IX

*L*ow clouds formed a roof over Geneva, glowing from the morning sun that hid behind them. The rain had stopped, but the air was heavy with water. Puddles gathered along the curb, so clear Grey could stick a straw in and drink.

He dragged down the sidewalk of a wide avenue. This early, the only people around were a few zealous businessmen and a hobo who was so well-dressed, Grey was well past him before he even realized that he was asking for money. There were tracks in the center of the road, and every five minutes a freshly-waxed tram rolled by. Nearly all of them were empty.

Grey wasn't meeting the Major until ten, so he killed time in three different diners and along the streets in between. Lack of sleep mixed with too much coffee twisted his stomach. He was tired of walking, so he headed to the lake.

He arrived at nine-thirty and found a bench with a view of the jet. In the daylight, the lake was clean and blue, and he could see distant hills on the far shore. Grey knew that behind the clouds to his left, a snow-capped Mont Blanc lurked over the city. He had been hearing about that mountain since he first set foot in Europe and wanted very much to see it at least once in his life. He stared in its direction, but it didn't peek out from the white sky. Not even once.

Right at ten, there was a terrible racket: a boisterous swan dashed across the lake, too cumbersome to get airborne. Its tremendous wings slapped against the water as its webbed feet pattered desperately over the surface.

There was still no sign of the Major, but the Major wasn't Swiss. He was Romanian, and Romanians did everything in their own time, not according to a wrist-watch. Grey worked himself to his feet and started around the lake. The Major had said to meet him on the walkway, and no doubt he wouldn't appear until Grey was already out there, exposed and trapped. But since Grey had asked for the meeting, he had little choice but to accommodate.

He turned down the walkway. Its tight-fitted flagstones looked waxed and the path was just wide enough for two people to pass, if both were willing to turn sideways. Grey was suddenly conscious of his clothing, the red-checkered pants and yellow shirt that he wore under his coat. They were a poor choice to be caught dead in.

He was past the fountain and halfway to the lighthouse when he felt the sudden urge to turn. A hulking man in a trench coat stepped off the shore onto the walkway, led by a squat dog on a leash. His movements were silent under the roar of the jet. That sound would cover a lot, Grey thought. Even a gunshot.

The man walked like he didn't have a care in the world, but that was far from the truth. He was Major Nicolae Dragos, and the list of countries that wanted him dead read like roll call at the United Nations.

Dragos was still just a baby when the Romanians had turned on their Nazi allies to join forces with the Russians. His father—a high-level member of the Nazi party—remained loyal to Hitler, but the Nazis executed him anyway. To say that Dragos had a deep-seated hate of Germans was an understatement.

As director of the Berlin operations for the KGB, Dragos was as famous for his cruelty as for his cunning. But after Grey's private manhunt wiped out his entire team, he defected to the States, claiming he feared for his life. His defection took some of the heat off Grey and probably saved his life. But then Dragos disappeared again. It turned out his defection had been a hoax; he fed the Americans a pack of carefully crafted lies in return for a whole lot of money.

The Russians had fully expected Dragos to return home with a pile of stolen intel, but his next stop was China, where he sold off secrets American and Russian alike. For the next five years, Dragos hop-scotched across the globe, pulling one grift after another until he had amassed a fortune. And then, just when it seemed like he had run out of countries that would take him, he showed up in Switzerland with an unlimited visa waiting for him—a neat trick that required as much influence as money.

He'd been here ever since, living on an estate somewhere north of Geneva. He pretended it was a secret location, but it really didn't matter. Pulling a job in Switzerland was a publicity nightmare that no country wanted, and none of them filed for extradition because the Swiss made it clear they wouldn't give one. So Dragos was safe, if trapped. Grey was sure he didn't care either way.

As the Major approached, Grey stuck his hand into his overcoat pocket, feeling the cool grip of the Berretta in his palm. Dragos, twenty paces away, noticed the movement and stopped. The small pig-like dog trotted forward, pulling the leash tight. Foam dripped from its mouth and pooled on the walkway.

The Major, much like his dog, had tiny legs set apart by wide hips. His gaunt face was the texture of a sponge, its deep pores frustrating his razor and leaving him with a permanent five-o'clock shadow. His massive jaw cut a wide arc around his face and his hair looked like polished iron. He was older than Grey had expected, older than he remembered. But even old men could fire a gun.

One hand held the leash, the other was in his pocket. He drew that hand out slowly: it was empty. He turned his palm upward, presenting it to Grey. He walked half the distance between them and shouted over the roar of the jet:

"Guten morgen, Stark."

"Major."

"It has been quite some time," the Major continued in German. It was the language-in-common between the two men, and, here in French-speaking Geneva, offered protection from prying ears. "You are not going to pretend you could actually hit me with that gun in your pocket, are you?"

Grey smiled despite himself. He drew his hand out, without the gun. Dragos nodded, closing the remaining distance. His pig-dog arrived first, sniffing Grey's boot and sizing it up as a toilet. The Major didn't offer his hand and Grey didn't offer his either. The Major spoke first:

"The CIA must be pretty desperate to put you on the job."

"I was just in the right place at the right time."

The general nodded as if this were some great wisdom. "Making much progress?"

"Would I be here?"

"Nein, you would not." The Major scanned the lake, stopping to squint at different points along the shoreline. Satisfied, he turned back to Grey. "They told me you were coming."

"Who did?"

"Vladimir, for one," Dragos shrugged. "And several others. They were all anxious to collect the bounty. You know that I've had a million-franc price on your head for decades now. Twice that if you were delivered to me for execution."

Grey paled and the Major chuckled harshly, like he was clearing his throat. He took advantage of the distraction and slipped his hand back into his coat. Grey winced, but the shot didn't come.

"Let's just say I am being cautious," the Major said, wiggling the gun in pocket.

Grey nodded gravely. The Major had the upper hand now; he would be able to shoot long before Grey could get his hand on his Beretta. And the Major was a keen shot, even from the hip.

"As for the bounty," the Major continued, "I am surprised you did not know about it. I did not think that Russians could keep secrets."

"Oh," Grey said, because he couldn't think of anything else.

"It is not that much money, really," the Major said, "but I have always felt I would take some pleasure to kill you."

"Don't let me stop you," Grey said bitterly, raising his arms. The Major hadn't been one to gloat, but time changes all things.

"Retirement gives one a lot of time to think," Dragos offered, as if bored by talk of Grey's death. "I hated you

Americans. *Blyad!* I hated you so much that I hated Russia when she gave up the fight against you. I had been a dedicated proletarian, risked my life many times for my country. Then one day, *wumf,* I have no more country.

"And the new government, they only wanted me to disappear. I was an embarrassment to them, a relic of a bygone era. They had no care for my years of loyal service. So I decided to retire myself, as you know."

The Major fondled his mouth, clutching for a cigar that wasn't there. Grey remembered that he used to smoke them.

"I do not think a government can be honest," the Major continued. "It is against their nature. I have learned that, even in the better days, my government lied to me immeasurably. As your government still lies to you."

Grey felt an insult rising in his throat, but the Major was faster: "They do lie to you, very much so. You will see."

Grey nodded; the Major was the one with the gun.

"Not so much happens here," he gestured back at the city. "I watch the world through the newspapers, but everything is so far away. I see what is happening, but there is no urgency to it, no immediacy. Current events feel like history, and all I see are countries struggling against one another, as they have since the dawn of time. Russia was once the greatest country in the world—it is true—but does that matter? Twenty years from now it will be China, two thousand years back it was Rome. And every country in the history of man believes that its way is the right way, and so the goal of every country is to remake the world in its own image. It is all just global domination, call it democracy or communism.

"The failure of any country is to doubt itself. When Mother Russia went democratic, what did she gain? A shit economy. Our most beautiful women sold off as prostitutes. And our former territories all gobbled up by the European Union."

"So America is no better than the U.S.S.R. was?" Grey asked. He tried to sound sarcastic, but his German wasn't what it used to be.

Dragos sighed, a deep sigh like he was trying to teach philosophy to a brick. "When we liberated Afghanistan, it was to stop them from slaughtering each other and to bring them a better way of life—our way of life. This is the same reason you are there now. But our war wasn't just against the Afghanis. America provided the Mujahideen with both arms and information. Because of this, we never brought them the peace we had intended to.

"But for you, they have rolled over. Is this because you are better than us? Because your cause is more righteous? You may believe such things, but, in truth, there is simply no one left to stop you."

"Your point of view, certainly," Grey said.

"Anyone who is left unchecked is going to assume his actions are correct. You speed and no one catches you, so you keep on speeding. Tell me, Stark, who is there now that could stop the Americans? They do what they want, lie as it suits them, and those who disagree grumble because they lack the strength to do anything else."

The Major dropped into silence. He looked expectant, but Grey wasn't sure for what. He replayed the Major's words in his head, and then it hit him. He said:

"You're telling me this was all a lie?"

The Major smiled. He drew his hand from his pocket, empty. He pulled something from his coat and offered it to Grey. "This might look familiar to you," he said.

It did. It was a leather-bound brief titled, *Report on the American-developed, Low-Reaction Nuclear Ordinance*, dated June 16th of 1988. It was the same report that Grey had held seventeen years before, sitting beside the bloody corpse of Katia the Cash Machine. The leather was chapped with age, the paper yellowed.

"We did manage to get one copy across, despite your efforts. I am one of the few who have actually seen it. Thanks to you, I am the only one still alive. Go ahead. Read it."

Grey looked at the report hesitantly. He had never looked inside before because he was ordered not to, at the cost of his life. The fear he had felt then was nothing compared with what he felt now. He drew the cover back.

The first page was a schematic of a device similar to the one Grey had seen in the bank five days ago. It was surrounded with technical notations that he didn't understand. The next page was more of the same. As was the one after that.

"Does not make any sense, does it?" the Major asked.

Grey shook his head.

"It is not meant to. It is *blödsinn*, complete gibberish. Project Deadfall wasn't a secret nuclear weapon, it was a bear trap. Your government decided to wipe out the entire Russian spy network in Berlin, so they invented a ploy to draw us out. It was the most terrible thing they could devise, a weapon that would obsolete our entire arsenal and end the Cold War. And then they gave us a chance to steal the plans for it.

Many of us suspected it was a trap, but that did not matter. The stakes were too high. If you truly possessed this weapon and we did not? Our way of life would be over. We were ordered to get the plans at all costs, and you were told to stop at nothing to keep them from us. And so both our sides chased these plans around Berlin, and many good people died."

The Major waited for a reply, but Grey had none. It was too vast to comprehend.

"Your own government set you up," the Major continued, "and now they would do it again, using the same lie. They will start a war, one that will kill thousands or millions, simply to get more oil." He leaned towards Grey and spoke in a conspiratorial whisper: "And who will stop them now if not us old warriors?"

The Major touched Grey's arm and he jumped. He looked at the old general's charcoal eyes, the deep cracks in his face. Grey nodded.

"I will verify this document," the Major said, "if that will help anything. The Kremlin will back me up. Your own people think that I will kill you, so they have not moved against you. But they are around here somewhere, watching us. You must get this report into the right hands, and quickly. You are only one and they are many. And now that I have given you this, you are their biggest liability."

Grey slipped the report in his coat, suddenly aware of the unseen eyes that the Major must have felt all along. He looked at his former adversary, unsure what to say.

"Thank you," he said finally.

"Don't thank *me*," the Major said, then turned and started back down the walkway. The pig-dog dashed though the Major's legs to take the lead, and the Major had to untangle himself from the leash before he could continue.

He watched the Major until he disappeared behind the mist of the water jet.

Grey looked at the city around him. Clean, untainted Switzerland. He'd been in its largest city for sixteen hours and the only police officer he'd seen was in customs. Geneva was an ideal city all right, just not his ideal.

He caught a cab to the train station and booked a ticket back to Lyon. His train arrived with such precision that he could have just stood by the track with his eyes closed and stepped forward the moment it was due.

He found an empty first-class cabin, sliding the glass doors shut behind him. He turned his back to the hallway and started to shudder. His face burned and water spilled down his cheek. He had come to Geneva prepared to give up what remained of his life. What he lost was everything it had ever meant.

BOOK
FIVE

1

*T*om McGareth balanced a cup of coffee in his shaky hand as he walked through the front doors of the DST's Paris headquarters. He hadn't been here in years, but the place still felt familiar. Or maybe it was just the jet lag. He walked slowly, swallowing as much of the hot coffee as he could.

The plane ride had been rough—a storm had chased them halfway across the Atlantic—and Tom wasn't even off the plane when Peerson called. He said there was important new information and that they needed to meet immediately. Tom had tipped the cab driver to get him to rush, but now regretted letting himself get riled. Peerson is not a colleague, he reminded himself, he is an adversary. Besides, it was Grey's neck on the line, not his own. He was only here to bring him in safely.

Tom passed quickly through security; Denis had granted him unrestricted access to the building years back. Looking down at the big room, he sensed the same change here as back at Langley: everyone was somber, exchanging tight-lipped nods instead of smiles. There was no light conversation about weekend adventures because most of them didn't plan to leave the building. Tom had seen this before. It was the cold wind that came before the war.

Everyone worked longer hours. Men didn't shave and women abstained from makeup. Lunches were spent hunched over paperwork. Any mistakes would be measured in lives lost, so work was checked and double-checked.

McGareth walked into a nearly empty conference room. It would seem that the meeting was to only include himself, Dr. Peerson, and the acting Director of Operations, Renard Faison. Tom couldn't remember meeting Faison before, and the man certainly didn't look like the ideal replacement for Denis. He was unattractive and unkempt. He looked at Tom with a smug sneer, and made no attempt to greet him. The job of host fell on Peerson, who bounced out of his chair and met him at the door.

"Ah, good, you're here," Peerson said, closing the door behind him. "Now we'll get started. As you can see, we are keeping this operation as small as possible. I can appreciate how embarrassing this must be for you."

Tom ignored the insinuation and took a seat by the door. "So what's the news," he asked.

"The news is that we've heard from Agent Stark. He checked in this morning."

Tom almost spit his coffee. "He did? What did he say?"

Peerson smiled; he enjoyed springing that on Tom. "Unfortunately, he didn't say much of anything. He phoned Operations, refused to take any of the messages waiting for him, and demanded to be connected to you. Of course, Operations told him you were unavailable, but he didn't seem to believe it. Turned into a bit of a screaming match, I'm told. Stark told them to have you call—you alone. He mentioned something about the bomb, but the operator didn't catch it."

"You're sure it was him?"

"It was a secure line, and he authenticated."

"Why did Operations call *you*?"

"You were in the air at the time."

"Planes have phones now."

"Unsecure phones. But that doesn't matter, I've given orders that all information relevant to Grey Stark be forwarded to me."

"On whose authority?" Tom pressed against the table; it was the only thing that kept him from tackling Peerson.

"Mine," Faison said, speaking for the first time, his squeaky voice no more appealing than the rest of him. "I'm the Director of Operations."

Faison spoke directly to the table, and Tom couldn't tell if he was introducing himself, or, for that matter, just talking to himself.

"Yes," Peerson said, giving Tom an apologetic shrug. "And Washington felt, what with the CIA being so embroiled in all of this, that it might be better if I were the point man for the American team. I hope you don't mind."

Peerson phrased it like a question, but it wasn't. Tom knew there was no point to checking with headquarters; this was the deal he had made to keep his job, and there was no point whining about it now.

"I'd like to hear the tape of Stark's phone call," he said.

"Certainly, I'll see what I can do. In the meantime, are you sure you wouldn't like to get some sleep? You look very tired—"

"I'm fine," Tom said, too sharply. Peerson's concern sounded genuine. Tom took a deep breath. "What's our next move?"

"Well…" Peerson said, as if contemplating the subject for the first time. "I think we should offer to buy the plans from Agent Stark. To see if he'll sell."

11

*G*rey again glanced at the pager on the dashboard; the screen was still blank. He steered the blue Peugeot rental down the now-familiar roads of the Lot region. He was so tired that he had to focus just to keep the gas pedal down. He wasn't speeding—he didn't want to draw the attention—but he also didn't want to waste a minute. While he trusted the doctor, there was only so much a man in his position could do if the DST came calling. So Grey was anxious to get back to the hospital.

The Major said they would move against him and Grey knew that Leigh would be a target. And he needed to be sure she was safe before he gave the plans to Tom. He couldn't bring himself to risk Leigh over this.

Grey hated himself for putting that much weight on his own needs when so many lives were at stake. He could only hope that he wouldn't have to make the choice. He wished Tom would page him, so he would have some idea of where he stood. Tom, he was certain, wouldn't lie to him.

Tom was the only one he could trust with the bomb's plans, and with the truth about where they came from. He had both the power and the inclination to do the right thing. Denis was out—he'd had Grey tailed and probably had men hunting him down right now. Tom might have played it loose with Grey, but he had also given Grey a chance when he needed it. So he would put the information in Tom's hands and hope for the best. After he collected Leigh.

The tires grinded against the shoulder and Grey jerked the wheel, pulling the car back onto the pavement. He was fading; it had been a long trip from Geneva.

His route back to France had been more direct than safe. When he arrived at Lyon, he tried to buy a ticket to Lisbon— a two-day journey that would pass right through Figeac—but Max Heiss's credit cards were frozen. Worried that the DST might be closer than he thought, he tried a different tack. He jumped the local to Clermont-Ferrand and checked into the nicest hotel he could find. He paid a three-day advance in cash and had the hotel clerk arrange a car rental for him, to be billed to his room. The car was dropped off thirty minutes later. He inquired about a good place for a late lunch, insisted on holding onto his room key—as many Americans do—and drove directly south.

It was dark by the time he got to Figeac. He parked in a moderately crowded apartment complex at the edge of town and went to the hospital on foot.

— — —

The prim nurse in reception didn't smile at him and opened her mouth only to lecture about visiting hours. Grey cut her off with his Paris police badge. It was a blunt instrument, and possibly foolish, but he planned to be long gone before any backlash.

"I'd like to speak to the doctor in charge," Grey said, hoping that she would be happy to pass him onto someone else. Nurses were creatures of habit and protocol; she would insist that the local police verify his identity before allowing him in. A doctor, on the other hand, was more likely to think for himself and might rather just skip the formalities to spare himself the hassle. He might even get lucky enough to get the same doctor, but he couldn't count on that.

It was too late at night to use the intercom, the nurse explained, so he had to wait while she went and found him. She went through red metal double doors that locked behind her. A half-inch gap between the doors revealed a simple beveled latch. Grey waited for the clicking of her heels to fade, then eased a credit card into the latch and slipped through the doors.

He moved cautiously down the white hallway and found the stairwell. He left his shoes inside the door and crept up three flights of stairs. He took the long way around to Intensive Care, sneaking behind the nurse's station. He entered the dark observation room, pulling the door shut. All three windows were curtained. He peeled them back and found nothing but empty beds.

Grey's heart raced. Maybe Leigh was doing better than expected and they moved her to a regular bed. But how would he find her? He didn't have much time before the nurse at reception noticed he was missing. Then his answer found him: the door opened and the lights switched on. Grey's hand went to his gun, but relaxed when he saw the one-armed doctor.

"Thought I might find you here," the doctor said. He didn't look pleased. The nurse from reception stood behind him, glaring with her arms crossed "C'est pas grave, Nancy," he said. "I was expecting him."

The nurse didn't budge. The doctor turned to her impatiently: "That will be all."

"Oui, docteur," she replied, backing out of the doorway. She might not call the police, but inside of ten minutes everyone in the building would know that Grey was here.

"Thank you," Grey said when she left. "I'm sorry, I don't even know your name."

"Which I find comforting. You have come back for your wife, but she is gone. A man showed up late last night, said he was your boss. He didn't look like it, but the truth becomes harder to recognize everyday. He at least brought the sheriff with him. He already knew your wife was here, and was most insistent that you weren't coming back. I didn't believe that I could be so lucky, and here you are." The doctor smiled, but it wasn't a happy smile.

"She was still in intensive care, but the man brought his own doctor. He said the threat to her life outweighed the risk of moving her. His doctor signed the discharge papers himself and pumped 100 milligrams of morphine into her—that is a lot. They took her away in a private ambulance. I couldn't have stopped them even if I had a reason to."

"What did this man look like?"

"Me describe your boss? You first."

Grey described Denis, but the doctor shook his head: "No. The height and figure is correct, but this one had dark skin and bleach-blond hair. Bleached teeth, as well."

"Australian accent?"

"I wouldn't know, but he had an accent."

Grey's heart fell three floors and landed in the hospital's basement. The floor turned to sponge and he grabbed the wall for balance. The Doctor waited, sympathetic but distant, as if watching an actor in a play.

"Any idea where they went?" Grey asked.

"The ambulance was registered in Toulouse." The doctor hesitated and then added: "I work with Toulouse frequently, but didn't recognize the driver."

Grey nodded. There was no optimistic way to look at it: they had her. Someone had her. Grey didn't even know what the sides were these days. He raised his cast: "Can you get this off me?"

"It is not advisable."

"It's necessary."

The doctor motioned with his head and led Grey out of the room.

Ten minutes later, Grey emerged from the hospital. His forearm was wrapped in elastic over thick gauze, allowing him to close his hand, but just barely. The damage to his arm, the doctor told him, wasn't just the loss of skin. He had a hairline fracture in his forearm. Too much pressure and it would snap in half. The doctor didn't know how much was too much. He recommended not trying to find out.

Grey walked back to the car and considered his next move. He had no more interest in saving the world. Right now, he didn't like it very much. It was three hours to Toulouse, but Leigh probably wasn't there. And if she was, Toulouse was a big city and he had no idea where to start looking. But he had to do something, and going to Toulouse was all he could think to do.

He backed the car out of its parking space and dropped it into first. It was then that he noticed the blinking orange light on the dash.

Someone had paged him.

<u>III</u>

*R*ichard leaned against the railing and stared out at the calm obsidian waters of the Mediterranean at night. The sea looked solid enough to walk on and Richard imagined what that would feel like.

He stood on the thin balcony attached to his apartment on the island of Frioul. A balcony such as his, facing toward the open sea, was less expensive than those turned toward the evocative hills of Marseille. But this view better suited his purposes, or at least what they had been, years back, when he had first leased the place.

From this balcony, he could spot the cargo ships loaded with Il Siyâh heroin and communicate with them undetected, using a pencil laser and Morse code, and arrange for them to unload in one of the endless coves around the island.

Frioul had been recommended to Richard by his local contacts and he immediately saw its potential. Most tourists never got past the castle on D'if and the harbor patrol rarely ventured west of the island. Even when they did, private yachts were never hassled. Once they got the dope ashore, Richard brought it by ferry to the mainland one briefcase at a time, under the guise of having business in the city. Frioul was the ideal smuggling point into Europe from any country with a border on the Mediterranean Sea. And that was a long list.

Il Siyâh used to send monthly shipments, but Richard was never sure when they would arrive. As a result, he would often be stuck out on this lonely island for up to a week. Worse still, by the end of the month he was usually broke, so he couldn't even ferry back to Marseille for a drink.

He gazed at the sea, but there would be no ships for him tonight. He had warned Il Siyâh off, telling them that there was trouble with the police and to suspend shipments for a while. A couple of months at least. They weren't happy about it, but Richard couldn't be here meeting the boat when he had more important things to attend to. He didn't even want to be here now, but this place was the perfect setup for what his employer wanted. And he wasn't getting paid until the bastard American agent was finally dead.

His telephone rang and he stepped into the apartment, sliding the glass door shut to keep the conversation from carrying out into the night.

"Has the package arrived?" a muffled voice asked. Richard knew the voice from a hundred phone calls. It was his contact, the man on the inside who was writing all the checks.

"Safe and sound," Richard replied, stretching the phone cord so he could open the bedroom door. The woman lay unconscious on the bed, covered with a thin blanket, looking more like a guest than a prisoner.

She had been easy to find; the American had practically drawn him a map. And with his employer's resources, it had been a snap to pull her out of the hospital and bring her here. Richard didn't need to check—she would be out for several more hours—but he enjoyed looking at her. He had seen women like this before, but they had disapproved if he gave them more than quick glance. This one he could stare at all day, and there was nothing she could do about it. His eyes ran up her body, lingering on the loose hospital gown that rose with each breath.

He shut the door so he could concentrate. "How are things progressing?" he asked.

"We expect to be contacted shortly," the man replied. "Is the tape prepared?"

"It's close."

"Finish it. We have to be ready when we get the call."

"Yes, of course. Anything else?"

"Any word from our compatriot?" He was referring to Amin.

Richard had scoured the countryside for his brother, checking every hospital and hotel. He even walked through the woods near the crash. There was no sign of him. The cars had collided over a deep gorge; he was certain that his brother had fallen in and his body carried off by the stream. He felt regret—a strange regret, as Amin's death had always been part of the plan.

"I think we can forget about him," Richard said.

"Good. We're well to be rid of him."

Richard's reply pinched off in his throat.

"That's all for now," the man continued. "Standby for the call."

"Yes, sir."

The line went dead. Richard pressed the phone back onto its cradle and sat down at his desk. He had been sent a laptop computer that plugged into his phone line. It had a microphone to pre-record his half of the conversation, after which he could record the other half and mix them together.

Richard picked up the script by the computer and found his place. He clicked the record button and read off the paper:

"We understand the Iranian offer was quite a bit lower than that…"

IV

It was 10:20 PM when Grey placed the call. He was standing at a phone booth in front of an abandoned gas station, somewhere in the middle of the countryside. He wasn't entirely sure where he was, and he hoped that made him hard to trace.

He had spent the last hundred miles preparing for the phone call, taking every random road that he could, and thinking through every curve ball Tom might throw at him. He knew that it would take some fast talking to convince Tom of the truth and Grey was too tired to think on his feet. So he wanted to have his thoughts in order beforehand. But nothing prepared him for what happened:

"Good evening, Agent Stark," the man on the phone said, picking up after one ring. "You are wondering about your wife?"

Grey knew the voice and the New Zealand accent, and the bleach-blond man to whom they belonged. His head reeled. This man had not only found Leigh, but also knew his classified pager number. Whoever he was up against had deep connections.

"Cat got your tongue?" the man prodded.

"No."

"Great to hear. Tell me this, do you have the plans?"

Grey nodded, then remembered to say it out loud: "I do. But they aren't—"

"I want the original copy," the man cut in.

"There's only one copy."

The man laughed shrilly. "You expect me to believe the Koreans made their bomb from the same copy you have?"

Grey pulled the phone back and looked at it. He had grown accustomed to the fact that the plans were fake; he had forgotten that most of the world still thought otherwise.

"Who are you?" Grey asked.

"I represent a private interest. I was contracted to get the plans from you. I don't want you to think I'm a bully. We're holding your wife—quite safely—but let's just call her insurance. We're also prepared to pay you seven million Euros for your trouble. We understand the Iranian offer was quite a bit lower than that…"

V

"We understand the Iranian offer was quite a bit lower than that," the man on the speakerphone said, "but we're anxious to have an exclusive deal. We'd like the originals."

Grey's phone call came in at exactly 10:40 PM. Tom was in the conference room, along with Peerson, Faison, and a stenographer. They were listening in while a DST agent negotiated with Grey for the bomb's plans. The DST agent, Tom had been told, had been operating in deep cover for years and there was no chance Grey would know him. The agent was stationed in Marseille, so they would lead Grey down there to make the exchange. If he took the bait.

Faison insisted there was no point in going down to Marseille until they knew what Grey was going to do. So they tied into the agent's phone line and the three of them listened remotely. Up until now, the conversation was indirect. But the agent just offered Grey money for the plans, and everyone in the room was holding his breath.

"How do we handle the exchange?" Grey asked.

So that was it, Tom thought. Grey really has betrayed them. He listened numbly as the agent rattled off instructions—which ferry to take to what island, and that he should sit where he could be seen. After he disembarked, and they were sure he was alone, they would wire the money to his Swiss account. He should call to verify the transfer, then call another number for instructions. Tom looked over at Peerson, who sighed appreciatively.

The DST didn't do much work out on the island of Frioul, so setting a trap was going to be quite a job; they had no base of operations down there and only fourteen hours to set one up. It would be tight. But the good side was—even if Grey suspected something was awry—he would never connect that location with them. That was important, because if he figured out that his own people were onto him, they would never hear from him again.

Tom suddenly had a thought: "Ask him about his wife," he said to Faison. "Tell him to bring her along."

Faison seemed unnerved by the request, but Tom marked him as the sort that who was unnerved easily. Faison looked to Peerson, who gave him a nod, then picked up a phone at his side and dialed. They heard the phone ring through the speakerphone. "Hang on just one moment," the agent said to Grey, and the line went silent.

While Faison whispered instructions to the agent, Peerson leaned over to Tom, a quizzical look on his face.

"He'll refuse, of course," Tom explained, "but if he thinks the buyer knows that she's traveling with him, he's less likely to put her at risk by bringing her along. I'd rather not see her involved in this." Peerson nodded, impressed.

After what felt like too much time, Faison put his hand over the phone and the agent came back on the speakerphone, telling Grey to bring Leigh along. There was a long silence.

"No," he said finally.

"We must insist," the agent replied.

"Who are you?" Grey asked, sounding suddenly addled. Peerson spun his finger impatiently and Faison whispered into the phone.

"You will find that out tomorrow," the agent said, and the phone went dead.

The conference room was silent as each man pondered what came next. Grey Stark had the plans for the Deadfall Device, and there could be no doubt that he had sold them to Il Siyâh and, in doing so, had jeopardized countless lives.

It was Peerson who finally broke the silence, speaking to Tom: "What do you think?"

Tom shrugged his shoulders. "I think we've only got fourteen hours, so let's go catch the bastard."

VI

*G*rey hung up the phone, clear now that he had escaped one trap only to fall into another. These people wanted to kill him. Even if he brought them the plans, there was no reason to let him go. This man and the 'private interest' he represented believed he had already sold a copy to the Koreans. They would assume he had more to sell and, if they left him alive, he would only diminish their investment.

They couldn't have picked a more ominous location than a nearly deserted island off the coast of Marseille. No people meant no witnesses. Hell, there was barely even any wildlife out there. The more he thought about it, the lower his hope of survival.

Still, he would go. There was a chance that he could save Leigh. A slim one, but it was there. They would assume he would try to save the both of them, so by accepting his own death from the onset he might be able to shield her.

Grey walked back to the Peugeot. The night air was suddenly cold and he felt eyes on his back. He knew no one was there, and resisted the urge to look.

Inside the car, he did some quick math. He had fifteen hours. It would only take him five to drive to Marseille. It was smarter to wait out here than where he might be spotted. He needed sleep, but he didn't expect he could. He could use a drink, but knew that wasn't a good idea. A friend would be nice, but there just wasn't anyone left.

So he just sat in the car, bundled up like it was snowing, staring at the bell-shaped lamp that hung off the power line. It cast light on the gas station and the pumps, and cast shadows everywhere else.

VII

*C*onsciousness came slowly, blurred white focusing into a naked light bulb. Leigh wore a hospital gown, but this wasn't a hospital. It looked like someone's house.

Her pain was missing, replaced by a warm fuzzy tingle all over her body, like she was being massaged with silk. The cynic in her suspected that she had been dosed with an opiate, but the rest of her didn't care.

She curled her legs and rocked to a sitting position. The movement drew an ethereal man into the room. He was wearing a white suit that matched his hair. He pounded across the floor and blocked out the light. He leered down at her, smelling of liquor.

"Will you be able to walk?" he asked gruffly.

Leigh drew a bare leg from under the covers and raised it into the air, stretching it out. She did the same with the other leg, and the man's jaw slackened. She grinned at him and said: "Sure thing, Doc."

The man's face tightened to a scowl, but Leigh knew she had gotten to him.

"I'm not the doctor," he barked. "My name is Richard Fiddich and you're my prisoner. One with a ransom beyond value."

"Oh," Leigh said, and then thought about it. "Am I worth that much?" she asked, stretching her arms up and out, popping the top snap on her gown. She tried to snap it again, holding the gown wide while she did, showing off deep cleavage. The man stared into the gown, transfixed. She gave up on the snap, heaving her chest with a sigh. The man averted his eyes.

"We're trading you to your husband," he said to the floor, failing to sound angry.

Leigh waited for the man to look up, then shook her head like he was being silly. "He wouldn't give you the plans," she said. "You're just setting him up."

"It's your husband who set us up, he sold us a weapon that—"

"He's my ex-husband." Leigh said, shaking her head. She switched to a sultry tone, emptying Richard's mind: "And he's far too stupid to set anyone up. He probably doesn't even know that we're together."

Richard raised a hand in protest; she took it in hers: "He's so desperate to find out who set him up, and here you are, the mastermind in the flesh."

Richard took a step backward and made his final stand. "I don't think you appreciate the position you're in," he said, attempting confidence he didn't have.

"Tell me," Leigh smiled, inviting. "Tell me."

"You are completely at my mercy."

Leigh pulled his hand and he came toward her. He raised his free arm to strike her. Leigh closed her eyes, angling her cheek toward the blow. It didn't come. She blinked, confused.

"Go on," she said. "I've been waiting for this." Leigh drew the edge of her tongue along her lips. "Hoping."

Richard bent his face towards hers, a clumsy romantic gesture. She pulled his hand through the top of her gown and pressed it firmly on her breast. The hand closed around it, felt the warm softness. Richard drew his thumb across the firm point, felt his mouth pulled to hers. A sharp pain in his lower lip: Leigh pulled it back between her teeth, then playfully let it snap to his face.

"You whore—" Richard said. Leigh pulled his hand back to her breast and sniffed his neck like a carnivore.

"Is that whiskey on your breath?" she whispered. Richard stammered, unable to reply. "Because I could certainly use a drink."

"Yes," he said, feeling dizzy, "yes." He sprang off the bed, racing to the kitchen. He grabbed a liter of Jameson off the counter. It was three-quarters full; he drank like he was just back from the desert. The whiskey stung his lip where the woman had bitten him, and it burned in his stomach. He felt his heart slow and his control return. He leaned against the counter, and put his thoughts straight. The woman was toying with him, no doubt thinking of escape. But she didn't fool him. And where could she go?

If she wanted to give herself to him, he'd be a fool not to take her. Yes, he decided, he would take her. It was what he deserved.

He took another swig from the bottle and started back to the bedroom.

VIII

*T*he ferry puttered through the deep canyon formed by the stone walls of the two forts. These forts had guarded over Marseille's harbor for centuries and, in the dark of night, musketeers could still be seen up on the parapets. When the boat emerged to the open sea, it turned west and accelerated, chopping against the waves.

Grey sat alone at the ship's bow, the metal bench radiating cold through his thin overcoat. The wet air cut to his skin, making him shiver and the fracture in his forearm ache. There were warmer seats in the back of the boat, but he'd been instructed to sit in plain sight. Besides, there were a few other people onboard and right now he preferred to be alone.

He held his hand out and tried to steady it; it shook from the cold or from the government-issued amphetamine he had taken—a clean upper that removed fatigue without clouding his mind or making him too cocky. The drug was extremely addictive, to be used only in cases of extreme emergency. But since he hadn't slept in days and his fate—and that of a million others—would be decided this very night, he figured this qualified.

The scant lights of Frioul peered at him from across the dark Mediterranean water, set against the even darker sky. The moon would come late tonight. The bench shook as the ferry rushed deeper into the sea.

This was the last ferry out tonight, and it would skip the island of D'if. There was nothing there but the castle, and by now all the tourists would be tucked into safe warm beds. Grey pulled the lapels of his overcoat up to his chin. It was cold tonight, even accounting for being at sea. Winter was coming.

Faison threw a switch on his binoculars as he raised them to his eyes. They vibrated—the optical stabilizers calibrating themselves—and he was rewarded with a green and white image of the ferry cruising out from the harbor. There was a figure on the bow. It should be Grey, but it would be a couple minutes before he would be close enough to be sure.

Faison stood on the upper deck of the deep-sea fishing boat that he had rented for the night. There was an undersized cabin set on the boat's front, looking like a Plexiglas outhouse. There were controls inside the cabin and another set on the upper deck, which was built on top of the cabin. The upper controls allowed the pilot to enjoy himself in fair weather; there wasn't much to this boat, and it was hard to imagine using it in anything but.

The Directorate kept a fleet of undercover boats, ranging from an ancient whaler up to a luxury yacht, but there was always a chance Grey might know them. Besides, there was nothing quite as innocuous as just hiring a boat right off the pier. The only thing that distinguished him from a recreational fisherman was the heavy chest he had wedged between the two swivel chairs at the back of the boat.

Faison leaned against the taught wire railing and waited. This wasn't how he had imagined his role in the operation, but he hadn't much choice. Peerson couldn't drive the boat because of his leg. Not that the fat bastard could even climb the ladder; he would need a ship big enough for an elevator.

Tom was out as well. Peerson wanted him on the island, to witness the exchange. And since Faison had promised not to use any more agents than necessary, it was just the three of them—Tom, Peerson and himself—and the undercover agent who was meeting Stark. Their team wasn't large enough to ensure his capture, but Faison had two boatloads of French Marines and a helicopter waiting ten miles up the coast, should he need them.

He was disappointed that, having finally become the Director of Operations, he was sidelined for his inaugural operation. But perhaps it was for the best. He wasn't much for fieldwork and, no matter what, the credit was still all his. Best to leave the dirty work to the foreigners.

Faison pulled the binoculars up, thumbing a small dial and digitally enlarging the image. Zooming in aggravated his attempts to steady the binoculars against the rolling waves, but he managed a glance at the ferry: Stark sat on the front deck, staring forward. The ferry bounced out of frame, but Faison didn't need to double check. He grabbed the radio and reported in.

"Roger. Move to second position," Tom said into the radio, and clipped the handset back to his jacket.

"He's on the ferry," he said unnecessarily; the room wasn't very large, and Peerson would have heard for himself. The large man stood at the window, practically blocking it out. He was staring at the sea through excessively large binoculars, like two wine bottles strapped together.

The two men were stationed in a small building set atop one of Frioul's hills, halfway between the harbor and the abandoned gun battery where Grey was to make the exchange. Finding this place had been a stroke of luck: it was right above the main path and offered a view of Grey's entire route.

The two-story square building was covered in polished marble, looking like a bank surrounded by a flat-walled moat. The place had been boarded up, but vandals had laid a makeshift bridge across the moat and had torn a hole in the doorway. The inside was canvassed with graffiti and smelled like a trash can. The two men had to clear the floor by kicking the liquor bottles, beer cans, and other debris into a corner. Tom had done most of the work, and his pant legs were filthy.

Tom stepped gently over to Peerson, the thin plywood floor flexing under his feet. Peerson watched Faison's boat motor past the harbor. If Grey suspected a trap, he would have an escape route planned. Faison was to cover the backside of the island, should he attempt a seaward flight.

"Are they ready up at the bunker?" Tom asked, letting his irritation show. For all their planning, he hadn't seen or heard any sign of the Directorate's undercover agent.

"I'm sure they are," Peerson said dismissively, as if the subject bored him. When Faison's boat disappeared behind the island, Peerson set the binoculars on the window sill.

"You're on edge this evening," he said, giving Tom a big smile.

"There's a lot riding on this."

"There's not much that can go wrong. The island is locked down. Once Stark sets foot on it, he's trapped."

"And if he doesn't take the bait? What if he didn't bring the plans with him?"

Peerson shook his head sadly. "We've got his confession on tape, we don't need any other evidence. It would be a shame if he didn't bring the plans, but we have ways of finding out where they are."

"You mean you'd torture him?"

Peerson gave Tom a patient look. "Our priority is to get the plans, but we also want the names of his cohorts. They will likely have their own copies, and Stark is our only way to find them. Once they learn we've taken him, they'll fade away."

Peerson pulled out his handkerchief and cleaned the binoculars' lenses. Then he wiped his forehead and carefully folded it into his breast pocket.

"That is my part of the job," Peerson concluded, "to be handled as I deem necessary. After that, well, he's CIA property. We'll turn him over to you." He lumbered to the opposite window, raising the binoculars to inspect Grey's final destination.

Tom stared out at the approaching ferry. What Jim had told him back in Washington was right: Peerson didn't want to kill Grey. He wanted a confession to wave around, to show the world that the CIA wasn't to be trusted. It was a bitter thought, poisonous, and in that moment Tom knew what he was going to do. What he had to do.

He slipped a forty-five automatic out of his shoulder holster, snapping the bolt back to load a bullet into the chamber. Peerson gave him a curious look, then turned back to the window.

Tom popped the clip out of the gun's handle and topped it off with another bullet. He raised the gun, feeling its familiar grip in his palm. He'd had this gun since Vietnam. The last time he killed anyone with it had been over two decades ago, in Berlin, under orders from the same man he was going to kill tonight.

Grey walked up the dock, sat on a dingy bench, and looked out at the harbor. The island behind him blocked the wind and the silence was unnerving, as if greater powers were at work. It was so quiet he could hear the faint whir of cars as they sped along the distant coastline, several miles away.

The ferry bellowed deeply to announce its departure. A minute later, it kicked away from the dock and started home for the night. Grey looked at his watch: it was quarter to nine. In ten minutes, he would go to the phone booth to call for further instructions.

He watched the full moon rise over the distant city, so huge and clear he could see every nick on its face. He wouldn't need a flashlight to see tonight. And neither would anyone else.

_IX_

A min stood back from the doorway and stared into the bedroom. Inside, the creature that was once his brother lay with an uncovered woman. She was laughing like a harlot and removing his shirt. They were speaking in French, too rapidly for Amin to understand. But he understood enough.

When he had woken in the forest, his mind was addled and he couldn't remember who he was, much less why he was there. But somewhere deep in his mind was this apartment, and the need to return here. It had been a two-day walk, during which he began to remember. He remembered that boats came to this place, boats that could take him home. The thought of going home pulled him along every step of a hundred miles; it kept him going when his body just wanted to lie down and die. But standing here now, he realized that it hadn't been his own desires that brought him here, but the hand of Allah guiding him, to show him the true color of his once-brother.

He slipped the gun from its holster and stepped into the room.

The drugs in Leigh's body were waning and the pain found its way in, stiffening her muscles. But she held her inviting smile, pressing her breasts to the blond man's bare chest and tickling her fingers down his back. This man—Richard he called himself—had been easy to crack. He had already given her a clear picture of the entire setup. Now she just needed to escape and find Grey.

She leaned back and traced a finger down the line of blond fleece on Richard's stomach, arriving at his belt buckle. She curved her hand around to the inside, her fingers brushing over his erection. Without the drugs it was harder to cover her revulsion.

She reached for the bottle of whiskey. It was nearly empty now; she had managed to get most of it inside Richard, but right now she needed a little herself, for what she had to do next. She drained the last slug from the bottle, then tossed it away. She put her hands on Richard's buckle and glanced up at him: the wide-eyed look on his face was not what she expected. He looked like he was staring at a ghost. She rose to comfort him, but there was a loud noise and his neck burst open. Richard moved his jaw, but no sound came out. Blood pulsed down his chest and sprayed over Leigh's naked body.

She turned to the doorway. The short Arab from the Mercedes in Paris held his giant revolver, creamy smoke rising from the barrel. In an instant, Leigh put it together: this was Richard's brother. Richard had mentioned him; he was supposed to be dead.

Half of his beard had been shaved and a long gash on his cheek was stitched up with blue thread. His left arm was slung from his neck by his unraveled turban. The entire top of his head was mutilated by an enormous scar, with only a small tuft of black hair that shot up as if electricity coursed through his body. His teeth were clenched tight enough to crush a walnut and his dark skin was pale. He could have just as easily risen from the grave as walked through the door.

Richard convulsed, falling to the floor. His brother watched his body grow still, seemingly drained by the effort of pulling the trigger. Leigh didn't know what the gunman planned to do next; she made a quick decision.

She tucked her knees up and rolled down the bed, going for her gun. Richard had been wearing it under his jacket, and had hung it on a chair while disrobing.

She sprang off the bed, hands reaching toward the white jacket. But her legs, weak from drugs or injury, buckled. She toppled to the floor, barely keeping her head from slamming against it. The man turned slowly. She lunged for the chair, her hand slipping into the white jacket and closing on the butt of her gun.

"No," the man said, training the revolver on her forehead. His aim was steady. Leigh removed her hand slowly, leaving the gun behind. Lacking other options, she tried charm.

"I was just going to cover myself," she said, with a smile that felt as ridiculous as her story.

The man motioned her back with the revolver's barrel, gently drawing his arm from the sling. Keeping an eye on Leigh, he crossed the room and pulled her gun from under the jacket. He inspected the large automatic and checked the clip—it was full. He backed up to the door and set the gun on a bureau.

He broke open the stock on his ancient revolver and tapped the cartridges out, sorting out the spent shells. There were only two bullets left. He slipped these into his pocket, leaving the gun and the empties on the bureau. He put Leigh's automatic in his shoulder holster and turned back to her. She was sprawled on the floor, wearing nothing but a film of blood.

"Whore or hostage?" he asked, his French so thick with accent it took Leigh nearly a minute to understand him.

"Hostage," she said.

The man accepted this with a nod and said: "You are the wife of the saboteur."

"Who?"

"The man who sabotaged the bomb. The man who denied me the Garden of Paradise."

"Grey didn't sabotage the bomb," Leigh said. "Didn't you hear what your brother was just saying—?"

"I have no brother!" the man boomed, unholy violence in his voice. His face twisted maniacally, sending a chill through Leigh. She pulled the sheet off the bed, covering her legs. The Arab walked out of the room. Leigh wanted to flee, but held still. Despite his harried look, he seemed to be in better shape than she was. And she didn't trust her legs to get her very far. The man returned and tossed an armful of clothing at Leigh.

"Make yourself decent," he said.

She used the sheet to wipe off what blood she could, then dug out a navy blue t-shirt and black men's pants—the darkest clothing that fit. After she dressed, the man spoke again:

"He is coming tonight?" It was barely a question. Leigh nodded.

"When and where?"

Before Leigh could reply, the phone rang. They waited in tense silence, neither sure what to do. On the third ring, the answering machine picked up. Richard's voice gave instructions, in French, on where to meet for the exchange. It said that he would be waiting there, along with his prisoner. The wild-eyed Arab listened carefully to the instructions and, when the message was over, drew the automatic from his holster.

"Let's go," he said, holding the door for Leigh.

X

Standing by the edge of the harbor, Grey listened to the recording and then set the pay phone gently on its hook. His instructions were simple: cross to the southern half of the island, then follow the trail west. At the end of the island, he would find an old gun battery. He should stand in plain sight and wait to be approached. In other words, he was to go to the remotest part of an already remote island and stand there like a paper target.

Grey walked along the barrier wall, crossing at the back of the harbor. The stiff Kevlar vest he wore under his shirt dug into his waist. He stopped at the trailhead, scanning the island while he nonchalantly wrapped his shirt-tail over the edge of the vest. His eye caught a distant glimmer, an optical lens flashing in the moonlight. Grey turned, finding the dark silhouette of a building up on the hill. They—whoever they were—were up there watching. Perhaps through the scope of a rifle.

Since no one shot him, he started up the trail. Whatever they were up to, there was nothing he could do about it. But he'd mention the building to Leigh. She would need to know about that for when she escaped.

The large waves of the open Mediterranean slapped against the boat as it chugged out to the far side of the island. The water was too deep here to drop anchor, so Faison swung back toward the island, adjusting the engine to a high idle and stabilizing his position against the outgoing tide. The boat see-sawed on the water, tossing him about the deck.

He leaned his chest against the wheel to hold it steady and inspected the sheer cliffs of Frioul's west coast, almost a half-mile away. He had driven out this far for two reasons: he was less obvious, and the angle allowed him to see over the top of the cliff, even if there wasn't much to see.

He raised his binoculars and scanned the ridgeline, stopping at the gun battery where the exchange would take place. From here, he could only see the three circular discs of cement that made up the roof. Sixty years ago, that roof protected a trio of fourteen-inch cannons—German, not French—that kept the allies at bay until they finally overran Marseille from land, coming south from Normandy. The batteries were silent now, stripped of their weapons and rendered meaningless in this nuclear world. On the other side, cement barracks lined up along a road. Faison couldn't see them from here, but that's where it would happen.

He sighed. It was all fine to pretend he had a reason to be out here, but he had been running planes over Frioul all day and not a single boat had come to port. Grey hadn't arranged for an escape boat and Faison wouldn't be doing much more tonight than just waiting it out. At least he was safe. Safe but useless.

He was just pulling the binoculars from his eyes when he saw something move along the ridgeline. It looked like two people struggling, but a wave jostled the boat and he lost focus. By the time he got it back, they were gone.

Faison reached for his radio, but stopped. He knew something was wrong, but he couldn't say what it was. He set the radio down; he had nothing to report. He cursed himself for slacking off and raised the binoculars back to the ridge.

Grey was winded by the time he crested the gentle hill. He bent over, putting his hands on his knees, and caught his breath. To wear out so easily made him feel old, but he knew it might only be the drugs—they might make him feel alert and strong, but it was a thin veneer. He needed real sleep, real soon. Now would be fine by him, but somewhere nearby a foot scraped on gravel. It was time.

A string of war-era cement barracks arced alongside the gravel road in front of him. Their doors had been pulled off, leaving gaping holes like well-formed caves. The road dead-ended at a rock wall, where two figures stood. It was hard to make them out in the moonlight, but Grey was certain that one of them was Leigh. Whoever else was standing there would be the least of his worries; it was always the flunky who got put in the line of fire. The higher-ups would be back with the snipers—if they were on the island at all.

The two figures made no move toward him, so Grey started down the road. He stopped within earshot. Nothing was said, so he continued forward. He walked slowly, spreading his hands out to show that they were empty. He stopped again when he could see Leigh's long hair blowing in the wind. He was maybe twenty feet away; that was plenty close. The other figure was a man—he could tell by the beard. He was hiding behind Leigh, using her as cover. Grey waited for him to speak. Or for anyone to speak. No one did.

Grey felt the back of his neck prickle. He stepped sideways, glancing at the road behind him. It was empty. What were they waiting for, he wondered. Was someone else coming? His hands began to shake; he was in no condition for a standoff.

"I'm here, just like you said," Grey called out. There was no response. "I'm all alone and unarmed."

That wasn't true; the Berretta was in his pocket and he had four knives spread around his body, but in situations like this, he always said he was unarmed. If things went badly, a fib like that wouldn't matter.

"I brought the plans." Grey reached into his jacket. A gun muzzle flashed three times, blinding in the darkness. His eyes were locked on Leigh, deadly afraid to see her collapse. Relief poured through him as he felt the bullets strike his own chest, knocking him backwards.

The force of the first bullet threw him against a concrete wall. The next two pounded his chest like blows from a sledgehammer. He couldn't tell if his vest had held or not. He couldn't breath and the salty smell of blood filled his nostrils. His knees went out and he dropped onto them. He struggled to hold onto consciousness.

He lost.

Leaning out of the window, McGareth had just raised his binoculars when the gun flashed. He brought Grey into focus just as he collapsed.

"What the hell?" he said, turning to Peerson. Peerson looked as shocked as Tom was, maybe more so.

Tom grabbed his gun and radio. "Let's go," he called out, leaping down the flimsy staircase and dashing over the bent plank that spanned the dry moat.

He barked into his radio, telling Faison to pull his boat around to the cove below the bunker. He looked up at the window, calling to Peerson, who was still staring through his oversized binoculars. Peerson dropped them and started down. Tom didn't want to wait, but this was a shooting match now and he would need the backup. Besides, Peerson was the only one who knew who the good guys were.

The NATO man appeared at the doorway, still hobbling on his cane. He moved gingerly across the plank, balancing with his arms out wide, a hippo in ballet shoes. McGareth couldn't wait any longer. He sprinted down the hill, taking tall steps so he wouldn't trip over anything.

Back at the barracks, Leigh was on her knees, sobbing quietly. She knew she had just watched Grey die. The Arab was a marksman—she had traded shots with him before—and he wouldn't have stopped at three shots if they hadn't done the job.

She fought to control herself, but despair ripped through her in waves. If he was going to kill her too, she wished he wouldn't put her through this first. But he didn't move.

Leigh spilled her tears onto the dusty road. The man stood beside her, waiting. Finally, she pushed herself up, feeling the stiff crust of Richard's blood under her clothing. She turned to Amin and straightened, daring him to finish what he had started. She didn't wipe her eyes; she didn't care.

"Can you drive a boat?" he asked.

"No," Leigh replied, hearing her voice tremble. She could, but knew she was safer on the island. Who knows where this man would take her.

Amin stared at the southern horizon. He said, "Then I must hide until the morning ferry comes."

"You don't have a boat?"

"There are many boats on this island, but I cannot use them." The man was unnaturally serene—that deep calm of the holy. Leigh picked nervously at the dried blood under her fingernails.

"What about me?" she asked.

He considered her question and said, "When we are back on land, you may go."

"You're not going to…" She couldn't finish the question. She didn't need to.

"I killed that man because he defied the will of Allah. In this matter you have helped me. Do not cause me trouble and I will not kill you."

His words struck her dumb: she had helped him, if in no other way than she hadn't even tried to stop him.

"Come," he said, walking down the road. Dread poured over her; they would pass right by Grey's body.

The man took three steps and stopped, raising his palm and pointing down the road. Two figures came out of the rocky shadows. One was lean and stealthy, the other, far behind, fleshy and imbalanced. Amin moved behind Leigh, resting his gun on her shoulder and drawing her back through the doorway of a concrete bunker.

McGareth crouched down in the middle of the road. He was at the exact spot he had seen Grey fall, but there was no body. He ran his hand over the gravel. It was dusty and dry, bloodless.

He glanced back and saw Peerson lumbering up. The large man gaped at the empty road like the earth itself had cracked open. After a full minute of thought, Peerson drew his gun. It was a nine-millimeter automatic, a target pistol with a long barrel for accuracy. Tom hadn't known Peerson was armed.

Peerson leaned down to Tom and whispered, "We're going to have to—" Then he stumbled back, his mouth slack and his face white. He pointed at something behind Tom.

Tom sprang to his feet, twisting around and raising his gun. All he saw was the dark road and the empty black doorways. An impact shot through his body; the road wobbled and he lost balance.

Hidden in the shadow of the bunker, Amin watched the men approach. They stopped at the road and looked around. He aimed his gun at the fitter of the two, tightening his finger on the trigger. Then he saw they weren't even looking for him, but searching for the saboteur. With a shock, he realized that there was no sign of him.

Amin suddenly felt trapped. He needed to move, to get off this dead-end road. He looked around; rebar rungs led up the barrack wall, through a hole in the roof. Amin motioned to the woman and was surprised to get a confirming nod. She must know who they are, Amin thought. He'd ask about them when they were safe.

The woman scurried up the ladder and disappeared into the roof. Amin chased after her, but by the time he poked his head into the room above, she was on the other side, heading up a stone staircase. Amin knew she would escape if she got the chance, but didn't dare call to her or fire a warning shot. He hurried after her as fast as he could.

The stairs led up to a large round room, a third of it open to the starry night. The woman stood on a cement walkway on the far side of the room, next to a small exit. She wasn't looking at him, and she wasn't moving. The floor between them was a glistening pool of black water, and the only way across was on two circular metal rails rising above the water, once used to pivot the enormous artillery that was housed here.

Amin stepped carefully onto the tracks—one foot on each—and eased forward. The woman turned, looking out the open wall. Amin followed her glance and saw the black sea, the moon dancing on its surface.

Something splashed into the water by his feet and adrenalin spiked in his blood. He dropped flat to the rails as gunshots echoed through the bunker. Cement shattered by his head and shards dug into his skin, but he felt no bullets.

The firing stopped. He heard an empty clip rattle on the ground. Amin hopped up and fired, but his leg slipped off the track. The automatic's trigger was a far more sensitive trigger than his revolver: it fired four bullets aimlessly into the dark. He holstered the gun and pulled at his leg; it had sunk deep into the sewage-thick water and came out slowly.

Amin only had one bullet left and couldn't see his assailant. The exit was clear, so he scrambled for it on all fours, his wet foot slipping on the rail. He dashed through the hole in the concrete and popped out into the night air.

He emerged into a rock-covered field that sloped down toward the ocean. He had seen this island many times from the smuggling boat; he knew that the ground ended suddenly at a cliff, with a steep drop to rocky breakers.

He ran to the right, along the backside of the cement barracks. The loose shale slipped under his feet and he kept his hands on the ground so that he wouldn't slide downhill. The field ended at a jagged barrier of rocks. He put his hands on one and swung his legs over. He landed harder than he wanted and needles prickled in his knee. He put his back to the wall, gun ready, and watched the bunker's exit. No one followed him.

Shots rang out and the rock by his head cracked open. He recognized the gun's report; it was the same one as in the cement building. He ducked down and waited. Thirty seconds passed quietly. He didn't know who was after him or how many they were, but he had lost the initiative. For now, to get away would be enough.

This side of the outcropping was grassy, and a dirt trail led down to the west. It was the wrong way to go—backing himself further into a corner and further from escape—but he knew that Allah would not lead him to a dead end.

He followed the trail down to a cove. Far below, he saw the white wake of a boat pulling up to the shore. God had sent him a way back home.

Faison's voice crackled on Tom's radio, reporting that he was in position. With some effort, Peerson crouched down and rolled Tom over, grabbing the radio and turning the top dial until it clicked off. Then he pried the gun from Tom's hand and tossed it into a gully. It skipped down the shale and disappeared from sight.

He pushed himself upright and wiped the stock of his cane with his handkerchief, removing all evidence of its impact with Tom's head. When the cane was clean, he tossed it after the gun.

He was still debating his next move when gunshots reported from the other side of the bunker. Raising his long-barreled automatic, he scurried down the road with surprising agility, keeping his large body flat against the concrete barracks.

Leigh raised her head slowly and peered down into the dark bunker. When the shooting had started, she hid by laying flat on the cement ledge that ran along the open wall. She watched the Arab flee, and now she wanted to find whoever was shooting at him.

She swung her legs down, hanging by her elbows while her feet probed for the raised rails. She found one and shifted her weight onto it. She kept a hand on the wall for balance as she worked her way around to where the floor rose out of the water, forming a small shelf. A man was slouched against the wall. He looked up as she approached and smiled weakly, his teeth spotted with blood. It was Grey. He was alive.

Leigh sailed across the floor without touching it, dropped to her knees and pulled him into an embrace. She felt the thick body armor under his jacket—a precaution she had never imagined he would take—and laughed. She felt something wet against her shirt. She pulled back: it was blood, coming from a dark patch on Grey's shoulder. Only then did she see how pale he was.

"He got you?" she asked.

"Just now. It must have bounced off the ceiling. Dumb luck. The other shots only cracked a few ribs."

Tears streamed down her face, but she couldn't stop smiling. "When did you start wearing vests?"

"About two hours ago," Grey smiled back. "I don't even own one; I swiped it out of a police car"

"You didn't."

Grey shrugged. "I remembered what a good shot that guy was."

"How bad is it?" she asked.

"That's a big gun he's got. Yours?" Leigh nodded. "Hit the bone right at the joint, but I think he missed the artery. Can't move my arm. Hell, I had to look just to be sure it was still there."

Leigh sobered up. He needed a hospital, but this was far from over. She noticed the gun in Grey's limp hand, the empty clip lying next to it. She peeled his fingers back and took the gun, then reached into his jacket for the spare clip. Grey winced. "Sorry," she whispered, kissing him on the forehead.

She counted the bullets. There were six. She held up the clip: "Should I even ask?"

"Just the one."

"At least you're consistent." Leigh pushed the clip in and jerked a bullet into the chamber. "You should stay here, out of sight. There are at least two other people on the island. They're not friends of the Arab, but that doesn't mean they like us, either." Nearby gunshots emphasized her point.

"They're after the plans," Grey said, pulling them from his jacket and holding them out to her.

"*Merde*. What a mess. You'd better keep those." Leigh pushed Grey's hand back. Grey dropped the plans and grabbed her forearm. "Don't go," he said, trying to find her eyes in the shadow of her hair.

Leigh felt her stomach quiver. "No choice," she said, pulling her arm away. His hand was too weak to stop her.

Leigh was out of the exit before Grey could say another word.

Grey watched her go. He wouldn't wait here, he decided, not if he could be any help. Even just as a target, to draw some of the fire away from her. He tucked the plans back into his jacket. He rose to his feet by kicking his legs and sliding his back up the wall. He tested his fractured arm—the only arm he had left now. It was stiff, but worked.

He drew the knife from his boot and lumbered after Leigh.

Faison stared at the high cliff walls that formed a horseshoe around the cove. The waves were calm here and the air still. He looked at his radio, hoping it would say something. He had checked in several minutes ago, as he was pulling into the cove, but no one responded. In fact, his radio had been silent ever since Tom's urgent request. That made him nervous enough, but on top of that he had heard gunfire a minute ago.

He couldn't guess what was happening, but he knew it was bad.

Someone appeared up on the ridgeline, backing toward him. He pulled his binoculars up, but he had disappeared behind a large rock. It could have been Tom McGareth. Faison picked up the radio and called for him. There was no reply.

There were plenty of reasons why McGareth might have his radio off, but Faison didn't like it. He considered calling in the Marines, but didn't. He was perfectly safe and if the others wanted help, they would let him know. He waited to see if the figure would appear again, but it didn't. He decided he might as well prepare for the worst.

He climbed down to the deck and crept out to the chest at the stern. He had to shake it a few times to pull it free from the chairs. He dragged it below the cover of the raised deck.

He popped the chest open. It was stuffed full of weapons, one of everything he could get his hands on. He unclipped a long-barreled Browning sniper's rifle from the lid. He dropped in a clip and worked the bolt, loading a bullet into the breech. He popped the cap off the massive infrared scope and focused it at the cliff. He still didn't see anyone.

Leaning the gun on the wall, he stepped into the small pilot's cabin. He threw a lever, switching the rudder control down from up top, straightened the wheel and slipped a loop of thick rope over it, holding it in place. Next he brought the throttle down a single click; the engine fired with a deep bellow. Faison stepped out to the deck and raised the gun. As the boat moved backward, his view rotated. He focused the gun on the rock where he last saw movement. He would soon see who was hiding behind it.

It wouldn't be McGareth; he would have signaled by now. He clicked off the gun's safety and set his finger on the trigger, as calm as a hunter. Whoever was up there, he wouldn't have anything bigger than a pistol. At this range, it would be useless. The best marksman wouldn't even be able to hit the boat.

The ground was dotted with tufts of firm grass that Leigh used as cover while she crawled toward the cliff's edge. She stopped and listened, trying to hear above the howling wind. She was taking her time, playing it safe. It would be hard enough to best the Arab in a fair fight.

Three shots rose from the cove. A single shot replied, startlingly close—only a few feet away. She rolled over, raising Grey's tiny gun, seeing nothing above the grass. The shot sounded like a forty-five caliber. As far as she knew, only one person on the island had a forty-five. She waited, gun raised, paralyzed by the fear that any movement would give her away.

No one appeared through the grass, and there was no more gunfire. Several minutes later, she heard an engine roaring, down in the cove. She forced herself to lower the gun and crawl forward.

She reached the cliff's rim and curled a hand over the cold stone, pulling her face through the grass. She looked down into the cove and saw a white fishing boat sputtering in the water, fifty feet below.

Amin was at the controls on the upper deck, his half-bald head obvious even from here. He ran the boat back and forth, gunning the engine and turning madly. The ship ignored his efforts to steer and traced back and forth in a straight line, offering no way out of the cove. A man lay at the back of the lower deck. He had the twisted look of death.

Leigh needed to act fast—it wouldn't take Amin long to figure out the boat's controls. She looked at the water far below, picking a spot free of the dark shadows of rocks that lurked beneath the surface. She rolled back from the cliff, rising to her feet. She took two steps forward and launched over the cliff in a swan dive. She pressed her thumb over the gun's muzzle, hoping to keep it dry.

Everything was silent in the rush of wind. The approaching water was beautiful, one of the most beautiful things she had ever seen in her life. Just before impact, she tucked her chin to her chest and clamped her eyes shut.

Grey had seen Leigh hop over the pointed rock outcropping a few minutes ago, and was making his way across the rocky field after her. But the stones shifted under his feet like marbles and it was slow going.

He had found spots where solid bedrock peeked through the shale and he was navigating the field by moving from one to the next, connecting the dots. It wasn't far now; he only needed one more patch of stable ground between himself and the outcropping. He saw it, a jagged boulder rising above the stone, and stepped forward.

The rocks slipped under his feet and he fell forward. The knife flew out of his hand. He landed hard on his elbow; pain rippled up his fractured arm. He lay there, waiting for the pain to subside, then crawled forward, tenderly leaning on his injured arm, the other one uselessly dragging on the ground. The rocks below him slipped away, becoming a small avalanche that poured over the edge of the island. Several seconds passed before he heard them rain into the water below. One wrong move and he would be joining them.

Grey had slid too far down the slope and had missed the boulder he was aiming for. He decided to try directly for the outcropping. As he crawled, he was slowly losing ground, sliding down the slope. The cliff's edge was getting close.

He had almost reached the jagged rocks when he saw something in the corner of his eye: a shadow rising on the hilltop. He turned to look and saw a flash of light. A bullet ripped into his neck and plunged down through the shoulder of his good arm. The impact flipped him onto his back and he slid down the hill.

His chest burned and pain coursed through his body. His arms flopped around uselessly. The cliff raced toward him.

Grey arched his back, digging his heels into the ground. Dust kicked up around him and rocks bashed into his head, pounding him senseless. His foot caught on something solid and his body spun. A stone bashed his ear to lettuce as he swung onto a flat rock the size of a mattress. He stopped.

He felt blood trickle from his ear, the rest of his body was numb. He was disoriented and his head was buzzing. Both his arms were limp, one of them hung down over the cliff's edge. He strained his neck, trying to find his assailant, but couldn't raise his head. All he could see was the bunker peering down from the top of the hill. It was very far away.

A round shadow appeared on the outcropping, wobbling on the uneven rocks as it made its way toward him. It was Peerson.

Peerson took his time getting over to Grey. There was no rush: the worst thing that could happen was that Grey might bleed to death before he got the chance to kill him.

The water hit Leigh like glass; it shattered painfully and she plunged into the dark depths. It was surprisingly quiet; the only sound was the few bubbles that escaped her clothing. She touched the bottom gently and let herself float in the serene isolation.

She had a sudden, overpowering urge to breathe. She fought it, kicking madly up to the surface. She burst into the air and gasped it in. An engine roared in her ear; she ducked back as the boat sped past her face, its wake dousing her with water.

She shook her head, clearing her eyes, but the boat was gone, hidden behind the high waves. She shifted Grey's gun to her mouth—clamping the barrel between her teeth and sealing the muzzle with her lips—then swam toward the sound of the engine. She drew long side-strokes so that she could keep her head up. Waves slapped her face and water sprayed up her nose, but after a few minutes, she caught sight of the ship.

The engine was smoking from the strain, and its noise provided all the cover that Leigh could want. She came up alongside the white foam of the boat's wake and it backed right up to her. She clamped her hands over the gunwale and was dragged backward. When the boat stopped to change directions, she eased herself up, peering over the side.

Amin was on the top deck, his back to her, struggling to turn the boat. He was making some progress, but it was probably just the current shifting.

Leigh drew herself out of the water and lay flat on the gunwale. She lowered her feet to the deck, keeping her eyes locked on the Arab. Her wet clothing squeaked on the fiberglass, but he didn't notice.

She pulled the gun from her mouth. The barrel was full of water. *Putain*, she thought, letting it drip quietly into her hand. She could only hope it would still fire; salt water was quick to jam guns. She glanced around the deck for another weapon but didn't see any. Her eyes stopped on the dead man. He was long and thin, his skin pasty even before death took him. His eyes were lifeless. He looked familiar, but Leigh couldn't place him. Dark blood was congealed on his chest, surrounding a single bullet hole in his breastbone. Leigh shuddered. The Arab had been right next to her when he took the shot. She thought that kind of accuracy was impossible. The cold night air soaked away her confidence.

The engine growled and the boat started forward. Leigh bent over and slipped her hand into the dead man's coat. She found a holster, but no gun. She frowned; she would have to try the Beretta.

She turned to Amin and raised the gun toward the back of his head. She tried to fire, but her finger wouldn't move. She found that she couldn't just shoot him in the back. She wasn't a secret agent—she was a cop. To kill a man in cold blood—no matter what he had done—was something she wasn't prepared to do. She watched as her arm lowered the gun. She had no idea what to do next. Then it was decided for her.

The man cursed loudly in Arabic, cranking the throttle down in frustration. The engine roared and the boat lurched forward. Leigh fell with a thump. The Beretta slipped out of her hand and bounced to the back of the deck, well out of reach.

Amin turned at the noise and they locked eyes. He reached into a steel chest at his feet and brought out a short-barreled machine gun. He drew back the hammer and aimed it right at her.

It took Peerson the better part of two minutes to stroll down the outcropping. He stopped to inspect every rock he passed like it was his job, and hummed to emphasize that he was in no hurry. He followed firm ground as far as he could, then hobbled over the loose stone to where Grey lay. He drew his gun out and trained it on Grey while he inspected his injuries. Grey lay still, conserving what little blood he had left.

"Do you have any idea what a complete pain in my ass you are?" Peerson asked, wiping his forehead with a handker-chief.

Grey could tell what was coming. Peerson, it would seem, was a braggart at heart. He was prepared to spare Grey a little time, providing they spent it stroking his ego. When one's accomplishments must be kept secret, no one better to tell than a dead man. Grey wasn't as pessimistic about his fate, so he obliged him:

"It was a setup from the start, wasn't it?"

"Figured that out, did you? What a good detective."

"Why?"

"Why?" Peerson tilted his head back and laughed at the moon. "Because we needed a reason to invade Iran. And a really good one, too. We lost some credibility when we didn't find any nukes in Iraq. This time, we made sure the evidence was there first."

"So you created a bomb so horrible everyone would be too scared to think straight," Grey said.

Peerson nodded vigorously, pride swelling his face to a pink marshmallow. "Yes. A very nice way to put it. And putting this weapon in France was a stroke of brilliance—not my own, I'm afraid. The British army was spent after our last war, but the French Legionnaires had abstained from Iraq, leaving them well-rested and ready for action. And what greater victory than to convince a doubter like France?"

"And grabbing power in the Directorate was just a perk."

Peerson shrugged. "An inevitability, really. Sadly, the best part of the plan fell apart here at the end. This," Peerson waved his arm around as if addressing an audience, "was where we were going to prove that the bomb's plans had been provided to Iran by none other than the venerable CIA. And I think, though I shall never be sure, that we'd even convinced your boss to kill you himself, just to keep that a secret."

Peerson stared at the horizon, wallowing in his disappointment. Then he donned a valiant smile. "But I feel the operation has been a success. The NSC has uncovered a traitor most foul and recovered the bomb's plans, while the

CIA and the Directorate have only fumbled about. But now I have a question for you:

"Major Dragos gave you a document when you met in Switzerland, did he not?" Grey didn't respond. Peerson waved his gun casually. "I'm going to search you after I kill you, so if you have it with you, and I think you do, we can make this quick and painless."

"It's in my coat pocket."

"Do you mind?"

Grey found he could still move his arm—the one that wasn't dangling over the cliff's edge. He brought it slowly and painfully into his jacket and retrieved the binder. He tried to toss it, but it didn't go further than his elbow. Peerson reached down for it, but changed his mind.

"You really were a tailor-made scapegoat," Peerson said. "A disgruntled agent who just happened to be involved in Operation Deadfall twenty-odd years back. You had every opportunity to keep a copy for yourself, knowing it would be useful one day. And now, after a couple decades of bitter captivity in Paris, you'd become a spiteful drunk. Your patriotism fermented, so you sold the bomb to Iran, telling yourself that you deserved the money for all of your years of loyal service."

"Except that the plans are fake."

Peerson wasn't as surprised as Grey would have liked. "Dragos told you that, did he? You should be damn glad you never got the chance to tell your wife. I'd hate for her to have to disappear."

"You're not going to kill her?"

"No," Peerson shook his head, "We have no reason to."

Grey knew he was lying, but he appreciated the courtesy. "But I'm a different story, right?"

"I'm afraid so," Peerson said. He removed the clip in his gun, unnecessarily inspecting the bullets inside. It was an opportunity, but he was too far away for Grey to take advantage of it.

"I'm afraid I've got to go now, Grey. Full day tomorrow." Peerson slid the clip back in and took aim at Grey's head. He held it there, leaning forward to grab the binder. "Mustn't get this soiled," he said. His hand was inches away, but Grey didn't move—Peerson would be ready for him.

Peerson straightened up and tucked the plans into his jacket, taking the time to button it back up. This took both hands, which was what Grey had been waiting for.

Bending at his torso, Grey kicked his right foot at Peerson's gun. It fired as it flew into the air, hitting nothing. The gun landed on the rocks and rattled over edge of the cliff, disappearing.

The effort brought Grey fresh pain, but he ignored it. He swung his foot back down, catching Peerson in the face and sending him over backwards.

Grey rocked up to a sitting position, bounced over to his knees and then up on his feet. He kicked with all his strength. Peerson's head was on the loose shale, so he had to settle for the ribs.

Grey got two solid kicks off before his head started to reel. The island spun around him. He shook his head, but it wouldn't stop. He was too old, too weak, and had too little blood in his body. He was already falling when the pain cut into his leg—Peerson drove a knife through Grey's calf.

Grey's knees buckled, and he dropped onto them. Peerson drove his fist into Grey's face—he wasn't very strong, but Grey went down hard. Grey raised his hand to stop the fall, but his fractured forearm snapped, folding in half, and his leg came down hard on the knife, driving the point out through his shin and spraying blood on Peerson's face. The knife's handle crunched against Grey's shin bone and stuck there.

The world around Grey sputtered; he struggled to keep his eyes open. Peerson picked up a large rock, testing its weight in his hand.

He crawled toward Grey.

The machine gun fired so rapidly that it seemed to explode in Amin's hands. Wood shattered at Leigh's feet as she sprang for the cover of the overhang. Something tugged on her foot and she knew she'd been shot. It was a small bullet, maybe only a five millimeter. A single bullet wouldn't do much damage, but the gun was spitting out a hundred a minute. They chased her across the boat, the last few thumping into the roof overhead.

An empty clip fell on the deck in front of her. She heard him load another. Leigh looked at the Berretta, lying in the far corner of the boat. She didn't know if it would fire, but it was her only hope. She stepped out and dove at it.

The machine gun cracked to life and bullets tore up the deck all around her, raising a cloud of splinters. She landed on her hands and did a cart-wheel, putting her right hand over the gun. Her fingers gripped the handle as a bullet grazed the inside of her arm, inches from her head.

Her legs flipped over her body and she snapped her torso up. She stood in mid-air, hovering over the boat. Amin gritted his teeth, his face lit by the strobe of the machine gun. Three or four tiny bullets drilled into her rib cage, climbing toward her head as gravity pulled her down. The boat drove out from under her and her feet touched the white foam behind it.

A bullet pounded into Leigh's shoulder, twisting her sideways. She snapped her arm out straight, pointing the Beretta at the man on the upper deck, twenty feet away. Her finger pulled the trigger and a small dot appeared on the bridge of Amin's nose and red sprayed from the back of his head. Her hand clipped the boat's stern, knocking the gun loose. It clattered to the deck as Leigh plunged into the sea.

She bobbed in the boat's wake as it raced toward the Mediterranean. It looked like it was going to make it, but then bounced off an underwater rock, turning straight into the cliff. The hull snapped in half. The motor growled, trying to push the boat up the cliff wall, but the water rose over the exhaust and it sputtered out. The boat slipped backward into the sea. It wasn't too deep here, Leigh thought. They could find it, if they ever wanted to.

Leigh spun around, inspecting the steep cove walls. There was no way back up. The bullets in her body all started to hurt at once, and the water around her was red in the moonlight. She tried to ignore the pain, and swam toward the cove's entrance. She went slowly, saving her energy for the rough waters on the other side. It was going to be a long swim.

Grey screamed as Peerson crawled on top of him, the deep scream of a man who had fought for his life down to the last inch and lost. Most men would be disturbed by such a noise, but Peerson seemed to relish it. He put a knee on Grey's chest and pressed broken ribs against his waning heart.

Grey's throat went dry and he gasped, the air suddenly thin. Peerson frowned sadly and maneuvered his knees onto Grey's shoulders, the left one directly on the wound his own bullet had made. He leaned his blood-spattered face to Grey's ear and whispered: "You needn't worry, it's almost over now."

Peerson took the rock in both hands, centered it on Grey's head and raised it high in the air. He leaned back to get the maximum swing.

Grey bent the knee of his good leg, bracing his foot flat on the rock. He used this as a lever, and swung his other leg upward, bringing it—along with the knife that stuck out of his shin—into the air. There was a sound like a nail being driven into wood, and his leg stuck to the back of Peerson's head. Peerson struggled, unsure why he couldn't move. Then his eyes rolled back into his head and he teetered.

The stone dropped from his hands and rolled down the side of his body. He brought his hands up behind his head and pushed Grey's leg back, freeing himself. Then he collapsed onto Grey, blood rising like oil from the back of his neck from the earth—ruby red mixed with clear spinal fluid.

Grey didn't see Peerson die; his own eyes were vacant, what was behind them had already left.

The two bodies lay motionless in the stone field, one stacked on the other. Their blood mixed together on the flat rock, forming a pool that dripped over the cliff's edge. Anyone who saw them would think they were two lovers in an embrace. But there was no one around. The island was as still as death itself.

XI

When Grey opened his eyes, it was snowing. Thick flakes swirled under a streetlight, dancing frantically in the strong winter winds. It was still night. Or maybe it was night again; it was too warm for snow and Peerson was gone. He realized he was in a room watching the snow through a window.

It was a small room. It was white. A lot of machines were in here, too. Medical equipment. The room had the mop-water smell of a hospital. There was a vase at the end of the bed, empty. He was all alone.

The bed was bent at his waist, affording him a view of himself. Three different tubes ran into his body: one each to arms so withered he couldn't believe they were his, and a thick one that snaked under the linens and went into his chest. His skin was as translucent as wax paper, showing off the veins underneath.

There was a clock on the wall. It was two in the morning. He watched it until three, when he was interrupted by a nurse.

She was small and thin, like a toothpick brought to life. She checked his chart and several of the machines before noticing that he was awake. She sent out a general alert.

The first to respond was the night-duty doctor. Grey smiled at him: he had learned to like doctors recently. Decent folk, doctors. This doctor, however, took Grey's smile as an invitation to shine a blinding light into his eyes. Back and forth and round and round the light went, as if the doctor were searching for a lost child in the caverns of Grey's skull. Then he decided he could get a better view through the ear. Whatever he hoped to find, Grey never learned.

The doctor gave up the search and shrugged at the nurse. He wrote some stuff on a clipboard and left. The nurse tidied up the already tidy linens and inspected his tubes for leaks. She was so attentive, Grey wondered if she was playing for a tip. When she was satisfied everything was in order, she smiled, patted his foot, and left him to stare at the clock.

The next person Grey saw was Leigh. She burst into the room, red-faced and out of breath. Her hair had been cut very short, spiked and bleached. She was wearing a shiny green-pastel suit that was cut for an old lady—loose with thick padded shoulders—meant to recreate the human shape that time had robbed. She was way too young for it, and it looked ridiculous on her. She looked at Grey, her face torn between respite and disbelief.

She caught her breath in the doorway, then walked softly to the bedside, as if the faintest noise might scare him away. She put her hand on his cheek and traced his cheekbone. Her fingers were searing hot, and nothing in Grey's whole life had ever felt as good.

Leigh sat in the chair by the bed with practiced ease. A thick book was split open by the armrest, but Leigh didn't read tonight. She only gazed at Grey's face. He did nothing but gaze back.

When the nurse returned, Leigh took her to the door and fed her some sharp words about the empty vase. It seemed that Leigh had filled it daily and the nurse had gotten a little too efficient about cleaning it out. It also seemed that most of the medical staff around here had no expectation that he would ever wake up. Grey heard the word vegetable thrown out and wondered if he was one. He thought about it for a while and decided there was no way to be sure. So instead he thought about the flowers. Had he smelled them while he was asleep? Were they in his dreams? But he couldn't remember his dreams. They were locked behind the grip of consciousness.

The first week Grey couldn't move at all. He drifted in and out of awareness, but was never quite asleep. He had slept plenty; over three months, he was told. That seemed like enough for now.

Leigh was always beside him, sometimes awake, sometimes asleep. Sometimes she read quietly, other times she would talk to him about nothing. She never mentioned the bomb, the plans, or the war. Every morning she brought him fresh flowers, though he never saw her leave to get them. The only time she left was when they came to clean him. And the first time they did, he could see why.

Cleaning happened twice a week. Two strong orderlies lifted him up and spread a vinyl sheet over his bed, then scrubbed him roughly. Underneath the linens, Grey's body was shriveled to the bone. Leigh was doing him a favor by leaving; he was ashamed of what he had become.

During the dayshift, he was attended by the doctor with the metal hook. "For you," the doctor told him, "I made the wrong decision. But for the world, I could have done no greater favor." The way he smiled at him, Grey felt this was a good thing. "Unfortunately," the doctor said, "I could not save your plaid pants. I hope they were not precious to you."

Grey laughed weakly, and suffered greatly for it.

At the end of the first week, some unseen signal was given and Leigh arrived with newspapers. Three months' worth, stacked so high she rolled them in on a hand-truck. She sat on the edge of the bed and read them out loud. Grey still couldn't talk, but managed to grunt expressively at what she said. It was progress.

The first paper was from the morning he had traveled to the island of Frioul. It had an update on the war and its various preparations. The next couple days had similar fare, but the fourth day opened with a catchy four-inch headline that read: "NUCLEAR BOMB A HOAX."

The story described how the CIA, led by Tom McGareth, uncovered proof that the fake bomb in Paris had been planted by a radical splinter of Il Siyâh in an attempt to provoke a war. McGareth received a minor concussion during the raid on the terrorist's stronghold, and two agents were killed. Grey wasn't mentioned, standard procedure for operatives, and he took that to mean they still considered him one. Or maybe he just didn't exist anymore—between Leigh's hair and her downturn in fashion, there was no doubt that they were hiding from someone.

The subsequent papers were filled with stories about the orderly pull-back from Iran's border, and about the troops that were returning home. A few people were unhappy about it, but none of them were soldiers.

A joint action was announced between France and Iran to hunt down those responsible, but Grey suspected it was just posturing. Cabinet members resigned in America and in France, and things went back to normal. The NSC, which had been cited in nearly every pre-war article, was mentioned only once, a page-six story about them appointing a new director. He was a former MI6 officer, a man of such little note that they ran facts about his wife and his dog just to fill out the article.

Jerard and Faison both got front page obituaries because of their "heroic roles" in uncovering the bomb hoax. Jerard was said to have been "the treasure of French intelligence, missed by every man in the department." Faison was listed as "Former Director of Operations for the DST." There was no mention of Denis.

Grey began physical therapy and started back on solid food. Leigh slipped him treats from the outside world and Grey's voice found the strength to thank her. He could read the paper himself now, but preferred to have Leigh read it to him. She did, too. She stopped bringing flowers, and started wearing perfume.

Grey continued to read the papers, but two weeks after the hoax was discovered, interest in the almost-war dropped below the fold. A week later, it was gone altogether. The paper was still good for the crossword, though, and Grey had plenty of time for that.

Soon all the intravenous tubes were gone. Grey had small exercise weights by the bed and he used them constantly. They were thick with foam so he didn't hurt himself when he dropped them, which was often. Slowly but surely, the shape in his arms came back.

One night Leigh told Grey she still loved him. Grey told her that he had never stopped. From then on, she curled up next to him in the small bed for at least an hour every night. The nurse would allow that much.

One afternoon, a month after he woke up, Tom McGareth arrived with a crew of agents in tow. He was well-dressed and well-manicured—sharp, like a politician. More or less, that's what he was now.

The agents swept his room for bugs and were surprised not to find any. McGareth sent them away and had a steak brought in for Grey's dinner. It had come all the way from Paris, he said. Tom also brought an expensive bottle of Kentucky bourbon, but for now, Grey was only allowed to smell.

McGareth chatted while Grey ate. Tom had been promoted, and was reportedly on the short list to replace the Deputy Director, who had retired to spend more time with his family. The CIA was back on top and NATO's commission had all but vanished. Best of all, he reported, his wife had brought the kids back from Germany.

It was only after Grey finished eating that Tom got to business: "I've been instructed to bring apologies from the highest levels."

Grey nodded, knowing it was just a formality; nobody that high up really gave a shit. "You've won a compliment of awards." Tom produced a small wooden box. "The trinkets are in here, the money is in your bank account." Grey nodded again.

"Have you given any thought to your future?" Tom asked.

"I'm sure you have," Grey said with a thin smile.

McGareth shrugged. He produced a thin yellow envelope and placed it on the nightstand. Grey glanced at Leigh before reaching for it.

"We have a safe house in Morocco," McGareth said. "It's a nice place, spacious, good view. We're more than willing to write it off, if it fits your needs."

Grey pulled his hand back from the envelope. "That's a very generous offer."

McGareth shook his head. "It doesn't come from me. The boys at the NSC asked me to set it up."

"In exchange for?"

"I got the impression that it's in exchange for you just going there and keeping your mouth shut."

Grey thought it through. He didn't know if he could trust McGareth anymore, but what else could he do. "It's not a setup?"

"I wouldn't think so. They've been panicking about your health ever since they got a hold of those plans you were carrying—they've got enough trouble without the world learning that they were the ones behind the bomb hoax. Their fear is that a clever man like yourself wouldn't have gone to Frioul without making arrangements for a copy of the plans to surface—in a very public way—should anything ever happen to you."

"And where would they have gotten that idea?"

"I think I gave it to them."

"It would be clever of me, wouldn't it?"

"It would. They traced back over your every move and haven't found so much as a hint of your private copy. And as long as they can't find it, there's no fear of them coming after you. In fact, I'm certain you can count on their protection."

McGareth picked up the envelope again. He eyed Grey from top to bottom. "You do have the plans well-hidden, don't you?"

"Extremely."

He set the envelope on Grey's chest. "Denis sends his regards. He's decided not to allow the DST to reinstate him. He's exploited the situation well. His grandchildren's grandchildren will be set for life, should he ever produce any. But he's lost his security clearance, so he won't be able to contact you. He knows that you made it; I made sure of that much."

Tom rose to leave, stopping at the door.

"They'll find another way, you know," he said. Grey didn't understand. "To get to Iran," Tom explained. "They're off about North Korea for now, but they'll be back."

"I think that will be someone else's problem," Grey said with a smile.

McGareth nodded, giving him one last look. "Good luck with whatever comes next."

"You, too."

When McGareth had left, Leigh took the envelope off Grey's chest and opened it. Inside were two passports—for a Mr. and Mrs. Torrance—and two first class tickets to Rabat leaving three weeks from today. There was also a ring with two house keys, and a piece of paper with a typewritten address. She held it all up for Grey to see.

"What, no car?" Grey said. This got him a laugh.

"Maybe it's in the garage."

"Maybe. I hate to think what kind of dive they're saddling me with."

"Only one way to find out."

Grey looked at Leigh, his face solemn. "Nobody's going to make you go. I'm the one they want to get rid of."

Leigh stared at him for a long time, her mouth pursed and her eyes narrow. "You are so stupid," she said, and kissed him on the lips.